TOMORROW'S PARTIES

TWELVE TOMORROWS SERIES

In 2011, *MIT Technology Review* produced an anthology of science fiction short stories, *TRSF*. Over the next years, *MIT Technology Review* produced three more volumes, renamed *Twelve Tomorrows*. Since 2018, the MIT Press has published *Twelve Tomorrows* in partnership with *MIT Technology Review*.

TRSF, 2011

TR Twelve Tomorrows 2013, edited by Stephen Cass

TR Twelve Tomorrows 2014, edited by Bruce Sterling

TR Twelve Tomorrows 2016, edited by Bruce Sterling

Twelve Tomorrows, edited by Wade Roush, 2018

Entanglements: Tomorrow's Lovers, Families, and Friends, edited by Sheila Williams, 2020

Make Shift: Dispatches from the Post-Pandemic Future, edited by Gideon Lichfield, 2021

Tomorrow's Parties: Life in the Anthropocene, edited by Jonathan Strahan, 2022

TOMORROW'S PARTIES

LIFE IN THE ANTHROPOCENE

EDITED BY JONATHAN STRAHAN

THE MIT PRESS
CAMBRIDGE, MASSACHUSETTS
LONDON, ENGLAND

This book was set in Dante MT Pro and PF DIN pro by New Best-set Typesetters Ltd. Printed and bound in the United States of America.

Library of Congress Cataloging-in-Publication Data

Names: Strahan, Jonathan, editor.
Title: Tomorrow's parties : life in the anthropocene / edited by Jonathan Strahan.
Description: Cambridge, Massachusetts : The MIT Press, [2022] | Series: Twelve tomorrows
Identifiers: LCCN 2021057613 | ISBN 9780262544436 (paperback)
Subjects: LCSH: Science fiction—21st century. | LCGFT: Short stories.
Classification: LCC PN6120.95.S33 T66 2022 | DDC 808.83/8762—dc23/eng/20220318
LC record available at https://lccn.loc.gov/2021057613

10 9 8 7 6 5 4 3 2 1

CONTENTS

INTRODUCTION: SCIENCE FICTION IN THE ANTHROPOCENE   vii
Jonathan Strahan

1   IT'S SCIENCE OVER CAPITALISM: KIM STANLEY ROBINSON AND THE IMPERATIVE OF HOPE   1
James Bradley

2   DRONE PIRATES OF SILICON VALLEY   11
Meg Elison

3   DOWN AND OUT IN EXILE PARK   27
Tade Thompson

4   ONCE UPON A FUTURE IN THE WEST   47
Daryl Gregory

5   CRISIS ACTORS   75
Greg Egan

6   WHEN THE TIDE RISES   95
Sarah Gailey

7   I GIVE YOU THE MOON   115
Justina Robson

8   DO YOU HEAR THE FUNGI SING?   135
Chen Qiufan, translated by Emily Jin

9   LEGION   157
Malka Older

10   THE FERRYMAN   173
Saad Z. Hossain

11   AFTER THE STORM   189
James Bradley

ARTWORK: SEAN BODLEY   213

ACKNOWLEDGMENTS   217
CONTRIBUTORS   219

INTRODUCTION: SCIENCE FICTION IN THE ANTHROPOCENE

Jonathan Strahan

LET'S START IN THE PAGES OF *MERRIAM-WEBSTER*, A DEFINITIVE SOURCE OF definitions since 1828. It defines *science fiction* as fiction that deals "principally with the impact of actual or imagined science on society or individuals or having a scientific factor as an essential orienting component." While there's a lot of science fiction that doesn't fit that definition too well, I wouldn't quibble overly with it. My feeling is that science fiction is fiction that looks at the problems of today through the lens of tomorrow in order to better understand the world we live in now. Not all of it does, of course, but that's the fun of defining science fiction, which could fill a book by itself.

Anyway, the world we live in is a bit of a mess right now. As I write, we are more than two years into a global pandemic that is only just beginning to show signs of abating and that has stretched science and society to the breaking point. And yet this pandemic, the COVID-19 pandemic, is a temporary problem. Global income equality, human rights issues, social justice issues, data privacy, and more affect us all, whether we're on the streets of New York or the streets of Lagos—but as serious and persistent as those problems are, I think it's fair to say they're not the *defining* problem of our time. That honor goes to man-made climate change.

We are living through a specific time in our planet's history. I'm sure J. R. R. Tolkien would have a fancier name for it, but consensus seems to be that it's to be called the Anthropocene, a period of time our old friends at *Merriam Webster* define as that "period of time during which human activities have had an environmental impact on the earth regarded as constituting a distinct geological age." It goes on to add that this began with the Industrial Revolution—which sounds right, but isn't directly relevant to what we're addressing here, which focuses on what's happening now and what might happen next.

The Anthropocene is characterized by warming oceans, melting ice caps, extreme weather events of all sorts (dry ones, wet ones, cold ones, hot ones), habitat loss, species extinction, and more. Fun! Well, really not fun. Rather terrifying, actually. It can be pretty hard to feel good, to see a way forward, when you feel that the world as you know it is actually dying around you.

But as Kim Stanley Robinson, who is interviewed by James Bradley in these pages, has said elsewhere, there's a moral imperative to be optimistic, to attempt to deal with climate change and the challenges it brings in a way that improves our situation, rather than giving in to despair. In fact, as he suggests in these pages, the COVID-19 pandemic shows that there's reason for some optimism in our situation. An optimism that people across the world can work together on a global scale in a way that might address the problems we face, can find ways for people to live and even thrive as the planet faces changes it cannot avoid.

And that's where *Tomorrow's Parties: Life in the Anthropocene* comes in. I wanted to give you a glimpse of what life might be like, however improbable, however bleak, as we live with climate change in the future. What, I asked, would education, raising a family, building a home, doing any of the small day-to-day parts of life look like? And I got some incredible responses. Ten stories by ten talented science fiction writers, fantastic art by Sean Bodley, and a terrific interview. These aren't hopepunk or material for doomscrolling; instead, they're engaging, wonderful—and admittedly sometimes very dark—stories set around the world in the nearish future, and they all show how we might just live with and even through this current age.

Tomorrow's Parties is part of the MIT Press's Twelve Tomorrows series, which has as its mission the exploration of the role and potential impact of developing technologies in the near and not-so-near future. The title is a nod both to the fine Velvet Underground song "All Tomorrow's Parties" and to the William Gibson novel of the same name. It seemed to fit this project, which in a way is a gathering of stories looking for spaces in which tomorrow's parties might happen—a little sad, a little elegiac, a little hopeful. I think these stories fulfill that mission and more, and I hope you enjoy them as much as I have.

Perth, Western Australia

March 2022

1 IT'S SCIENCE OVER CAPITALISM: KIM STANLEY ROBINSON AND THE IMPERATIVE OF HOPE

James Bradley

THERE IS NO QUESTION KIM STANLEY ROBINSON IS ONE OF THE MOST IMPORTANT writers working today. Across almost four decades and more than twenty novels, his scrupulously imagined fiction has consistently explored questions of social justice, political and environmental economy, and utopian possibility.

Robinson is probably best known for his Mars trilogy, which envisions the settlement and transformation of Mars over several centuries, and the ethical and political challenges of building a new society. Yet it is possible his most significant legacy will turn out to be the remarkable sequence of novels that began with *2312*. Published across less than a decade, these six books reimagine both our past and our future in startlingly new ways, emphasizing the indivisibility of ecological and economic systems and placing the climate emergency center stage.

The most recent, *The Ministry for the Future*, published in 2020, is a work of extraordinary scale and ambition. Simultaneously a deeply confronting vision of the true scale of the climate crisis, a future history of the next fifty years, and a manifesto outlining the revolutionary change that will be necessary to avert catastrophe, it is by turns terrifying, exhilarating, and finally, perhaps surprisingly, guardedly hopeful. It is also one of the most important books published in recent years.

This interview was conducted between January and March 2021, beginning in the immediate aftermath of the attack on the United States Capitol and the inauguration of President Biden, and ending as a second wave of the COVID pandemic began to gather pace in many countries around the world. As we bounced questions back and forth across the Pacific, a drumbeat of impending disaster grew louder by the day: atmospheric carbon dioxide reached 417 ppm, a level 50 percent higher than preindustrial levels; a study showed the current system responsible for the relative warmth of the Northern Hemisphere—the Atlantic meridional overturning circulation—at its weakest level in a thousand years; and Kyoto's cherry blossoms bloomed earlier than they have at any time since records began in the ninth century CE.

JB: In several of your recent novels, you've characterized the first few decades of the twenty-first century as a time of inaction and indecision—in *2312*, for instance, you called them "the Dithering"—but in *The Ministry for the Future*, you talk about the 2030s as "the zombie years," a moment when "civilisation had been killed but it kept walking the Earth, staggering toward some fate even worse than death." I wonder whether you could talk a little bit about that idea. What's brought us to this point? And what does it mean for a civilization to be dead?

2

KSR: I'm thinking now that my sense of our global civilization dithering, and also trying to operate on old ideas and systems that are clearly inadequate to the present crisis, has been radically impacted by the COVID pandemic, which I think has been somewhat of a wake-up call for everyone—showing that we are indeed in a global civilization in every important sense (food supply, for instance), and also that we are utterly dependent on science and technology to keep eight billion people alive.

So *2312* was written in 2010. In that novel, I provided a timeline of sorts, looking backward from 2312, that was notional and intended to shock, also to fill the many decades it takes to make three centuries, and in a way that got my story in place the way I wanted it. In other words, it was a literary device, not a prediction. But it's interesting now to look back and see me describing "the Dithering" as lasting so long. These are all affect states, not chronological predictions; I think it's very important to emphasize science fiction's double action, as both prophecy and metaphor for our present. As prophecy, SF is always wrong; as metaphor, it is always right, being an expression of the feeling of the time of writing.

So following that, *The Ministry for the Future* was written in 2019, before the pandemic. It expresses both fears and hopes specific to 2019—and now, because of the shock of the pandemic, it can serve as an image of "how it felt before." It's already a historical artifact. That's fine, and I think it might be possible that the book can be read better now than it could have been in January 2020 when I finished it.

Now I don't think there will be a period of "zombie years," and certainly not the 2030s. The pandemic as a shock has sped up civilization's awareness of the existential dangers of climate change. Now, post COVID, a fictional future history might speak of the "Trembling Twenties" as it's described in *The Ministry for the Future*, but it also seems it will be a period of galvanized, spasmodic, intense struggle for control over history, starting right now. With that new feeing, the 2030s seem very far off and impossible to predict at all.

JB: In *The Ministry for the Future*, the thing that finally triggers change is the catastrophic heat wave that opens the book. It's a profoundly upsetting and very powerful piece of writing, partly because an event of the sort it depicts is likely to be a reality within a decade or so. But as somebody whose country

JAMES BRADLEY

has already experienced catastrophic climate disaster in the form of fire and flood and seen little or no change in our political discourse, I found myself wondering whether the idea such a disaster would trigger change mightn't be too optimistic. Do you think it will take catastrophe to create real change? Or will the impetus come from elsewhere?

KSR: People are good at imagining the catastrophe will always happen somewhere else and to other people. Thus in Australia, people will tend to think, "But it never could happen in Sydney, in Melbourne, in Perth." Even though it could. So it won't be catastrophe per se that changes people's politics and their votes. The impetus comes from ideology, from one's invented imaginary relationship to the real situation. Here the discursive battle is paramount. The stories we tell each other will make the difference. The scientific community keeps telling us a story: that if we continue burning carbon into the atmosphere, and otherwise wrecking the biosphere, we will crash as a species. This story is making headway; I've seen the headway, everyone has, in the last two decades. A tipping point will arrive soon where it is the obvious story that everyone accepts as real; it will become hegemonic. And the sooner the better.

The radically cold temperatures hitting the US as I write this are located in many of the "red states" that voted for Trump, especially Texas. Voting Republican now is in effect a vote against science, a denial of science. So as I write, everyone in those regions without electrical power has to contemplate that in fact they depend completely on science and technology to stay alive. Will that change their thinking and their votes? Probably not—not all of them, and not immediately. But repeated shocks from reality will soon change the window of acceptable discourse, and then the hegemonic space. We are utterly dependent on the science and technology that is both civilization's invention and its enabling device. This story needs to be insisted on. One way I try to do this is to remind everyone that when you're sick and scared for your life, you run to a scientist, which is to say your doctor. That's proof of what you really believe, more than your vote or your words.

In Australia, I can only say I'm mystified. Thirty million is a small population to include so many science deniers. An advanced, developed, rich nation, but also an island that can feel separate from the rest of the world—who knows? No one can understand other political entities from the outside. Even inside them, they are mysterious. But I'd have expected your science deniers and coal burners to be defeated at the polls by now. Maybe that will happen. Maybe electing an idiot like Trump helped to speed the process here.

JB: Part of the process of change has to be about rethinking our relationship with the past and the future. The idea of how we reimagine our relationship with the future is one you return to often: in *The Ministry for the Future*, your characters discuss the way economists discount the value of future lives when making decisions now, and the entire plot of *Aurora* is driven by the failure of people in the present to consider the effect of their actions on the lives of their descendants. But in an odd way, aren't these questions about the future the easy ones? Because it's the poisonous legacies of the past, of racism, slavery, colonialism, and extractivism, and their human and environmental costs, that are really intractable. Can we solve those questions of the future without solving the problems of the past? Or is that a false dichotomy?

KSR: This question reminds me of a slogan one sees in Marx, also Tolkien: we have to deal with the historical situation we've been given. Things could have been different, but they're not—so on we go, free to act, and obliged to act, but not in a situation of our choosing.

That's not to suggest we ignore history. Studying it teaches a lot (maybe everything) about where we are now. Seeing how we got to this moment—which is to say arguing about how we got to this moment—is part of the discursive battle about what to do now.

So there are indeed poisonous legacies of the past, inscribed into current practices, hegemonic beliefs, structures of feeling, and laws. The dead hand of the past, trying to strangle the new baby future that we, in the present, midwife. What I often feel that one can see very clearly is two major strands, braided together although often in direct conflict. I call it science versus capitalism. It's like Australian economist Dick Bryan once said to me about finance and the state: they are hand in hand, but they're arm-wrestling for control.

So the project becomes to strengthen the strand that is working for justice and a sustainable balance with the biosphere—I call that science, though it has to be admitted that this is a signaling word for a whole strand of history, which includes in it democracy, justice, progress, etcetera. Then, against that, there's capitalism, again a signal word for feudalism, patriarchy, and all the older power systems of the few over the many, most of which emerged with agriculture about ten thousand years ago. That power system has an ancient lineage and is hard to beat.

Into this mythic dualism, lots of elements of history can be slotted, but it is a view from space, or a sock puppet play, very Manichean, and maybe often unhelpful. Maybe it's my own false dichotomy, but I still feel it has some explanatory power. So it's not the future over the past, except as a version of this: it's science over capitalism.

JB: I'm interested by your decision to define the conflict as science versus capitalism, because it forces us to think about a lot of these questions differently and to recognize that many things we don't usually think of as technologies—economic policy, finance, social justice, education, and all the other drivers of social change—can be usefully treated as precisely that. But doesn't it also demand we recognize the real challenge isn't electrifying the grid or rolling out solar panels, it's a much more fundamental realignment of political power?

KSR: Yes, I think that's right. Technology can be thought of as machinery only, but here computers are really helpful as an analogy; they have to have both hardware and software. In civilization as a technology, as with computers, the software is crucial; otherwise it's just an inert hunk of metal and plastic. So in this case, we need to focus on software technologies like finance, economics, law, and politics. Then justice becomes a technology, and language itself. This blows up questions like, "Can there be a technological solution without political reform?" Maybe people are there asking, "Could we just make new machines that would overcome the disastrous effects of our unjust and unsustainable political economy, which is to say neoliberal capitalism?"

I think the answer to that is no. We need to change our political economy so that a single index, profit, isn't our measure of doing well. We need to figure out a financial system that pays us for doing things good for the biosphere, including all its citizens, human and not—this would be safest, and indeed it's necessary for humans—rather than rewarding activities that hurt people and biosphere, which profit-seeking will do.

Capital gets invested at the highest rate of return. That's the law, often literally the law. Repairing the biosphere and creating justice among humans is not the highest rate of return now. So it won't happen. End of story.

Or beginning of new chapter. This is what we're seeing in new terms like *Modern Monetary Theory, full employment, carbon quantitative easing,* the *social cost of carbon, universal basic income and services, Half Earth plans,* and *wage parity.* Also in the return of older terms like *socialism,* or *social security.* All these ideas or systems or software technologies are being proposed to get out of the death spiral of neoliberal capitalism. What I find interesting and really encouraging is that these ideas are being discussed by people in the central banks and the national governments and the international diplomatic community. Even among economists, who for the most part have devoted all their work to an analysis of capitalism. These are no longer marginal or science fictional ideas; they are on the table as potential legislation.

JB: Those ideas and that sense a new world is being brought into being around us is very much a part of *The Ministry for the Future*, which, despite the grief and anger that make it so wrenching to read, shares the essentially utopian vision of your work in general. But it's often not easy to see how much change is afoot, if only because, as Mark Fisher put it, capitalism occupies the horizons of the thinkable. Do you think this difficulty contributes to the sense of despair and powerlessness so many people feel at the moment?

KSR: Yes. I think of it in terms known to many now: ideology, hegemony, structure of feeling, capitalist realism: "There is no alternative." And so on. It's been forty years of a dominant political economy, following a couple of centuries of expanding capitalist power over world history, so it's hard to imagine how that could change. Thus the famous Jameson/Zizek slogan: "Easier to imagine the end of the world than the end of capitalism."

But I think now there's also a widespread feeling that it can't go on. And what can't go on won't go on. Capitalism is breaking the system, meaning people's lives and the biosphere. We're on the brink of causing a mass extinction event that will hammer humans, too; it's not just climate change, which can be imagined as a matter of turning down the thermostat, but a much wider habitat collapse—our only habitat.

Given that feeling, people are looking for a way out of the current system and also for some ideas as to what that next system might look like. Even at the heart of the capitalist order—which is to say the central banks, the big corporations and investment firms, and in governments from local to nation-state level—there

5

is talk of change. Of course, very often many of those speaking are hoping to manage change while retaining power. But some very interesting changes are part of that discussion. So I think the feeling of a massive immovable system has begun to creak, shift, crack, and let in new light.

JB: There's a question here about how the change takes place, though, isn't there? Especially given the power of the interests that oppose it. In *New York 2140*, you imagine a kind of Velvet Revolution, a peaceful reorganization of society and the economy, but in *The Ministry for the Future* you quote Keynes's line about the euthanasia of the rentiers. Do you think we'll see an acceleration of violent resistance as the climate crisis intensifies? And how should we think about that?

KSR: I'm not sure about this. In *The Ministry for the Future*, I described all kinds of political violence and also sabotage against fossil fuel or antihuman infrastructures. The novel was an attempt to describe the next three decades in terms that were antidystopian, but also plausible given the world of stark disagreements that we live in. If people see their families die as a result of climate change impacts, then the slow violence of capitalism will spark the fast violence of spasmodic revolt. Very often these violent acts of resistance do little good; the resistance fighters are killed or jailed, and the oppressive system doubles down in its oppression.

So I am among many who are trying to imagine ways of gaining the good results of a revolution without going through the trauma of old-style violent revolutions, which very often backfire anyway. Some better way to a better situation, which can be imagined in the realms of the discursive battle (Can we get more persuasive?); the political battle (Can we win a working majority?); the legislative battle (Can we pass laws that will help?);and then, also, sabotage of life-destroying machinery, mass civil disobedience, and alternative systems of governance that are simply lived outside the current nation-state system—and so on. The list could be extended.

My objections to violent resistance are both moral and tactical: First, it isn't right to hurt other human beings, if not being attacked by them and defending oneself. Then, tactically, violence often seems to backfire and increase the misery being resisted. This is either because the state monopoly on violence is jealously held (and possibly a good thing) or because even if you seem to succeed by violence, you fail in the long run because the effort has used bad means, and the most violent among the revolutionaries tend to seize power and then use that same violence against any dissent of any kind.

This isn't the whole story of history, obviously, but it's the way it feels to me now, in our current situation. So a very rapid, stepwise, legal reformist revolution seems to me the best thing to try now. Later, if we get into the 2030s without meaningful progress on the various justice and sustainability fronts, I think more violent forms of resistance are more likely and maybe more justified. We're in a closing window of opportunity for peaceful tactics to work.

JB: That closing window of opportunity means some very radical ideas are now on the table, some of which—such as proposals to dim the sun or seed the

oceans with iron—are likely to have significant side effects. The idea humans might terraform or reengineer the environment in this way is central to your Mars trilogy and plays a big role in *2312*, *Green Earth*, and *The Ministry for the Future*. Do you think we're now at a point where some of these sorts of schemes have to be seriously entertained? And to what extent should we see them as a symptom of the failure of democratic means?

KSR: We're in an all-hands-on-deck situation, so all these radical ideas need to be explored to see if they might help in safe ways. Geoengineering has been defined in advance as "doing dangerous things to save capitalism," so naturally people tend to be wary of it. But everything humans do at scale has planetary effects and could be called geoengineering in some literal sense. Maximizing women's education and political power worldwide could be called geoengineering because it would slow the population rise as a result of increased human agency, and this would have biosphere effects we could measure. As it's a good and needed thing in and of itself, its ancillary benefits to the biosphere make it a double good.

So at that point the term *geoengineering* is exploded, and if you wanted to discuss it further it should be on a case-by-case basis. Deflecting some sunlight away by casting dust into the atmosphere (solar radiation management), if the dust were not volcanic but chosen for its inertness (like limestone dust), would reduce temperatures slightly for a few years—then the dust would fall to Earth, and the results of the act could be evaluated. If it was done by international agreement, then it would be the result of representative governments. It would be an experiment. Seeding the ocean with iron dust to create algal blooms, which would then die and fall to the sea floor, taking their carbon with them—well, the oceans are already sick because of our carbon burn, plastic pollution, bottom dragging, and overfishing. Doing more to it seems stupid to me, but on the other hand, a single experiment wouldn't change much and might teach us some things. On this particular tactic, I'm like most people in thinking there's got to be a better, safer way.

But this discussion is part of what it means to be in the Anthropocene— we've damaged the biosphere so badly that we now have to work at repairing it, without knowing enough to be sure how to do that well. Still, some actions are obvious. Stop emitting carbon dioxide into the atmosphere. Stop destroying habitat. Invent regenerative agriculture. End poverty and extend equal rights and education to all. These good acts will all have positive biosphere effects. The various emergency actions being discussed are marginal to these big, obvious things we need to do. You asked if I thought we were already at the point where we will need to do these things; I don't think so. But we're close. And if millions die in a wet bulb 35°C heat wave, then the nation-state where that happens may take matters into their own hands. No one in the developed world will have any right to object to that.

JB: The vision of our future you articulate in *The Ministry for the Future* is deeply confronting, but also, ultimately, hopeful in that it runs counter to the growing belief in the developed world that collapse is inevitable. Do you see hope as an imperative?

KSR: Yes, I do. Also, it's very natural and biological; life hopes, hunger is a hope. Again, it's too big a word to help much. Is it good to be alive? Do you hope to go on living therefore? That kind of hope is very persistent.

But then also there is fear. And there are reasons for fear. Is there a growing belief in the developed world that collapse is inevitable? I'm not so sure. And what would collapse mean? That you have to live like people in the Global South live now? Or that three-quarters of all humans will suddenly die in a spasm of civilizational incompetence? These are very different kinds of collapse. So hopes and fears, we always have them in a great overflow.

What I like about science is the way it tries to get particular. Is enough food being grown to feed everyone on Earth? Yes. Is it automatic that that continues? No. Is wilderness a good idea or a bad one? (This is one I'm thinking about now.) Well, scientists involved would ask which of the eight or ten definitions of wilderness you're talking about. I like that kind of specificity.

But I think with this question you're inquiring about our culture's structure of feeling, the vibe, how the young feel, what the internet is saying if you just link around reading, and so on. There, in the realm of the general intellect or the feeling of our time, we're inside a ringing bell. There is a great roaring, a cacophony. You can pull out the sounds you want to hear and call it an accidental symphony of sorts, and then get on with what needs doing. Your hopes and fears will still keep you awake at night. Meanwhile, the work goes on. People want their children to have a good life. Capitalism isn't working, and what can't go on won't go on. So we'll be experimenting our way into a different political economy. Hopefully we'll dodge a mass extinction event, and then all kinds of good possibilities will open up. I think it really is a crux moment in history. The 2020s are going to be wild.

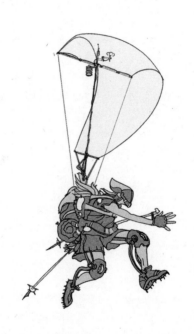

Meg Elison

FIRST GAME OF THE BASEBALL SEASON, AND FATHER AND SON GO TO THE GAME.
Spring in Palo Alto is pale and sterile on the concrete, but at least it isn't
hot. The crowd packed into the stadium with their hats already on and
sunscreen applied in thick coats. Publicity about the new Dodger Dog had
been absolutely everywhere: LED billboards along every freeway, tweets
and TV commercials, unstoppable direct device ads on mobiles and wear-
ables anywhere in Santa Clara County.

"This hotdog had better give me a handjob and then drive us home,"
said Elliot Famberg with a chuckle. He tapped his dermal RFID credit
against the pad display at the ticket booth and the display showed his tick-
ets, bright and immediate.

"Welcome Mx. FAMBERG. You and DANIEL FAMBERG (CHILD
TICKET) will have a great time today!"

The door gave an electronic beep and Elliot passed through slowly, sunglasses in hand, letting the facial recognition program get a good look at
him.

Danny waited, watching his dad go through the ordering process.
They were both impatient, but both very interested. The lintech confirmed
Elliot's identity and Danny stepped through next.

"Honestly, they should update this obsolete lintech system. Whatever
else they've added, this is the infrastructure. You know?" Elliot looked up
at the top of the doorway and saw a crisscross of red lines under the glass.

"It's like the fucking Stone Age, I swear to god." Danny loved agreeing
with his dad at moments like these. It was as much fun to trash bad design
as it was to make something new.

He made a caveman face at the scanner, brow furrowed and lower jaw
thrust out.

The door beeped equally, not caring what faces Danny made at it.
Elliot was already a few paces ahead.

"Come on, Danny, hustle. And don't say 'fuck,' your mother will kill me."

"Mom says 'fuck' all the time," Danny said, but he was distracted by his phone. He was receiving ghostchat videos from his two best friends. Ava was at the beach today. She said she had slipped out in the wee small hours so she could surf alone. Her scuffed old board stood up in the sand and she was showing him the surf. It looked like a good day to be out.

Jayden's videos were from hours before, filmed in the near dark of his bedroom. He pulled back the bedspread and the growlights under the bed flashed out so bright that the phone couldn't capture anything for a few seconds. When the image resolved, Danny saw that his weedlings were doing very well.

He grinned and let the ghostchats die. He clued in that his dad was talking and joined the conversation already in progress.

". . . a grownup means knowing when it's OK to say 'fuck' and when you ought to keep your mouth shut. You say it anytime, everywhere. It's gonna bite you in the ass someday."

"Fuck yeah, Dad." Danny grinned and his father grinned back.

They were climbing the dark metal stairwell to their seats, halfway up behind the foul ball pole. When they reached the top, the sun was blinding after the semidark and Elliot threw a hand up in front of his eyes.

"Fuck," he said as he fumbled for his sunglasses.

Danny's glasses transitioned slowly, darkening until they were as good as sunglasses. He was used to it, having worn lenses since he was a baby. Their seats were on the aisle and Elliot waited for Danny to go in first.

"I'll sit on the outside so I can handle the hot dog situation, whatever it turns out to be."

"Okay." Danny fidgeted in his seat and browsed the internet on his phone. Danny liked baseball and knew that once the game began, he'd be able to put his phone away and pay attention.

But waiting with nothing to do was torture. He replayed his friends' ghost chats. Ava's wetsuit didn't fit right, he realized. He wondered if she inherited it from someone taller.

Danny thumbed past yet another ad for the Dodger Dog stunt and didn't really notice it. Beside him, Elliot was on his own phone, reading an email from work.

"If we can nail this presentation, we can make more money than god," he muttered.

Danny didn't look over. "The delivery drones?"

"That's the ticket. We're presenting tomorrow on the liability structure, that's the thing the insurance guys wanna hear. After that, it's all gravy, all the time." Elliot was talking to himself, his thumbs already gliding with a terrible fury over the lights of his keyboard.

Danny was used to this, too. Elliot had been with Babazon since before Danny was born. Danny's mother was his father's third wife, and she had been a minor movie star, once upon a time. People at school were shocked and a little weird about it when they realized who his parents were, but his school in Palo Alto had parents richer and more famous than them. Last year a kid had left two weeks into being a senior because he had gotten his startup bought out by Fizzle. It was just that kind of place.

Ava sent another ghostchat, this time a selfie of her in her wetsuit. Her black hair was shaved on one side, but the part that was still long was wet and shiny, tousled by the waves. He could see sand on her upper lip.

The caption read WIPED THE FUCK OUT in neon green across her torso. He grinned and ghosted her back, a quick pan of the stadium that ended with his smiling face.

i'm just here for the hotdogs

He plastered four hotdog emoji across the bottom and hit send to both Ava and Jayden.

Jayden answered right away, with fourteen baseball emoji. *You love that shit and we all know it. Say hi to Daddy Bigbucks for us.* Danny smiled, but didn't respond.

Elliot handed him a ball cap. Danny took it, still smiling. He knew it would be a brand-new Dodger blue cap that his dad had bought for this game. He always got a new cap when they went to the ballpark. The newness of the cap was stiff and scratchy like always. Elliot and Danny both worked their caps in their hands, breaking them in. Once they were better, they put them on. Elliot grinned and dragged his son in for a selfie.

"Dad, come on." But Danny was laughing already.

"SMILE, DANNY."

Danny tried to smile like an adult. Elliot showed off his flawless veneers, very white in his tanned face. In the picture, Danny looked like a miniature version of his father. He wished he had his mother's blue eyes or even her full lips, girls seemed to love that kind of thing. But he might as well have been named Elliot 2: The Return of Elliot.

Elliot sent the picture to his assistant for her to post on his affable guy social media presence across a few platforms he didn't want to bother with himself. He stuffed the phone back into his stiff new jeans and leaned back in his seat.

Five minutes before the game was scheduled to start, Danny stood up and stretched in front of his seat.

"I'm out of content," he said, looking out over the ball field.

"How can you be out of content? The internet is literally endless." Elliot was back to staring at his own phone.

"It's endless, but not all of it is interesting."

Elliot stood up and stretched, too. "It's almost time," he said, glancing at his smart watch. He dismissed a reminder absently and folded his arms.

Just as Danny was about to huff out an ostentatious sigh, music poured from the speakers and the scoreboard lit up. Dancing hotdogs appeared at the top and bottom of the screen while words in Dodger blue flew out of the right and bounced into lines.

The announcer's voice boomed out of speakers all around them. Danny jumped a little in his seat and sat up straight, looking around.

"IIIIIT'S TIME, DODGER FANS! The moment you've ALL been WAITING for! Who's ready for a DODGER DOG?"

All around, people whooped and whistled. Elliot joined them, with a look of boyish enthusiasm.

"Jesus, Dad. You act like you never had a hotdog before in your life." Danny was excited, too. But this was still embarrassing.

"Come on, Danny. This is gonna be great!"

It was great, Danny realized. He put his arm around his dad's shoulders and smiled at him. His dad smiled back.

The cheery, booming voice of the announcer told them all to use the app they had downloaded, or to download it now. Danny looked over his dad's shoulder and saw him building two dogs the way they always had them: ebeef with mustard, white onion, and celery salt. Elliot had already entered his blockchain ID, so the whole process took only a few seconds.

Danny popped his chin toward his dad's phone. "The UI is really good. Smooth. Looks slick."

"Easy to use," agreed Elliot. "Perfect proof of concept for the big one, when we pull it off. Maybe I'll order a couple more during the seventh inning stretch?"

"Maybe? I can eat two any day."

"Now let's see them add beer to the same app and I'll be a happy man," Elliot said, glancing up toward the tunnel into which he would have to walk in order to get a beer. "The law says we can't drone alcohol or weed. For now." He sighed and stayed put.

The game began and Danny and his dad watched the Dodgers begin the simple task of beating the Diamondbacks. Danny was grateful for his hat as the sun crested over the eastern side of the stadium.

Ava sent him another ghost of herself eating a massive burrito at a little table, the ocean at her back. His stomach growled. He looked around anxiously, hoping to see some sign of the coming of their Dodger Dogs.

He saw nothing.

The second inning ended and Danny was certain he was going to starve to death. He waited for his dad to give up and go to get a beer, and then he would tell him how badly he needed a plate of overpriced nachos.

As Elliot stood, something caught his attention. Danny saw his dad whip off his sunglasses and stare down toward the ball field.

"Here they come!" Elliot's voice spiraled up with excitement as music blared out of the speakers once more and a strange high buzzing filled the air. The sound reminded Danny of his quadcopter at home, a present from two years ago. He had added a few things to it and kept it tuned up for fun, but it had never been really useful. Just a toy.

The microdrones came up as one, rising in a mathematically perfect disk from everywhere at once. As they rose to the level of the first row of seats, they smoothly broke formation and started to locate people in their seats.

Their tinny, beeping voices rose all around them and Danny craned his neck, half-standing in his seat to see. The man in front of Danny stood straight up, blocking the view in every direction with his six feet of height and almost the same amount of width.

Danny huffed and tried looking right or left. As he leaned closer to his dad, one of the drones leveled with Elliot's face.

"Mx. Elliot Famberg, please accept two ebeef Dodger Dogs with mustard, white onion, and celery salt."

Elliot took off his cap and stared at the machine hovering in front of his face. It was about the size of a man's shoe, with no visible means of propulsion. Tiny red and green lights blinked on its underside.

When its cargo area slid open in a series of oculus-shaped shells, Elliot nearly jumped back. Inside, two Dodger Dogs sat packed tight together in paper sleeves. Danny could see condensation beading on the inside of the drone from the heat of the food. They both stood there, unsure what to do. The drone repeated itself.

Danny reached out to take the dogs and the machine neatly feinted away from him. "Please do not touch the Dodger Dog Drone," the tinny voice said as it gyroscopically kept the dogs level and presented itself once again to Elliot.

"Mx. Famberg, do you wish to cancel your order?"

Elliot was peering keenly at the design. He turned to Danny, speaking out of the side of his mouth. "See how it's balanced? Even when its load moves . . . they must have given it some kind of shifting ballast to compensate . . ."

When he realized the waiting machine was beeping toward cancellation, he snapped back into the conversation. "Uh . . . no. No thank you. Thank you." He took the dogs as gently as one would pick up a baby bird in lightly curved hands. The microdrone beeped and sailed off, arcing high above people's heads to return to its station.

"Can you believe that? Look at them go. They're gonna be delivering for us soon. All over the world. Everything you order, pizza to car parts. By the time you have a license, there will be no more trucks on the road, guzzling gas and pumping out exhaust. It would have happened a long time ago, if not for the auto lobby. But we're beating them the same way we beat the labor people. With real progress." Elliot was beaming when he handed the hot dog over to Danny. Danny accepted, but he didn't take a bite. He was watching, two rows down, where a big kid had just swiped the Dodger Dog Drone out of the air and swiped its cargo in front of a smaller kid who could only be his brother. Big guy let the drone go and bit in. The little kid began to cry to their dad to fix it.

Watching this scene unfold, Danny was seized with the idea that would change his bored rich scion's destiny. He didn't want a hotdog. For the first time, he understood that he wanted much more than that.

"IT'S NOT LIKE THEY REGISTER A STANDARD FLIGHT PLAN," AVA WAS TELLING DANNY as they worked together over the crisscrossed diagram of the drone traffic in Danny's neighborhood one year later. "The Dodger Dog Drones had a limited area to work in, and their range of motion was circumscribed by the edge of the stadium."

"Actually, according to my dad's files their routes are really limited. If we focus entirely on traffic in and out of Atherton, the routes are all narrowed down to five feet right here," he said. He was tapping the screen where the lines converged, making a throat they could cut like real pirates.

"According to what I read, the liability is almost limitless for that neighborhood. They expect the volume to be so big that it's way cheaper to just ship replacements than to track down most mistakes."

"Right," Ava said forcefully. "But. They've got to be programmed to avoid hazards, right? They can dodge just about anything. Light poles. Birds. Other drones. They have a lot of autonomy when it comes to obstacles."

"They do," Danny agreed. "But it's all automated. No eyes on them. So they won't know why something never showed up. Just that it didn't."

"Won't they come looking for the lost drone? Those can't be cheap." Ava was chewing on her right pinky nail. Danny hardly ever saw her nervous. He didn't know where it was coming from.

"We're going to dump them at the Babazon return center, just like it says on their bellies. If found, please return. Right? It's foolproof."

"If we don't get caught. If we don't create patterns that they can see. If we stay random." Ava noticed him watching her chew and she dropped her finger, her smile brightening once more.

"So, how do we scuttle?" Her voice was cheerful again, back on the high seas of her spirits. Danny liked to hear it there.

"What if we used a material they don't see very well?" Jayden's voice was low and barely audible. He was rummaging in Danny's trunk of unused parts and 3D print filament.

"We know they can see organic and inorganic stuff," Danny said. "We don't know if they're using something like sonar or simple visual scanning input."

"That part was sealed in the reports," Danny admitted. "Sorry."

"Trial and error," Ava said at once, diving in where she could see Danny felt insecure. "I've got my net prototype. Danny, you've got what?"

"Signal interruption," Danny said. "I still think that's better than any physical barrier or weapon." He pulled his tablet closer and clicked over to the screen where he had written the code. "We're gonna have to cage our phones when I broadcast this," he said. "It's gonna jam up everything. Probably fuck the Wi-Fi in any surrounding houses."

"Ok," Ava said, nodding. "And Jayden, what's it gonna be?"

Jayden pulled his head out of the trunk, his wispy freshman mustache curled upward with his smile. "Lucite," he said. He held in his hands a clear box intended to house a bot that made too much noise, to dampen it without obstructing its view. "I bet you our first score that it can't see its way through this."

"How do we even get that within range?" Danny was thinking it through, looking idly up at the ceiling to imagine the sky. "You'd need to raise up a sheet or a block of Lucite quickly and accurately to interrupt flight."

"Ahaaa." Jayden grinned. "My drone flies above the delivery drone, matches its trajectory, and dangles a Lucite cage from a cable. It lowers down and encases the whole thing. Could force a landing, even if it doesn't interrupt flight."

"What about retrieval?" Ava was working on next steps, always before her friends. "We're going to need nets. Hooks. Grabbers. Some way to fetch the ones that fall in random backyards or on rooftops."

She showed them her ideas for capture, which included retrieval baked into them. "Simple physical interference. We fire a net from a cannon when we're within range. We use a telescoping snag hook, the whole thing is lightweight aluminum. We pull what we want to us, and disable the drone."

But each of their plans were needed, when it came to the trial runs. Danny's signal interruption was necessary to make sure no one could track the drones once downed. Jayden's Lucite escort proved useful in catching anything that evaded net and hook. And Ava alone ensured retrieval, every time.

The first time they actually caught one, the process was a mess. Jayden flew his cage drone above the one from Babazon—Danny identified it through his binoculars and gave the coordinates.

Jayden, tongue jammed in the corner of his mouth, maneuvered free-hand with the joystick before handing over control to the computer. "I was doing better on my own," he muttered, watching the machine wobble as it righted itself. The Lucite box was heavy and the drone wasn't built to compensate. It came down too fast and merely winged its target.

"I'm on it," Danny was already saying before Jayden sucked his teeth. He turned his powerful antenna up and over toward the drone, sending the first jamming signals he thought might work based on the specs he had seen. The drone was impervious, flitting onward to its delivery.

"You better hope it's not broadcasting a distress signal," Ava said through clenched teeth.

"It's not!" Danny did not actually know this for sure.

Ava yanked back the catapult lever that locked her net into place, pulled the tracker app up on her phone, eyeballed it, and fired.

The net sprang apart in the air, as nimble and as bizarre as the wings of a bat in full daylight. The net caught the small craft and it came down, falling like a stone.

Danny's algorithm to make the drone surrender its cargo worked the first time. Jayden's plan to Faraday-cage the little beast to keep its GPS from working was airtight.

Ava's suggestions kept them safe. They didn't start their raids on the first day Atherton's drone service went live. They waited almost a month, into the height of summer when no one was out at midday. They avoided dog walkers' hours and they came and went separately from the throat where they could scuttle drones. They each had a plausible and simple excuse for the equipment they carried.

Jayden's drone and Lucite was for wildlife photography. He had pictures of feral cats and a racoon inside his cube in his gallery, just in case.

19

Danny's drone and laptop were for his research into being just like his dad—and who would hear the name Famberg and ask for more than that?

Ava's net rig traveled compact but looked like a mortar launcher. She had thought long and hard about it, then put it in a red wagon beneath tripods and props for a photo shoot. She was just doing it for the ghostgram. Before they left the throat each time, she would lie in the dust, wreathed in flowers. She would pose with an afghan dappling the sun over her beautiful face and a book. A girl's vanity can hide a secret of almost any size.

None of them was old enough to get into real trouble, even if they got caught. This was their catechism, every day. Like a catechism, some of the belief was real, and some of it was just knowing how to say the words. Like catechism, judgement was waiting.

That first drone that they freed from Ava's net turned out to be delivering a six-pack of IceAde and a case of sweet Thai chili flavored snack mix. They lay back in the yellow grass on their hillside, hidden from the road, and feasted. They twisted the IceAde bottles, watching them do their patented slush-freeze. They drank deep and ate until their lips went numb. It was the perfect plunder; nothing to hide. They disposed of their trash and Jayden took the drone to the Babazon return center on his way home.

The person who had ordered the IceAde and snacks in Atherton waited less than fifteen minutes before reporting the failure. She had a new shipment in under an hour. The irregularity was hardly noted anywhere, by any system. Such things just happened.

Danny walked in the door of his house, stowing the drone in the mudroom where his parents kept their jogging shoes and lightweight windbreakers and fleece vests.

He caught his dad in the kitchen, making eye contact as he realized his dad was, as usual, on the phone.

"Vulnerabilities? Like what?"

Danny's face was hot so he opened the fridge and pretended to look for a snack. He knew there would be nothing but raw fish and vegetables in there, and he'd already done so much snacking that he thought he might never eat again.

"You're telling me that crackerjack team of yours is worried about a labor strike? Listen, we have systematically routed out anyone with union ties. Anyone with a hammer and sickle avi. Anyone who is related to or in a relationship with a known leftist. There is no will at all in these workers. They get what they get, and they don't get upset. I know it chaps your ass to admit I'm right, Ahmet. You're gonna have to get over it. Yeah? Yeah, me too."

Elliot tapped the side of his throat to hang up his vox implant and he pulled the phone from his pocket to check his texts.

"Hey, buddy boy. What all did you do today?"

"Just walking in the hills," Danny told him, diffidently. "Playing with my drone. Hey, Dad? Are you really not worried about people refusing to work for Babazon or whatever? Like couldn't they just walk out?"

Elliot leaned forward and put his elbows on the counter to look Danny in the eye. "So, used to be you could lose your shirt if a single worker decided that the restroom wasn't clean enough. Or that their pay was too low. But we fixed all that with uniformity. Everybody makes the same, everybody sleeps in the same dorm. Everybody has the same debts to pay off, the same access to daycare at the same cost. All it took was equality. You understand, Danny?"

Danny was nodding. He understood what he needed to. He knew that he and his friends were not vulnerable. Not at all. But in the back of his mind, he wondered whether his dad was right.

It had been Ava who had started calling them pirates. Neither of the boys had made the connection, but she talked about it nonstop while she built her netapult. "They mostly just robbed the rich," she said. "Their biggest enemies were like the East India Trading Company, merchants like that. They were privateers, getting rich off bigger privateers. We're doing the same thing that Babazon does, just at a smaller scale."

"I don't know about that," Danny said doubtfully. "Babazon doesn't steal from anybody."

"Bullshit," Ava said at once. "Those distribution centers in Fremont and Hayward, all those people who work there? They get their pay docked for room and board. Most of them are in debt to Babazon. They're paying it off with their labor, at less than minimum wage since Babazon houses them."

"My dad says those dorms are really nice," Danny said uncertainly.

"Then why don't you live there? Why doesn't Babazon keep all their important employees in the dorm, too?"

"Well . . . because . . ." Danny had no answer.

"The people who live there, their kids go to Babazon school, where they basically just learn to do the same thing. They can read and write code, but they don't learn about any other kind of life. They don't get to build robots or study languages like we do. Babazon is stealing from them, same as if they were slaves."

Jayden had piped up at that. "It's not like they can't leave. They can leave anytime."

"Sure," Ava agreed. "And go where? Live on what? Take their kids to what school? Ours?"

"There are scholarship kids," Jayden said. "You should know, Ava."

The air between them grew thick. This was the one thing they never talked about. They hung out together at Danny's house, at Jayden's. Never at Ava's. Neither of them knew where Ava lived, or what her parents did for a living. She never talked about it. They both assumed she was a scholarship student at Astra Academy; she hadn't been part of their middle school class and they saw her get on the bus after school on days that they didn't hang out. She was one of the best in the robotics program; if anyone could earn a scholarship it would be her.

Ava's mouth hardened and her full lips almost disappeared. "Maybe that's why you two don't understand my interest in piracy. You're too busy shipping tea for the queen."

She hadn't revealed anything about herself that day. She had quieted her chatter about pirates, but only a little. Whenever the opportunity arose to refer to herself as a pirate, she took it. She did not apply the same stories, the same words to them.

But pirates they were, and their booty grew more difficult to hide as their treasure grew. Following Ava's example, both boys had gotten themselves a wagon and dragged them into the hills on days they went scuttling drones. They spaced these out, choosing at random between weekdays and weekends. They kept mostly to the afternoons, with Jayden creeping out for a few night raids on his own.

21

"My dad is working on a side project," he said. "He told me not to knock on the door of his office unless the house was on fire. So he doesn't notice at all if I go out. Look at what I got the other night!"

Jayden pulled back the towel he had laid over his wagon and showed them a large cache of vintage muscleman magazines. "Look at this. Look how hot." He ran his fingers over a yellowed image from the seventies.

"Those are probably pretty rare by now," Danny said, biting his lip. "Those won't be as easy to replace as the usual stuff we take."

"Who cares?" Jayden was running his eyes over the pile again. "I'm gonna hang them up all over my room. My mom says it's OK as long as they're not showing meat."

"Ew," Ava said.

"I don't ew the shit you like," Jayden retorted.

"You ew girls all the time," Ava said dismissively. "And I just meant ew to calling it 'meat.'"

"But we are meat," Jayden said, piloting his drone up out of its cradle. "Meat that conquers drones."

Ava watched his drone go up and cocked her netapult into place. "I really want to bring down a PL9," she said. "I have no idea how we'd hide it."

"If we get a PL9," Danny said, "that's all you. Jayden and I both already have one. You can borrow games!"

They brought down their first kill of the afternoon and were disappointed to find it contained only an order of tampons.

"I'll put it in the low value pile," Ava said. She always took care of this kind of stuff: dish soap and toothpaste and Band-Aids and baby food. She carted it away every time it passed through Jayden's hands and Danny's, both of them declaring it worthless.

Everything they hauled down that day was low value, ending on a disappointing box with six tubes of rash cream in it.

"Man," Jayden almost yelled. "Doesn't anybody order cool sunglasses?"

"Or electronics," Danny muttered. Almost everything he had claimed from their prizes had been something he wanted to take apart. He and Ava had fought over a minicomputer that could be used to automate digital signage or hack billboards. In the end, he had let her have it because he already had one. It was just old. Ava had none at all, and he realized she probably couldn't get her dad to buy her one.

"Tell your dad you want Heliobates," Danny said. "Your birthday is coming up."

"Yeah," Jayden said. "But fuck that. I wanted to get a pair for myself. Like a proper pirate, right Ava?"

Ava laughed a little, looking at her phone. "Right."

They split up soon after. It was late, but at this time in the summer the sun was still up until nearly bedtime. It was easy for Danny to tail Ava, with their shadows growing long. She seemed very tired and he knew why when they went past the bus depot.

"She can't get on the bus with the wagon," he muttered to himself. "What a pain in the ass." He knew that meant he might have to walk back, or call his dad's driver to get him. It did not dissuade him from following her.

By the time they made it to the edge of the woods, she had turned and noticed him. She stopped at the first line of trees and faced him, her mouth turned down at the corners.

"What are you doing?"

He grinned a little, feeling the sunburn on his face as his cheeks stretched. "Learning more about being a pirate. Come on. Show me."

He didn't even know what he wanted her to show him. She looked him over, then shrugged. She pulled her wagon along a dirt path, and he followed behind with his.

The camp was simpler and more rustic than he had expected. There were rumors that people lived in these woods, people who had been purged for organizing labor, or people who had left the Babazon warehouse dorm. In his mind, he had thought it would be orderly, like a trailer park or a network of tree houses. In reality, many of them lived in tents or sheds made of corrugated metal and plywood. The people looked clean as they moved through the trees, going about their business of getting ready for bed. Danny saw a man toweling off a toddler who had just been washed with cold water from a bag. He did not know where to look after the baby's red face.

"Ava!" An older woman called as she emerged from the darkness in the woods, deeper than the twilight they had left behind. "Did you bring us something?"

"Just low-value goods," Ava said with a grin. She pulled back the old blanket she kept on her wagon and handed out her haul: the tampons and salves, the Band-Aids and other things Jayden and Danny had not wanted.

When the wagon was cleaned out, Danny came to her side to speak to her. "Why don't you sell all that? Or trade it? There's a lot of people who need stuff like this."

She turned on him. "The people who need stuff like this are right here. Look around. Does it look like they have anything to trade? You think they have crypto-credit I can use?"

Danny was ashamed and wished he wasn't. He felt like he had done this to her, personally somehow. He reached for anything to make himself feel less guilty.

"Well at least I told you all the stuff that I know about these drones," he said. "I'm doing my part."

Her smile brightened to something catlike, something that was more hunger than humor.

"You are definitely doing your part," she said. She took him by the hand. They left their wagons on the ground and she led him up a ladder to a tree house. Inside, forty small versions of her netapult were laid out on the ground in various states of construction.

"I took everything you told me, plus all the data I have from our scuttles. I've been teaching people to do what we do. Teaching piracy."

Danny was nodding. "That's good," he said. "Your camp can certainly use a lot of the stuff we're getting. But they're—they're not pirating in Atherton, right? That might get noticed, I mean . . . if too many people do what we do . . ."

As he trailed off, Ava was pulling out her phone to show him a map. It was password-protected even after it read her face on the ocular scan. "These are the camps I've taught this to," she said, pointing out red dots on the page. All over the Bay, from Oakland to Vallejo, he could see drone-downing activities.

"When a pirate was in command of a ship, she was called captain," Ava said in a low voice. "When she commanded several ships, she was a commodore. That's my handle on our server. Commodore 64."

"Why 64?"

She shook her head. "It's from the history of machines," she said. "It's not important. What is important is information. We need more of it. We need all that you can get."

"Why?" Danny looked at the intensity of her brown eyes and he couldn't begin to guess what she wanted. In the space of the last few minutes, she had made him feel very small and very lost. He was displaced from the center of the story. He was no one. He was a drone, here only for delivery, and in the morning she would dump him at Babazon returns.

"Because this is just the beginning," she said. "It's not about stealing from them. It's about getting back everything they took."

Danny couldn't speak. He could barely think. He nodded to her, then walked out of the woods. He left his wagon behind. When he reached a road that seemed safe to be on, he tapped his implant to ask his father's driver to pick him up from his tagged location.

All through the dark car ride home, he tried to make sense of it. He tried to understand how the dad that took him to ball games and taught him to program could be part of something as bad as Ava had made the company sound. He couldn't wrap his head around it. He stumbled out of the car bone-tired, thinking of when he was smaller and his dad would carry him to bed when they got home.

In the morning, he waited until his dad left the house before diving back into the files that had given him his start as a pirate. He nosed those aside, digging instead for the folders containing statistics on the Babazon warehouse. Evictions. Terminations. The numbers swam through him like fish through cannon holes in the hull of a ship.

He sent Ava a ghostchat of the screen in front of him. "Tell me what you can use."

3 DOWN AND OUT IN EXILE PARK

Tade Thompson

I HADN'T HEARD FROM COSMO FOR TWELVE YEARS, SO SEEING HIM ON MY DOOR stoop was . . . an event. With the bushy, uncombed hair, ratty beard, Steelers T-shirt, battered jeans, and army boots on his feet, any change in the wind blessed me with a pungent smell that told me his relationship with soap was tenuous.

"Can you do me a favor, Francis?" he said, like we were midconversation, like he hadn't fallen off the edge of the map over a decade ago, like we were still friends.

"Really? No 'hi, how are you?' Cosmo?"

"It's been a long time, Francis Cotillard. How are you? How's the family? Can I ask you a favor?" Delivered in a flat monotone. He'd never been a warm, fuzzy person to start with.

"You coming in?"

He seemed to hesitate, but then he stepped past me into the house.

"Where've you been?" I asked.

"Exile Park."

I fed him.

Exile Park. The rock bottom of rock bottom. I knew Cosmo had things bad, but this was a surprise.

I watched him shovel down the food. Microwaved rice and tilapia stew. He ate like people in war zones do, soldiers, correspondents, and the like, not pausing to speak, not fully chewing the food, just getting it into the stomach as efficiently as possible. I got him seconds before he could ask. I sat across from him, smoking.

Cosmo Adepitan. We went to university together, though always at the periphery of friendship. He was always the friend of a friend, so our orbits overlapped, and we knew of each other rather than knew each other. He was a socialist, maybe an anarchist back then, I can't remember. I know his girlfriend at the time had a sugar daddy who happened to be an officer in the military. I know soldiers with guns came for him one night and he disappeared. Whether it was his politics or his woman that led to the attack was unclear, but he was never seen or heard from again. People thought he had been Erased.

"Nobody gets rich until nobody is poor," I said.

"What?" asked Cosmo.

"Isn't that what you say in Exile Park? Nobody gets rich until nobody is poor?"

Cosmo swallowed the last morsel the way he did the first, savoring nothing. He wiped his mouth against the back of his right hand and turned to me.

"Francis, can I ask a favor?"

I nodded.

"I need you to come see something."

"In the Park?"

"Yes."

"I'm never setting foot in there, Cosmo. Donna would kill me."

"Bring her," said Cosmo. "We could use her expertise."

"It's not that simple. We have a child now."

"There are children in Exile Park. Your child won't burst into flames."

I giggled. "You clearly don't know Janet."

"Will you come?" Cosmo was always so earnest and he hadn't changed.

"Can you tell me what it's about?"

"I'll tell you when you get there."

I laughed, dragged on my cigarette.

"Well?"

"Let me talk to my family."

"NO," SAID DONNA. "THAT PLACE IS MADE OF PLASTIC. NO. THERE'S MICROFIBERS IN the water, even. No."

OKAY, EXILE PARK IS AND ISN'T MADE OF PLASTIC.

Back in 2077, we had plastic mega-islets. Don't ask me why they didn't just call them islands. The convention was the country in whose national waters the mega-islet drifted was responsible for cleaning it up. Which sounded fair, but wasn't. Most of the plastic came from highly industrialized nations, and when one drifted close to Lagos, Nigeria simply refused to play ball. They disavowed the mega-islet and the entire area, which was a risky thing to do. Anyone could plant a flag on it and claim the waters. Nobody did, but they could have.

This thing drifted sluggishly in the Gulf of Guinea for years. It was so big, you could see it from Tarkwa Bay and Victoria Island. It had its own ecosystem and the ocean flora and fauna, who waste nothing, accreted, claimed it as home, further tied it together. A lot of that part of Lagos was full of reclaimed land anyway, so you can see where this is going.

DONNA WAS A CONSULTANT IN PUBLIC HEALTH OR COMMUNITY MEDICINE AS SHE insisted on calling it. Cosmo knew this.

True story, Donna proposed to me by miming Marva Whitney's *What Do I Have to Do to Prove My Love to You*. You had to be here. She was such a serious person most of the time, and I didn't even know she took me that seriously in our sporadic relationship.

"You can come with me," I said to her. "You'll keep me out of trouble."

"Where are we going?" asked Janet, sweeping in.

And that is how Cosmo got three of us to follow him back to Exile Park.

THE ONE THING I REMEMBERED ABOUT COSMO IS HE HAD A PROBLEM WITH FIGURATIVE speech. He didn't get metaphor. He had no imagination and I think he had no mental imagery at all. Aphantasia. As we made our way over water, Janet sketched his profile a number of times. She was excited and not taking no for an answer and I should have been harsher in my discipline, but I wasn't. Life was hard enough and she was just a few bus stops away from adulthood where the usual horrors awaited. I would give her the things she asked for that I could give, all under Donna's disapproving glances.

There were no checkpoints. The coast guard was not in evidence, and even if they were, nobody harassed those coming from or going to Exile Park, not even bribe-hungry Nigerian officials.

When the islet loomed, Janet changed her subject from Cosmo to the edifice. We were headed south and it was sunset, the dying light casting an orange hue on the west side, leaving much of the rest in shadow.

From this direction, at this distance, at this time of day, it looked like a natural rock formation poking accusingly into the sky. At God, maybe. A multitude of antennae gave it a hairy appearance, with solar panels forming bald spots of sorts. The buildings grew organically, sideways, and one upon the other, rising from the plastic foundation. Each living space was boxlike, rhomboid in cross-section, and precarious. No architect had planned this, no municipal services from the mainland had contributed.

Getting closer, the external surface was covered in bamboo scaffolding from which cables and wires hung. Thicker cables plunged into the sea and, at some distance, towers for tidal energy plants loomed in silhouette. Exile Park did not admit to siphoning power from the mainland, but it was rumored to be a significant percentage of their energy use. I couldn't see it, though. It seemed such an undertaking would be impractical.

Closer still we encountered other boats returning to the mainland after a busy working day. Whatever else it may have been, Exile Park was a market and people plied their trade while floating in the artificial bay created by plastic arms. Commerce must commerce. These boat traders were never allowed on the island. On the other hand, fishing boats returned to the island in the same direction as us, tooting horns and ringing bells, maybe to warn loved ones of their impending arrival.

Perhaps because of Cosmo, other vessels parted to let us dock first. We ducked under the chicken wire that skirts the structure like an apron, and on which rubbish had accumulated, no doubt thrown from above.

"Follow me," said Cosmo. "Don't stop for anybody. Don't answer any questions."

I brought up the rear so I could keep an eye on Janet and Donna. We were in a tunnel, wet floor, moist air, dimly lit for the most part. The floor inclined upward and every few yards or so there would be two steps. The cables coiled in at the entrance and stuck to the ceiling except where they broke off into a doorway or inexplicably dropped to the floor and continued up. Donna crouched quickly and was up before anyone but me could notice, but I'm sure she just took a sample. I heard talking drums start up a beat and hand it off on each floor, following our party. I didn't know what they said, being white and an outsider, but I could see how they were once used to send coded messages in ancient times.

Without warning Cosmo stopped and opened a door to our left.

It wasn't bad, as such things go. It was a square space, two single beds on opposite sides, a window, walls of indeterminate color, a cooking unit of some kind in a corner, a wooden table on which a table fan labored ineffectively. A door led into what I hoped was a bathroom.

"I'm sorry, but this is all we have," said Cosmo. "I know it's nothing like your home, but you won't be here long."

"It's perfectly fine," said Donna. No strain in her voice. Hmm.

Janet was quiet, but took pictures. That child can be a pain, but she knows when to shut up, bless her.

"Cosmo—" I said.

"I know, why are you here? You're here because of crime."

SIX WEEKS AGO . . .

On the various roofs of Exile Park there is grass, more like scrub, but enough to nourish livestock like goats and dwarf cows. The soil was brought to the island in buckets and bowls and bags, all from the mainland. There was, of course, more than enough organic waste for bespoke fertilizer. The raised edges of the roof helped to minimize wind erosion, and the entire windward side was shielded with a metal screen.

On any given day the roof would be calming, with ruminants chewing either fresh grass or the cud. Baby goats frolicked in their way.

On this day, there was no eating or gamboling. The animals all collected on one side of the west roof. On the other side, blood-smeared grass, blood-dampened soil, and a body hacked to pieces.

"I'M NOT A DETECTIVE," I SAID.

"Oh, we don't want you to solve individual crimes. This is as close to a sealed environment that you can get. We already know the culprits. That's not the problem."

"So what do you—"

"I want you to look at a population effect. Numbers. Quantitative analysis with some qualitative detail. I don't want to tell you what to look for, because I don't want to prejudice your findings." Cosmo handed me a Portable. I hadn't been sure they had those here.

"The toilet's weird!" Janet shouted from somewhere. Donna shushed her.

"I could have looked at numbers at home," I said.

"Look at the numbers first," said Cosmo. "We'll talk tomorrow."

"How do I reach you?"

"Three-oh-one," he said. He pointed to the corner. On a rude stand, a wired phone. I tracked the cable down the floor and into a hole in the wall.

After Cosmo left we bedded down for the night to the sound of Exile Park groaning and settling like an old house.

I GOT UP EARLY AND SAT AT THE TABLE, GOING THROUGH THE PORTABLE.

The pattern was easy to see.

There were raw numbers and narrative contextuals. The amount and ferocity of crime in Exile Park had increased at an alarming rate, although they did not call it crime. They had a term, social harm. This is one of the things that confounds outsiders about Exile Park. It's portrayed in Nigerian media as lawless, and this is technically true, but only because there are no laws. Exile Park didn't count crime, it counted Acts of Social Harm, ASH. In Nigeria, crime is about violation of criminal law and law is defined by the State. A corporation might cause widespread contamination of the environment, which may not be a crime, but it's social harm, and the founders of Exile Park were fans of zemiology. They build their society on a foundation of minimizing social harm. But no matter which way you cut it, a person dead at the hand of another could not go unanswered.

Violence in the last year of Exile Park exceeded that of its entire history combined.

TETHERED TO THE BAMBOO SCAFFOLDING, AANU OLOJA SCRAMBLED ABOUT ON THE leeside of Exile Park, which faced the inlet and Lagos. Beneath her, desalination complexes, netting, and seawater. A comms engineer, Aanu connected customers to wireless networks for entertainment and learning. It was steady work, and required maintenance because the exposure to the elements wasn't conducive to antenna placement, but she enjoyed it and was unbothered by heights.

Any given day her tiny figure could be seen orchestrating insane goings-on with cables and multimeters, with her apprentice Benjamin Woo calling the plays over the radio. What happened next was unclear. Witnesses gave differing accounts, although that wasn't unusual.

Aanu grabbed a live wire and got electrocuted. It was, as such things go, not a lethal dose of electricity. She fell and should have been pulled up short by her tethers. She wasn't. All three of her tethers snapped and the discombobulated Aanu plunged into the deep.

Her body was never recovered.

"WE COULD NEVER PROVE IT, BUT WE THINK HER LINES WERE SABOTAGED," SAID Cosmo. "Aanu weighed nothing. It's often wet out there and she'd lost her footing thousands of times, no problem. She's as Spider-Man out there."

"You suspect Benjamin Woo?" I asked.

"Folks in the flats nearby said they heard Aanu confirming the status of the cables with him. He assured her the line was inert."

"The cables look pretty messy and disorganized."

"To outsiders," said Cosmo. "Woo's the comms engineer now, with an apprentice of his own just in case he takes a swan dive."

I nodded. I pointed to the figures. "You wanted me to confirm your findings. Violent crime, violent ASH is up. The figures do not provide me with an explanation. There's no bump in population. I don't know if there are deprivation changes."

Cosmo stands. "Come with me. It's time to show you."

JANET WANDERED DOWN WHERE THE MOISTURE INCREASED WITH THE WIDTH OF THE passage, taking photographs as she went. Everyone she encountered had well-insulated, water resistant safety boots, the kind she associated with offshore oil workers. They didn't stare at her. She saw no children, but it was morning, and she assumed they were in school. The wall indicated she was on or near Column III. Janet took a picture of the sign.

The ground lurched, and a heavy vibration rumbled through. Janet grabbed a hold of a cable to keep upright. It sounded like a train, but they didn't have trains on Exile Park, did they? The sound of metal groaning descended on her and thoughts of a tsunami or undersea earthquake played with her calm. The whole thing lasted eight minutes—she counted. She was rattled, but she had ambitions of being a photojournalist, of not depending on drones and being in the heart of the action herself. This was nothing.

She briefly considered going back to the flat, but continued downward instead.

I TRIED TO KEEP TRACK OF WHERE COSMO TOOK ME. THE SIGNAGE ON THE WALL seemed arcane, but he barely glanced at it. At times people would stop and ask him something and he would answer in soft, rapid tones that I could not keep up with.

As if reading my mind, he said, "There's a local shorthand we use in speech that might be difficult for you. Everybody speaks pidgin in addition, and most speak English, so don't be concerned."

This was a wider passageway than any of the others. It could easily accommodate seven people walking abreast. There were more people too, although it seemed to me like they were loitering, which wasn't something I had seen in Exile Park. The air was fresher, colors brighter. It was all a kind of green-grey wash of some kind, but the impressions were sharper. Even my own skin seemed radiant. I passed my hands in front of my face and I felt a strong urge to laugh. They strobed.

"It can be disorienting at first," said Cosmo.

"What can?"

"The euphoria, the sense of well-being."

I laughed. It came out as a bark. "I have no idea what you're talking about."

The low hum of people talking. They seemed cheerful, like the crowd fifteen minutes before a concert. I decided this feeling was abnormal and I started looking for ventilation.

"Are they . . . is someone . . . this is pharmaceutical," I said.

"You're not used to it, so it's affecting you more, that's all. Nobody from the outside has ever been this close."

"To what?"

Cosmo points. "To her."

The passage curved slightly and terminated in a dais on which she was suspended in a glass room. I say "she" because Cosmo did. There was no way of telling. She was old, skinny, and every inch of her skin was covered in visible veins, so much so her skin seemed green on first glance. The skin itself was composed of commodious redundant folds that created sulci, giving it a striped pattern in some areas, reticulate in others. It reminded me of the surface of the brain.

In my mind, I knew there should be some revulsion, but I couldn't feel it. That sense of well-being from before persisted and became stronger. I looked at Cosmo and . . . Was that a smile on his face? This whole thing felt like religious awe, like I was in the presence of a god.

With great effort I said, "I would like to leave this place, Cosmo."

CONTRARY TO WHAT MY BRAIN WAS TELLING ME, I HAD AN APPETITE AND ATE THREE fried eggs, two chicken wings, and two large slices of bread and butter. Cosmo drank coffee and watched me, our roles on the mainland reversed.

"What was that? Who was that?" I spoke with my mouth full.

We were in someone's flat. Hunger was my first sensation after seeing the god, and when I told Cosmo he started looking at doorways to flats. At first they had seemed similar to me, but now I could see subtle differences, and not just aesthetic ones. Beside each door, for example, was a panel, six by twelve inches. There was a column of glyphs, some lit up, others dark. We passed three before we saw one with the combination of glyphs Cosmo sought. This, he explained, was how nobody ever starved and food didn't go to waste. Those with excess announced it with the glyphs and literally anybody could come in for a meal.

"That was Olokun. Not sure if that's her real name, but it's *a* name we use for her." Cosmo sipped coffee. "She's been here from the beginning."

The host added another fried egg to my plate and I thanked him. "What happens when nobody is hungry for the excess?"

"Livestock, pets, composting," said Cosmo. "No hunger, no waste."

"What is Olokun?" I asked. "She's not human."

"She's human."

"Cosmo, I'm not stupid. I know what I saw, and what I felt."

"It's hormones, Cotillard."

"Explain."

"Olokun secrets agreeableness hormones into the air from her skin and from her bodily fluids. I can get you the studies, but last count she had forty-three volatile and two hundred nonvolatile hormones that she exposed all of us to."

"How?"

"As far as I know she was born that way. The folds of her skin increase the surface area of secretion. The veins efficiently transport her blood."

"That's amazing," I said. Then something occurred to me. "She's sick, isn't she? That's why you brought me here. Her volatile secretions are . . . my god, they've kept the cohesion of your little experiment. Now she's sick, it's not working, and people are getting violent with each other."

"She's not sick," said Cosmo. He dragged his chair back and stuck a cigarette in his mouth. "She's dying."

He left the room to smoke.

DONNA TOOK A SHITLOAD OF BLOOD FROM ME FOR TESTING.

"I'm fine," I said.

"You've been exposed to god knows what compounds that made you euphoric and then gave you the munchies. You are not fine until I say you're fine," said Donna.

"You're overreacting. The folks here are exposed to this every day," I said.

"Where's the child?" Donna liked to change the subject when she didn't like the direction.

"Off taking photos. Her beacon is loud and clear. I think you should examine Olokun."

"If I get protective wear. Why does Cosmo want you here?"

"He wants to know what happens when Olokun dies. He wants to know if this place will disintegrate into chaos. He wants to know what to do about it."

I could smell her hair and see the hair follicles on her skin as she worked. I experienced a sudden and powerful urge. "You know, Janet's going to be gone a while—"

"From the results I'm looking at, your arousal is not because of me. You're feeling frisky because there's a chemical in your system that causes a sexual response. I'm not sleeping with you, Francis."

"What? No, I'm just watching an intelligent, powerful, competent woman doing intelligent, competent, powerful things. It's a turn on."

"No."

"Fine. Don't blame me if I go and have wanton sex with the socialists, woman," I said.

"Be sure to get me some genital swabs if you do," said Donna. "I'm going to see if I can isolate a marker whose concentration I can measure in the air. What are you going to do, besides taking a cold shower?"

"Cosmo wants me to attend their parliament."

"They have a parliament?"

"Euphemistically, yes. For one thing anybody over sixteen can attend, comment, and vote. It's not based on representation at all. No one person outranks any other, except by competence. Competence means you get listened to and your opinion is weighted in your area of expertise. But only in your areas of expertise."

"Smart. No halo effect."

"So it would seem."

IT WAS A WARMER NIGHT. WARM NIGHTS IN EXILE PARK WERE NOISY AFFAIRS because a million air conditioners would come on at once. Most of the flats had no windows and had two, sometimes three air conditioners with no soundproofing. We got used to it, by which I mean Donna and Janet got used to it. I couldn't sleep so I poked through Janet's photos. Her camera had a device that sent all her photos to me and I told Janet she could disable it but she didn't. She wanted me to think she didn't care about what I saw, and I wanted to see what she was up to. Win win.

Janet and about seven of the local kids. Arms around each other's necks and carefree like only youngsters can be. One or two of them had the bowlegs that told me they weren't getting enough sunlight, but not as many as I would have expected. They seemed happy and well-nourished, for the most part. Good skin, too. Their clothes were clean, but I noticed signs of repair and reuse, which was good, I supposed.

She took a close-up of the ubiquitous collections of cables. They were bound together in places by wire, duct tape, even cloth. Sometimes alone, sometimes yoked with water pipes and slapdash signage.

She got shots of the massive support columns and their numbering. How far did that child wander? Most of the external walls of Exile Park weren't load-bearing. The flats and box-dwellings all connected to each other, but the weight was transferred to gigantic columns numbered I to VI. Each was ribbed with heavy-duty bridge cables, some of which coiled away and disappeared into walls and ceilings.

Janet even got into nurseries for the roof farms. Powerful lights shone down, ersatz sunlight for the delicate budding vegetation. The farmers smiled up at the camera.

She took a selfie and it made me sit up. I had to look at her asleep to assure myself she was safe. In the photo, behind and above her, hidden between girders on the ceiling, was a face.

PARLIAMENT.

Since everybody was allowed, I brought Janet and Donna with me. The room had a capacity of a few dozen, but it was also streamed through closed-circuit. Nobody sat in particularly lofty positions and there was no sense of rank or office. I did my thesis based on original fieldwork with fringe religions in Nigeria like Ekcankar, Guru Maharaji, and the Quakers. This was a free-form, no agenda meeting, like the Quakers. Silence, then someone speaks, then response, then silence as responses died down, then someone would suggest voting, they would vote, and the motion is dealt with. The only consistent action came from the people taking the minutes.

Cosmo stood up in a lull and introduced my family. "For recognition, Cosmo Adepitan. I introduce Francis Cotillard, invited by majority vote of this house on the Olokun matter. Accompanied by Dr. Donna Cotillard and Ms. Janet Cotillard."

All present banged their chairs, a welcome gesture.

"Do you feel up to giving your opinion on the data?" asked Cosmo.

I did.

My report, though dull, technical, and full of caveats, surprised nobody. I confirmed what they all suspected, and demurred when they asked for recommendations.

They adjourned, and we had the rest of the day to ourselves.

Donna, in spite of anything she might have said before, was intrigued by Olokun and, clad in protective wear, examined the god. Independent air tank, no part of her skin exposed, it looked like Donna was cleaning nuclear fallout. I didn't think it was necessary. Exile Park had its own doctors and nurses, and they'd already examined their god. Donna liked first-hand information and primary sources. She wasn't going to stop now.

"I estimate her body surface area is 300 percent that of a person of her average mass. The folds of skin can be stretched and the veins are pulsatile," said Donna.

We talked through a radio she rigged. I was walking the passageways looking up. Janet was off doing some busywork I gave her—photograph the ships coming in, something like that.

"Pulsatile?" I wasn't paying full attention, but I had read somewhere that if you repeat the last word someone says, they think you're listening.

"I know you're not listening, Francis," said Donna.

Shit.

"I really want to know. Why is pulsatile noteworthy?" I shone a torch between the cables on the ceiling. There seemed to be space there.

"Superficial veins don't usually have a pulse. Arteries do. There are exceptions, but I think this is an adaptation of some kind. The high pressure helps force out the hormones."

"The hormones, huh?" There was space up there, a gap between cable bundles and hard ceiling, one that a man could hide in. But why?

"Hepatomegaly. Liver's large," said Donna. Mostly to herself.

"Does she not mind you poking about her innards?" I asked.

"I don't think she's even aware I'm here. Her eyes aren't tracking me. Her motor reflexes are barely there."

I tried to find a foothold. I jumped, grabbed the wrong pipe, and screamed.

"What?" said Donna. Concern now.

"Stupid. Hot water pipe. Nothing to worry about." I was definitely expecting a scald on my left palm. If it was that hot, then anybody crawling around up there would have to know what to avoid. It didn't make sense, but the face was there. I didn't draw Donna or Janet's attention to it.

"Douse it in cold water as soon as you can," said Donna. "I think I'm done here."

AT NIGHT, OUTSIDE, IN WHAT PASSED FOR A BAY, PEOPLE SET UP FLAME GRILLS AND sold the day's catch as fried fish snacks. Donna, Janet, Cosmo, and I sat on an iron bench, eating piping hot fish and watching the lights. Drums played, people sang.

Cosmo, who had looked derelict when he came inland, cleaned up well. He was like a different person, although still driven.

"Does she ever talk?" asked Donna.

Cosmo shook his head. "No. The last coherent word from her was fifteen years ago. There's a book floating around, *Awon Oro Olokun*, but I think some of it is cribbed from Nietzsche."

"I agree with your doctors, Cosmo. She's dying," said Donna. "And soon. The marker I set up . . . well, the levels are falling precipitously."

"If the hormones Olokun releases are what keep us . . . docile, will our way of life survive her death?"

"That's a question for Francis," said Donna. "But you have options."

"Such as?" Cosmo seemed to have blocked out every other stimulus except Donna.

"Life-support machine, keep her alive indefinitely," said Donna.

"Doesn't she have to consent to that?" asked Cosmo.

Donna shrugged. "I'm a 'needs of the many outweigh that of the individual' kind of person."

"Here we value both the individual and the many equally. We take individual freedoms seriously. The collective won't want to survive by trampling on the rights of the individual."

"I'm just naming options," said Donna. "Francis? Wanna weigh in?"

"I'm thinking."

I looked out at the lights of Lagos, twinkling, reflected on the sea, beckoning with the simplicity of my normal life. I fiddled with the bandage on my left hand.

"I'm thinking."

THEY TOLD ME THEIR STORIES, THE PEOPLE OF EXILE PARK. THE GAY COUPLE WHO had escaped stoning in the North. The one who had dared run against the president as an independent. The man who, inspired by Reich, rigged up an orgone energy transmitter on the highest roof. The ones who provided a free internet plug-in that thwarted surveillance. The repentant gun runners. The journalists, the many, many journalists. The osu, outcasts from the East, a resurgence of something thought forgotten. The painter of a hundred Madonnas, all subversive in some way or the other, either of corrupt visage, or corrupt implications, tainted halos, sexualized, covered in filth, cadaverous. A guy shot to death and dropped in the sea who washed up stuck on a plastic rock in the inlet, twenty-seven bullet holes in him, but still alive. People like Cosmo who escaped assassins. People who *were* assassins, reformed of course. The people who fled rival gangs. The people driven out by aggressive developers. Filmmakers who made films of the wrong kind, political or pornographic. Or both. The thug who had knuckle tattoos; THOUGHTS on the right, PRAYERS on the left.

They all heard of Exile Park by word of mouth and risked everything to get here. Everything was forgiven once you were doused in brine and passed through the pearly gates of the inlet and took the communion of Olokun, the plastic god of exiled Nigerians.

I SHOWED COSMO THE PHOTO, FOCUSING ON THE FACE.

"I don't know who that is, or why he is up there," he said.

"Do you have dissidents? Insurgents? Sexual predators?" I asked. "Is there an underclass here that I don't know about?"

"This is new," he said. "I'll flush him out. It might be an example of the new aggression."

Cosmo gives me a copy of *The Words of Olokun*, the English translation of *Awon Oro Olokun*.

"Great. Homework," I said.

THE YOUNG OLOKUN GOT AROUND.

She visited the north of Nigeria, where there was a persistent rash of suicide bombings. She quietly moved into an abandoned property and waited. They stopped within a week, according to her.

She traveled the world, masked, robed, because she was self-conscious about her looks.

She did know love. All who came close to her loved her, and the ones she chose for physical pleasure almost died of it. Some went mad from too much dopamine, and she realized she could not tell those who loved her for herself from those who just reacted to the chemicals she secreted. She restricted herself to carnal pleasures and left her heart untouched.

Back to the south, but warned by the Nigerian government. Stay out of our affairs. She could have brought peace to the whole nation, but that wasn't what they wanted. So she left. She had to keep moving. Egypt, Tanzania, Ghana, DRC, even Cape Town. If she stayed too long, people suffocated her without knowing why they were drawn to her.

Everywhere I went, there were those who were drawn to me and those sent by the State to follow me. I was an antidote to the war machines, which meant some factions would not make money out of manufactured outrage. They sent assassins after me. Tearfully, each of the killers confessed to me and asked for my forgiveness. One of them dedicated a shrine to me in Cuilacán.

But it was exhausting for her, and lonely. She wanted to disappear and rest.

Exile Park was perfect. When she heard of the disputed plastic mass, she moved there and settled. She had purpose.

It might be that the translation was off, but Olokun seemed to say a lot about peace.

This is my total art.

I am your kick start. What you do next is up to you. My gift is peace, a moment to breathe.

What do you do with the gift of peace?

Total art.

Did she know she was dying? There was no indication in her writings.

Reminded me of an architecture term, gesamtkunstwerk. Is the society in Exile Park Olokun's art? How will it continue without the hormones?

Tremors. The rattle woke Janet briefly, then she turned over and was asleep again. Donna didn't stir. Both of them, the sum total of my love.

I went back to reading.

COSMO HAD BEEN EXPLORING THE ROOF AND CABLE SYSTEMS FOR TWO HOURS when I joined him.

"Can't sleep," I said.

Cosmo shrugged. "I've been over this length and breadth. Nothing yet."

Janet's photos were geotagged, however, and I took Cosmo to the exact spot the photo was taken. Cosmo stared. Then he looked at my belly, checking how fit I was. Not very.

"I'm going up there," he said. "Give me a boost."

"Watch out for the hot water pipe," I said.

Cosmo pulled himself up and I watched his boots disappear into a tangle of black, grey, and red serpentine shit.

Silence, then scuffling sounds.

"*Oh, fuck!*" Not Cosmo's voice.

I was still trying to decide what to do. Who do I call? I couldn't get up there without help.

"Francis! Look out!" yelled Cosmo.

"What?" I asked.

I heard a creak, then a loud vibration. Cracks appeared in the ceiling and it ruptured, caved. Dust, water from burst pipes, sparks from electric cords. The lights in the corridor flickered. And a compact camouflage-green jeep fell out of the roof into the passageway right in front of me. It bounced on its springs before coming to rest. Internal combustion energy, two-seater, madman in the driving seat. The engine was running and acrid exhaust filled the corridor. Screeching as the wheels spun. It came for me. I made myself small on the side wall and it spun me around as it passed. The driver's eyes . . . same as in the photo.

It gunned down the corridor, hit one of the corners, corrected itself, powered on out of sight.

Talking drums broke my spell and people started to arrive. Did they have police in Exile Park?

"Francis," yelled Cosmo from upstairs. "You're going to want to see this."

ACCORDING TO ACCOUNTS THAT I PIECED TOGETHER LATER THE JEEP WENT ALL THE way down, scratching the walls, hitting four men and two women in its path till it smashed into the netting at the exit. It hung over the water for a time, but the net couldn't hold its weight and it broke free with a generous section of the barrier before it plunged into the dark waters.

Nobody dove after, even though I know they have an on-call rescue team. Emphasis was on looking after the injured and repairing the fence.

Everybody kept looking out for a floater over the next few days, then weeks, but nothing came back up or clogged the pumps. People assumed the driver escaped by some other means or a bloated body was trapped in the car on the seabed. Which was a shame. I had many questions for him.

Cosmo told me people spotted Nigerian gunboats hovering a few nautical miles out, but never engaging. There were stories of special forces diving, maybe searching for the body, but the tales were as substantial as smoke.

THEY EXPELLED US FROM EXILE PARK. HERE'S WHY.

I crawled up into the space Cosmo invited me to. It was . . . a nest, I guess. A spy's nest. Saboteur. Saboteur-spy. In the nest were charts, sixteen high-quality cylindrical tanks with timers, and keypad security. High-gain radio hardware. No identifying information, some coded writing that the best cryptographers Exile Park had to offer couldn't crack. There were some diagrams, though, that very clearly spoke to the support structure of the plastic island. All the columns identified, plus how to reach their lowermost points, where they sank into the island's "crust."

The one word that was recognizable out of all this guy's shit was ideonella, and that scared folks, for good reason. Way back in 2016, before living memory, scientists discovered *ideonella sakaiensis*, a bacterium that digested common bottle plastic. Prior to that plastic had been thought to be nonbiodegradable. We've come a long way since then, and though it's hellishly expensive, with the help of *ideonella* species variants, we can digest most plastic polymers now.

Including the ones that formed Exile Park.

It seemed our saboteur was an agent of the Nigerian government, although we couldn't prove it.

I followed the expedition into the bowels of the island, at the bases of the columns, and there were plastic liquefaction pools everywhere. Columns III and IV were out of alignment, the engineers said.

Parliament was packed full, oversubscribed. Panic first, then anger, then calm.

Could the damage be reversed or would they have to evacuate the Park? The vote against exodus was almost unanimous. They would fix the problem or die. Nobody wanted to go back to Nigeria.

"But we have to be more careful of outsiders," said a vocal fifteen-year-old.

Everyone turned to me and my family. I had seen it coming and I didn't wait for it to be put to vote.

In three hours Exile Park receded in the view above the frothy wake of Cosmo's skiff.

Janet took no pictures.

I WROTE A STRONGLY WORDED ESSAY ABOUT EXILE PARK WHEN I GOT BACK TO THE world. It was published, but nobody read it. I was critical of the Nigerian government, but I don't think they throttled it. I think most people were uninterested in what was an artefact of disobedience at best, an example of an anarcho-socialist existence that worked. So unthreatening was my article that nobody came for me in the night, or summoned me to CID at Alagbon Close.

Cosmo contacted me a few months later, told me Olokun died, sent me some screen grabs of her funeral at sea. That left me deeply sad for some reason.

I wrote this out of that grief, to purge it, and to create some kind of record.

It didn't work.

I'D FORGOTTEN ALL ABOUT THE PARK, AND I WASN'T PAYING ATTENTION WHEN Janet selected shots for her latest exhibition. She talked it over with Donna, though.

I wore my good suit. I shouldn't have because everyone else was casual, including Donna.

She called it *Down and Out in Exile Park*. Ironic, of course, because of the joy on the faces of the subjects. One hundred shots, half of those in black and white. She had an eye, that offspring of mine.

She brought a tear to my eye with the final piece: A six-foot shot of Cosmo in his skiff at sunset, looking toward Exile Park, squinting from the ocean spray, and a plaque with excerpts from my essay.

Home that night and I did a search to find out what happened to Exile Park. Not only was it still going on strong, it had inspired the Exile Park Experiment, spaces in seventeen countries where communities were built along Exile Park lines. They seemed to be thriving.

Olokun's dream.

She would be proud.

Daryl Gregory

The Country Doctor

THE DOCTOR'S PERPETUALLY SHORT ON SLEEP, SO SHE'S NOT HAPPY TO BE WOKEN up by the rumble of the garage door. That's an alarming sound for a woman who lives alone with a kid too young to drive. She lurches groggily to the window, looks down. Her car, a white Audi, glides out of the garage, its high beams diffused by the smoke.

She shouts, wide awake now, and throws herself down the stairs. Gets stymied for a moment by all the locks on the front door. Why did she install so many? Finally she's out, the dry grass pricking her bare feet. The taillights are moving away through the gritty smog. The car's going slow, obeying the neighborhood speed limit. She runs after it, shouting. The air rasps her throat, and the campfire smell fills her nose. She shouldn't be out here without a mask, much less be sprinting. Or what if the robbers decide to shoot her?

The car reaches the intersection, pauses cautiously. She's going to catch it! Then it turns left and accelerates away.

There's no one behind the wheel. The Doctor screams a few curse words.

She goes back inside, slams the door shut, then coughs and spits ash. The campfire smell is in her nostrils. The AQI seems worse than yesterday. She tells the house to turn up the air purifiers and call the police.

The 911 bot asks her what her emergency is. She tells it she needs to contact police, human police, live police. Her car's been hijacked.

The chatbot apologizes. "All of our officers are busy helping other customers. The wait to speak to an officer is currently . . ." The slightest pause. "Indefinite. If you have a premium customer code, speak it now."

"Fuck you," the Doctor says. This is not a premium customer code.

The Doctor's daughter comes downstairs, still in pajamas though she looks like she's been awake for some time. The girl starts to list all the major fires currently burning in Northern California.

"Not now," the Doctor says. The girl isn't wearing her Miss Mote glasses, so there's no app to tell her that the expression on her mother's face is a mix of worry and frustration, on top of the usual layer of long-term anxiety and low-grade depression—and no app to prompt her to say something kind. No, it's Doctor Soothe Thyself time, and the Doctor's not sure she's up for it. Too much is happening, all at once: the divorce, the move south to this suburb of a suburb, the new job, all in the middle of fire season. Her daughter needs to be in her sixth-grade class in ten minutes, and her patients are waiting for her. She needs her fucking car!

Her daughter's staring at her. The Doctor feels bad for snapping at her. "Audi Murphy's been hacked," the Doctor says, using the name the girl's other parent gave the car. "Either that, or it's decided to run away from home."

"This isn't home," the daughter says.

The Last Cowboy

THE LAST COWBOY NOSES HIS TRUCK FORWARD, TOWARD THE DOZEN OR SO protestors blocking the farm gate. He's barely moving but he does not stop completely, and soon he's surrounded. They're waving their umbrellas and chanting about sentience and complicity and suffering. The faces on the umbrellas are also chanting. The roar of his air conditioning is drowning out a lot of the words, but it seems they also do not like his truck, a gas burner.

He keeps his eyes straight ahead, nursing the brake, and his right hand rests on the butt of his pistol. A pair of women who look like twins in their white shirts and matching sunglasses stand their ground, their backs to the metal gate topped with razor wire. That metal surface is glowing like a stove in the bright sun. The Cowboy has no respect for the virtual protestors on the umbrellas, but he's got to tip his hat to these in-person folks braving the 125-degree heat.

A minute into this slow-motion confrontation, his grill's practically touching the women, their heads looking at him over the hood. He squints and nudges the vehicle forward. The gate starts to swing open behind the women, and the farmer is there, holding a shotgun. The women can either back up onto the farmer's property—a risky move—or get out of the way. One of them slams the hood of his truck and shouts something about his parenthood. Then they move aside.

Once the gate's closed behind him he lets the farmer climb into the cab. The Last Cowboy asks her, "That happen every day, or did they know I was coming?"

"Every damn day," the farmer says. She's a clear-eyed woman with a ruddy face. She directs him down a long road through empty, grassy fields that once fed thousands of cattle. She complains about taxes, especially the carbon impact tax and the new one, the suffering tax. "What about *my* suffering?" the farmer asks.

"I hear you," the Cowboy says. He eases the truck into the barn. The farmer hops out to close the doors behind them, to give them privacy from telephoto lenses and protestor's drones. The farmer wants only her own barn cameras to document this moment.

Two huge electric coolers sit on the floor, already loaded and sealed. The Cowboy asks to open them; he likes to set eyes on what he's hauling. She presses a thumb to the first cooler's lock and pushes up the lid.

The beef carcass is a big 'un, seven to eight hundred pounds hanging weight, and gorgeous. Fresh pink muscle, white marbled fat. Worth $30K, unprocessed. The second carcass is just as big and just as pretty. The farmer shakes her head. "You know my kids won't even eat real meat? Not that I can afford it. But they won't even try."

The Cowboy agrees that this is a damn shame.

"I just don't know how it all changed so fast," the farmer says. "I ate meat every day growing up. Sure, there were vegans and vegetarians, but most people loved a good steak or a chicken dinner, but now . . . ?" She shakes her head. "I think it's the schools."

The Cowboy has had some variation of this conversation with every rancher he's worked with. It's the schools, or the government, or the media. Maybe all of them. One day not long ago, more people started eating soy meat and potato meat and lab-grown abominations than the real stuff—and then that's all people were eating.

"Thank God for the billionaires," the farmer says. "If it wasn't for them, this whole way of life would be over." The Cowboy's aware of the cameras and wonders if she's performing for her clients. Was this really anything like the old way of ranching? Bespoke beef, each steer as fussed over as a child star, filmed nonstop from birth to death, the videos and copyright part of the purchase price.

The farmer climbs into a forklift and loads the coolers into the bed of the Cowboy's truck. The vehicle sinks low on its shocks, very near its max

49

payload. The Cowboy throws a tarp over the coolers, and they stack up crates of carrots around them as a disguise.

The farmer wants to make sure the Cowboy can make it to the meat processor by end of day—the contract depends on it. To complicate things, the processor's up north, near the forest fires. "You catch on fire, we'll both be toast."

"I'll get there," the Cowboy says. "My word is my bond."

"No," the farmer says. "Your bond is your bond."

The Cowboy forces a chuckle. He doesn't mention that he can't afford insurance anymore. He'll be dead broke if he loses this load.

"One question," he says. "You got another way off this farm?"

The Prospector and the Gambler

THE PROSPECTOR AND THE GAMBLER ARE LONG-TIME PARTNERS WHO'VE MADE A lot of money together over the years. Like a lot of partners, they quarrel constantly. Most of the arguments boil down to attention management. What should they pay attention to, and when? Money. Safety. Love. Health. The usual.

They are also reconciled to the fact that they're stuck with each other. The Prospector and the Gambler are two modes of thought, two sets of ingrained habits, and two genders, inhabiting one person. They share a brain, a set of hands, and an ass that spends too much time in a chair. They are not insane. They know that biologically and legally they are a single individual, albeit one who prefers to think of themselves as a multiple and use the plural pronoun. The Prospector, however, has argued that since they started spending all their time alone these past two months, they're certainly *flirting* with crazy.

The Prospector is the practical one. Fiscally conservative, hardworking, unafraid of commitment. They also make most of the income, that's just a fact. It's the Prospector's efforts that fund the activities of the Gambler, a financial daredevil whose exploits sometimes pay off in spectacular fashion, but often go up in flames.

The Gambler, however, has more fun. And it's their turn in the chair this morning, so sit down and shut up, Prospector, it's playtime.

Oh, but what game to play? The options are endless. In the past hundred years, humans had turned every material and immaterial object into both a stock market and a futures market. Want to encode your own genome into the blockchain and sell it to pharmaceutical companies? No problem. Want to own shares in a million other people's genomes? Knock yourself out. If commodities weren't your thing, you could bet on events, anything from a soccer tournament to a political election to the date when the Greenland ice sheet calved from the Arctic. (Too late on that one, but you get the idea.) New commodities and events were invented all the time.

Take NFT ponies. The idea is decades-old: virtual horses, represented as unique variations of an algorithm stored in a blockchain, could be bought, sold, traded, "mated" with other algorithms—and raced, of course.

The track software simulated a thousand races between a set of contenders to develop the odds. Say that a horse named Nature's Miracle won two hundred of those sim races, making it a strong favorite. The track would then randomly select one of those thousand races to be the "real" race. But of course the track had an 80 percent chance of picking one of the eight hundred races Nature's Miracle didn't win. A bit of pari-mutuel fun. Years ago the Gambler spent a couple months developing statistical models that averaged a 4 percent monthly ROI.

At that point the betting became suitable for automation, and therefore a job, and therefore boring. The Gambler turned it over to the Prospector. The Prospector's job? Keep mining that seam until it tapped out—which indeed it did a few years later. A bunch of AI-driven smart money apps had jumped into the betting pools, shrinking the Prospector's share. The ROI went negative, so the Prospector pruned the project from their portfolio and moved on.

But while Gambler and the Prospector weren't paying attention, the digital thoroughbred game evolved into something positively baroque. The horse algorithms had been upgraded to full genomes, some based on real-life horses, which could be grown in virtual wombs, cared for in virtual barns, trained by either AIs or actual human beings, and then put out to stud. They'd even built a market for virtual jockeys. In short, the number of variables had exploded to the point that it had become a whole new game. In any betting environment this complicated, there's a preponderance of chalk players—bettors who merely accepted the track odds and bet on the favorites—and outright suckers. Their dollars swell the pari-mutuel pools and entice sharks.

Sharks like the Gambler. They'd woken up with some ideas for new atomic statistical terms that might play well with their old models. They demanded the chair from the Prospector and set to work.

The Gambler's elbow-deep in the code when Arty, their helper AI, makes a polite coughing sound.

"I told you, no interruptions, no exceptions," the Gambler says.

"My apologies," Arty says. "But you did say I should tell you when the nearest fire was less than ten miles away. The Belden fire just crossed that mark." The AI then spews details about wind speed, wind direction, and rate of progress.

"Let us know if it gets to five miles," the Gambler says, and keeps typing.

"There's one other thing," Arty says. "You asked me to monitor blue-chip stocks on the reputation markets." The Gambler thinks, we did? They don't remember it, but it does seem like something the Gambler would ask for. "One of the highest valued persons is the subject of a video posted on Chateau Marmont—and has seen extremely high engagement for the last fifteen minutes."

"Who?"

"Trading symbol THX."

"Well now."

Last year the Gambler had paid the monstrous subscription fee to get into Chateau Marmont, an exclusive social network popular among Hollywood types and tech billionaires. The celebrities there assumed they were talking amongst themselves, though the juiciest items always managed to leak to the public networks eventually. The key word is eventually. The Gambler had set Arty to lurk there to find actionable information, early.

"Fine, we have to pee," the Gambler says. "Put the video on in the bathroom." On the other side of the dark room, the bathroom light turns on. The work wing of the house was custom designed for efficiency. The 1,500 square feet are windowless, the walls thickly insulated, the air cool and pure. There's no sound except the murmur of the computer fans and the hum of the HVAC. The solid-state batteries in the floors make no noise. The fiber lines below the batteries ferry silent photons back and forth to a level 3 hub five miles away, a fat pipe with such low latency that the Prospector and the Gambler can do high-frequency trading with all the big exchanges—New York, London, Japan—all while keeping in constant communication with Arty. No human voices disturb them when they're working, not anymore. The Prospector has been morose about that, but the Gambler has argued that it's been great for their productivity. Look, they can pee and work at the same time—without even closing the bathroom door.

The Prospector and the Gambler sit on the perfectly warmed toilet seat and Arty lights up the wall. The video:

An old white man stands in a dimly lit kitchen. He's in his nineties but spry and handsome. You can see the movie star still in him. He walks over to a long countertop, where the body of a dark-headed younger man, in his thirties or forties, lies on his back, his face slightly turned away from the camera. His skin is blue-tinged, the lips washed out. The old man reaches into a drawer and takes out a kitchen knife. Shows it to the camera. The twinkle in his eye is familiar from dozens of movies. Then he plunges the knife into the young man's chest.

The Gambler and the Prospector yelp.

Over the course of four minutes, the old man proceeds to do severe things to the body. Near the end of the video, someone offscreen, probably the person holding the camera, laughs. The old man smiles his famous smile: bemused, almost a smirk.

The Prospector and the Gambler realize their heart is racing. They've never been good at parsing their own emotions, but they do recognize shock. They grew up watching that old man. He's widely regarded as the most beloved man in Hollywood.

"Arty, is this real?" they ask.

"Analysis so far reveals find no artifacts or evidence of manipulation."

"And it's really him?"

"Multiple facial, gait, and body recognition systems concur." Arty isn't one program, but a loose confederation of dozens of core services—natural language parsers, data miners, weather monitors, statistical analysis engines—each with their own dependent services handling many smaller, more specific jobs. (And each one consuming a tiny fraction of a dollar from their account every second it runs.) The thing the Gambler and the Prospector call Arty is an orchestrator who manages context and memory and mood modulators. It had turned out that AI orchestras fared much better with their own analogs to mood. "Fear" and its compadres—concern, doubt, outright paranoia—were useful inputs for all risk calculations. As was confidence.

"So you're sure," the Prospector says.

"Very close to sure," Arty replies. "The person in the video is almost certainly the person who matches trading symbol THX, who has one of the top moral ratings for the last five years."

"Holy shit," the Gambler and the Prospector say as one.

Tom Hanks is a cannibal.

The Country Doctor

THE POLICE ARE SUPPOSED TO CALL THE DOCTOR BACK WHEN THEY'RE FREE, BUT she can't waste any more mental energy worrying about the car right now—school's in session and her patients are waiting. She hands her daughter her standard breakfast, toast with olive oil and Manchego cheese (a concoction she's insisted on eating every morning since she was six) and sends her up to her room to change clothes and turn on her cameras—one before the other, please! Thank goodness the girl's twists are tight and she looks presentable.

The Doctor, however, is definitely not presentable. She throws on yesterday's top and last week's salwar, then runs to the living room and logs in to work.

The calendar starts a session with her first patient of the day. He/him, sixty-five, Huntington's disease, living in Modesto, fifteen miles from here. He's one of her few patients who can go outside on his own, even do his own shopping, but nobody's going out in this smoke. The room behind him looks clean and tidy. She asks how he's feeling and he says, "Just fine, Doc." She doesn't correct him. Stopped trying weeks ago. Legally she's not a doctor here—she's still waiting for her California Physician's and Surgeon's License—but she's the only medical professional her patients see on a regular basis. All the clients the insurance company has assigned to her have some type of dementia—Huntington's, Alzheimer's disease, Lewy body dementia, Wernicke-Korsakoff syndrome, FTD, CJD, NPH . . . the rainbow of cognitive disorders. If calling her Doc or Doctor reassures the patient, she's not going to take that away from them.

For a while, she forgot she was a doctor herself. Back east and twenty years ago, before she got married, and became other things. A ranch owner. A mother. A woman who had time to *crochet*. This VHV job's not close to perfect, but it's something. She likes being of use. What she doesn't like is starting the day so overwhelmed.

She runs through the checklist with the patient, covering everything from movement symptoms to mood. He has difficulty with words but manages to answer all her questions. Then he says, "How are *you* doing, Doc?" There's concern in his voice.

"Fine," she lies. "Thanks for asking."

The Doctor gets off the line three minutes early. She finds the Audi app, but it doesn't recognize her face, retina, or skin—and refuses to open. What the fuck? She's seen her ex use the app, and knows there are all kinds of useful widgets in there—Find My Car would be especially handy right now—but she's never had a reason to try them before now.

She's out of time. She visits the next patient, and the next. Then it's on to one of her favorites, Colleen: she/her, eighty-two, Lewy body dementia. She's the only patient who lives in the Doctor's town.

Colleen is not waiting in front of the camera. The Doctor clicks through the alternate views, and can't see the woman in any of them. She calls out, "Colleen! Are you in the bathroom?" It's the only room without a camera. The Doctor puts in a call to Audi while she waits. It's the same automated hell as it was with the cops: The bot can't help her, no one's available, would she like someone to call her back?

Colleen still hasn't appeared. The Doctor calls up the tracker. The woman's wristband is supposedly in her bedroom, but it's not visible on the camera. Did she somehow manage to take it off, or is Colleen hiding in the closet or something? The Doctor hopes the device is still on her body. Colleen's prone to both hallucinations and wandering. Several afternoons she's attempted to walk back to her old office at Indiana University—2,000 miles east. What if she's gotten out again? The Doctor calls her name for another minute, with no response.

She checks the map. Colleen's apartment is 1.4 miles away. If it were twenty a visit would be out of the question. If it were two blocks it wouldn't even be a question—the Doctor would just pop over. But this middle distance, in this weather, is simply questionable.

Legally the Doctor is not allowed to make non-virtual home visits—that first V in VHV is strictly enforced. The Doctor certainly won't be paid for any. If she believes a patient is having an emergency, the protocol is to call 911. Police and medical service providers who respond to the call will bill the insurer, who is also the Doctor's employer. Employees who call 911 do not stay employed.

Colleen has still not appeared on camera.

Okay, maybe the Doctor could zip over there and zip back. The only bus service in town runs to Modesto, so she starts checking on-demand cars—and is reminded why she took the Audi in the divorce. The rental prices are astronomical. Worse, the shortest estimated wait time right now is over an hour. How is an hour "on demand"? That's like walking into an Italian restaurant and demanding a cold lasagna.

She's going to have to walk.

Fuck.

And the Air Quality Index is 180.

Double fuck.

The Doctor jogs upstairs. She changes into more professional clothes, grabs a filtered mask, and slaps a screen on her arm. Then she walks into her daughter's room to tell her the situation—and sees that the girl's not in class. Her screens show only weather maps and live feeds of forest fires.

"Hey!" the Doctor says. Her daughter does not look away from the fire. "Put on your glasses and look at me."

The girl sighs, slips on the Miss Motes. Looks her mother up and down. "So," she says. "You're angry."

"You bet I am."

"The Mods are in danger," the daughter says. Mods is her name for her other parent: Moms or Dads, feminine one moment, masculine the next, always plural. The girl's never been good at reading human faces for emotion, but she's always had an instinctive understanding of her parents' flexible pronouns.

"I'm sure they're on top of it," the Doctor says. "Did you message them?"

"I didn't get a response."

"What a surprise," the Doctor says.

"Sarcasm," the girl says.

The Doctor feels bad about talking down her ex, especially in front of her daughter. She'd promised herself she wouldn't do that. "Listen, you get back in class. I've got to go take care of something. I'll be back in an hour. Maybe two."

"You're leaving the house?" Her voice rises.

"You'll be fine," the Doctor says. "The fires are two hundred miles from here. It's just smoke."

"*No*," the girl says, furious. "I am going with you." Spitting each word.

The girl has always had problems with emotion regulation. Even in the best of times, alterations to her routine could set her off, but since the divorce and the move she's been a four-foot-two Vesuvius. The fight could go on all day. The Doctor doesn't have all day.

"Fine," the Doctor says. "Get your mask and grab a liter of water."

The Last Cowboy

THE LAST COWBOY'S HANDS ARE SLICK ON THE WHEEL, AND HIS EYES ARE ITCHY. The farther north he drives, the thicker the smoke. The truck's air conditioner is blasting but particulates are leaking into the cab and he can smell the burning pine. The trusty Ford is laboring as it climbs into the mountains. The load is heavy and the gas tank's needle is dropping fast.

He gets out his phone, a rectangle of metal and glass separate from all other devices as God intended. He starts scrolling through the map, looking for a gas station along his path. It's slim pickings. California's gotten hostile to the old ways, especially NorCal. But he finds a station twenty miles up and not too far off the highway, so he makes it for it.

The smoke blocks the sun and obscures the road—the false twilight of fire season. The Cowboy's going slow, his fog lights on. Electric cars zoom up in his rearview and zip past him, their radar and lidars and whatnot unbothered by the grit. Reckless, he thinks.

He exits the highway where the map tells him, but sees nothing. Finally he spots the orange sign of the 76 station, struggling to be seen through the ashy soup. The station's nothing but a tiny store, a single traditional pump, and a mess of charging plates.

He pulls his bandanna up around his mouth and climbs down from the truck. The heat drops on him like an anvil. He keeps one hand on his holster, the other on his phone. Waves the screen at the pump. Nothing happens. Waves it again and a message appears on the pump's screen.

Hi, this planet-killing poison dispenser has been commandeered by Ethical Earth. Pay $250 now to unlock, and we'll make a donation in your name to a local charity that supports climate-change refugees.

What in tarnation? "No," the Cowboy says to the pump. "Hell no."

He marches over to the little store but there's no one inside, not even room for an attendant. It's wall-to-wall vending machines. What's the world coming to? Outside, a car rolls onto one of the plates, and the plate lights up. Of course *those* are working.

The Cowboy considers asking for help from the car's driver. It goes against his nature. But maybe the driver's a local and knows what's up. Maybe the Cowboy's using the wrong app. And he needs the gas.

He ambles toward the car, a white coupe turned gray with ash. He pulls down his bandanna and taps on the driver's side window. There's nobody in the front seats. He cups his hand to the window and peers into the back.

The car horn blares and he jumps back. The headlights flash.

"God damn it, I'm not trying to steal you," the Cowboy says.

The car lurches off the plate and flees toward the exit, skittish as a colt.

The Cowboy's alone at the station. He looks at the gas pump. Pictures shooting it.

He gets back in the truck, fuming. Scrolls his phone for more gas stations. There's another one forty or so miles down the road. He might could make it. Or he could get there and the pumps could also be locked up with ransomware.

A man can't be expected stand for this, the Last Cowboy thinks. It's literally highway robbery. But he can't risk running out of gas. He has meat to deliver.

He steps out to the truck and waves his phone at the pump.

Welcome back! The minimum donation is now $400. You should have paid the first time!

The Prospector and the Gambler

"DO YOU WANT ME TO PLAY IT AGAIN?" THE AI ASKS.

Of course the Prospector and the Gambler want to watch the video again, but there's no time. Footage like this will leak to the public networks any minute. If they're going to act, the Gambler thinks, they have to act now.

The Prospector has doubts. Even if the video is unaltered, what if it's just for some movie? What if the body's a prop?

If it is, the Gambler thinks, it's a fucking realistic one. The body had *depth*. Bones. Congealed blood. Removable organs. The question, the Gambler argues, is not whether the video or the body is real or fake. The question is whether it'll affect THX's reputation. A real video can look fake and do little damage. A fake video, even a crude fake, will cripple a sterling reputation if it confirms something the public already suspects. The Gambler believes that in this case there are two dueling beliefs in play. It's *Tom Hanks Is a National Treasure* versus *All Celebrities Are Depraved*. The reputation markets exist so you can bet on those beliefs like they're boxers.

But is this how *we* want to make our money? the Prospector asks. We *like* Tom Hanks.

Of course we do, the Gambler retorts. That's beside the point.

The Gambler changes tack. Look, this film is getting out, no matter what we do. Somebody is going to make money from the almost-sure drop in reputation—why not us?

But it's just not believable, the Prospector says. Hanks is too beloved for anyone to doubt him for long. And he has all his old charisma. Once he gets back in front of the cameras to explain himself, he'll win the doubters back. There'll be a rally, and his reputation will be right back where it started, maybe higher.

Ah, but the gap! the Gambler says, triumphant. Just give us a couple hours. A couple hours to work the doubt, and we'll make a shit ton of cash.

We're sure?

Almost certain.

The Gambler lives in almosts. They make money in the tipping points, when Almost Definitely So suddenly becomes Almost Definitely Not, and Not becomes So. The trick is spotting the shift and knowing when to jump sides. Most people pick a side and cling to it. This thoroughbred is unbeatable. California real estate always earns out. You will never leave me. They hang on until popular opinion shifts or their lives are in tatters. Most people, in short, are chalk players. Outright suckers.

The Prospector finally raises their figurative hands in surrender. Fine. Risk our hard-earned money.

The Gambler whoops in excitement. "Arty, what's the current price on THX?"

"853 per share, down from 858 a half hour ago."

"Borrow fifteen thousand shares, wherever you can get them," the Gambler tells the AI. "Then sell them all immediately."

Arty does not execute the command, but instead expresses concern, per the emotional settings the Gambler and the Prospector specified long ago. "That's nearly 12.8 million dollars," Arty says. "Do you really want to do this?"

The Prospector is distressed. If the stock goes down, they'll make a profit, yes, and if the stock goes up, they'll lose money—but there's no limit to the upper price of a stock. If it goes *way* up, they'll lose their proverbial shirt, and perhaps also pants and underwear—the entire proverbial wardrobe.

Arty makes a polite throat-clearing noise.

"Confirmed," the Gambler says. "Let's short America's Dad."

The Country Doctor

THE DOCTOR FIGHTS THE URGE TO HOLD HER DAUGHTER'S HAND AS THEY WALK. THE girl's never been a fan of physical contact, but if she were a couple years younger the Doctor would have held onto her just to keep her on the sidewalk. The smoke has become a dense, sandpaper fog. Trees materialize in their path. Ghost houses seem to drift forward like the hulls of great ships, their top floors lost in ashy clouds. The sun's been reduced to a faint orange haze—and yet it's still brutally hot.

The Doctor says, "How did it get bad so fast?"

"Adults ruined the planet," her daughter says.

"I mean since this morning."

"The wind's shifted. The Belden fire's just joined with the Meadows fire." This is a weather report from two hundred miles north. The girl's wearing her Miss Motes above her filter mask, but the Doctor suspects she's keeping them on not because she wants to engage more effectively with humans but so she can watch the screens while she walks. She's inherited an obsessive streak, and today her monofocus is trained on the forest fires burning near their former home.

"Don't worry," the Doctor says. "Fire season comes every year. The Mods will be fine."

She wishes she felt as confident about her patient, Colleen. If the woman is out in this heat and smoke, it could kill her.

The Doctor's shirt is ringing. She flicks the sleeve and a voice too soothing to be human thanks her for calling Audi-Volkswagen-Tata. The bot wants to know why she contacted the police first. The Doctor's annoyed that they know this. Does the police AI gossip with the Audi AI? Or are they one and the same?

"My car's been stolen," the Doctor says. Her voice is a little muffled by the mask. "I want to stop it."

The bot explains that for safety reasons they cannot stop the car while it's moving, but the primary owner may control many car functions through the app, such as flashing the lights, beeping the horn . . . the list goes on for some time.

"Fine, let me do that, then."

"Only the primary owner of the car can use those functions."

"I am the primary owner."

The bot explains that while she's a *registered* owner, she's not the primary one.

"What are you talking about? I own the title. It's *my car*."

Yes, she owns the physical car, the bot explains, but not the car's software subscription. And no, the car does not function without a subscription, and the transfer to a new subscriber cannot take place without the consent of the previous owner.

The Doctor screams, hangs up, and screams again.

Her daughter regards her through the Miss Motes.

"That's an appropriate response to tech support," the Doctor says.

"The glasses can't tell if you're making a joke."

"I'm dead serious."

"Noted."

The Doctor doesn't believe her ex deliberately sabotaged the car. Her former partner is many things, a lot of them contradictory: brilliant yet obtuse, obsessed with work yet eager for new experiences, emotionally distant yet suddenly effusive, hypercompetitive yet disdainful of status. They were a loving parent except when they forgot they were a parent. The one thing they're not is deliberately cruel. If the Doctor called them (and managed to get past their fucking AI butler) their ex would no doubt help her out. But Jesus Christ, during the whole damn divorce, they couldn't remember to turn over a fucking login?

The Doctor needs to calm down, but it's hard to take a calming breath when she's wearing a mask and the world is on fire. She walks in silence until the map shows that they've reached Colleen's apartment building. The ash is crusting her nostrils. She takes a long swig of water, then makes her daughter do the same.

"Ready for some old timey doctorin'?" the Doctor says with forced good humor. She hopes the glasses can't pick up on the falsity. "We're about to make what the history books refer to as a house call."

"Yee haw," the girl says.

The Last Cowboy

THE COWBOY'S BEHIND SCHEDULE, AND HE'S PUSHING THE TRUCK HARD NOW TO make it to the meat processor before closing time. The engines rev up the mountain. Headlights plow the smoke. He's mad at himself for driving so cautiously through the valley fog early in the day—that smoke seems like nothing now that he's in the mountains and hitting the thick stuff. He's mad at himself for paying the ransom, though he doesn't know what he could've done different. And maybe he's mad that he took the job at all.

The processor is in a tiny town called Belden, high up on Feather River Highway. The two-lane road's winding and narrow, sheer, dynamite-blasted rock on one side and a wall of pines on the other. He can't help but see the trees as latent fuel. California, he suspects, is itching to turn him and his sides of beef into barbecue.

What in hell is he doing out here?

This isn't the life he wanted. Everything's too complicated, changing too fast. He was born in the first pandemic and missed most of high school because of the second. Maybe that's why he never cared for people much.

His dad was an HR benefits specialist and his mom was a brand consultant. They were happy, but their lives weren't for him. He longed to live back in the days of his grandfather, in the 1980s. Grandad had two acres, a gas lawn mower, and three channels on the TV. A man didn't need more than that.

A shape rushes through the smoke from his left. No, many shapes.

The first body hits the side of his truck. He stomps the brakes and a mass of fur and antlers tumbles over the hood and smashes into his windshield. The airbag explodes—knocks his hands from the wheel, presses him back into the seat. The road drops away under his front wheels and the truck plunges down, then tilts sideways.

The Cowboy's head strikes the side window, and then there's a tremendous bang. The truck has smashed into something solid—a tree? Boulder? He stares through the starry windshield. The animal he struck has slid off. He can see nothing but trees and smoke. His ears are ringing.

The driver's door is jammed, but he climbs up and out through the passenger side. The heat has gotten worse. There's a sound in the air, a distant roar, like radio static. The sound of a forest burning.

He's standing in some kind of depression, not quite a ravine, deeper than a ditch. The truck's leaning on its side. One of the coolers sits ten feet away, ejected from the bed. The lid looks secure.

Well, shit.

There are headlights on the road above him. A car has stopped. A voice calls, "You down there! Is everyone okay?"

The Cowboy starts climbing up the bank. It's not easy. His eyes are blurry and he's pulled a muscle in his chest. A trim, white-haired man wearing a mask extends a hand and helps him up.

"A whole herd of deer," the Cowboy says. "They came out of nowhere."

"Running from the fire I expect," the old man says. "You all right? You bumped your noggin."

The Cowboy touches his forehead, and the fingers come away bloody. He's coming to terms with new facts. The fire is close, closer than he knew. And his truck and those coolers are not coming out of that ditch without a tow truck.

"Huh," the Cowboy says. "I guess I'm screwed."

"You're still breathing," the old man says. "Though we should probably get a move on."

Inside the car, the old man takes off his mask. He's older than the Cowboy expected, eighty at least. The electric car's not new, either, but it's

American-made. The old man does his own driving. They head south and downhill, away from the fires. The man tells him his house is the nearest place to stop that's out of the fire zone. They can patch him up there, and figure out how to get his truck. The Cowboy's not one for accepting charity from strangers, but this man has a kind, open face, and seems oddly familiar.

The old man turns off the highway onto a one-lane road that snakes down through the trees. He asks where the Cowboy was headed in this weather. The Cowboy's usually reluctant to talk about his work. There's a lot of anti-meat sentiment out there. But the driver seems like someone who respects tradition.

"Guess you could say I'm on a cattle drive." The old man is interested, and asks intelligent questions. The conversation keeps coming back to the Cowboy's dismay at how fast the old ways have disappeared. Hundreds of years of eating meat, now suddenly it's a social crime?

"That's the way it always is," the old man says. "When I was a young man, there wasn't any gay marriage. People thought it would never happen. A boy in a dress was something to laugh at on TV. Then suddenly gay folks getting married is not only inevitable, it seems obvious."

"Well of course anybody can marry anybody else," the Cowboy says. "That's not what I'm talking about."

"Okay then, marijuana. Psychedelics. Assisted suicide. Nobody in my day thought those would be legalized, certainly not in every state."

"But those are just . . ." There's a headache growing behind the Cowboy's eyes, and he's having trouble ordering his thoughts. "Those are just common sense."

"It always seems that way after the turning of the tide."

"I'm talking about something spiritual." He's surprised to hear those words come out of his mouth. He's not the poetic type. "It's sacred, one life giving itself to feed another. People don't understand what we're losing. Plant meat, lab meat, it ain't the same. It's soulless. I can sure taste the difference. I bet you can, too."

The old man gives him a long look. Turns his attention back to the road. "Maybe so," he says. "Maybe so."

They're on an even smaller gravel road now. The Cowboy hadn't noticed the transition. The drive ends in a large, empty field, the brown grass cut short, smart for fire season. In the center of the field is a sprawling ranch house guarded by a wide apron of cement. The smoke seems thinner here. The afternoon sun a little brighter, hurting his eyes.

At the door the old man says, "I do have some house rules." He nods at the holster on the Cowboy's hip. "If you don't mind."

The Cowboy doesn't like this. But a man's home, and so forth. He surrenders his piece, and the old man puts it in a large plastic box full of gardening tools. Closes the lid.

"I hope you'll excuse the mess," the old man says. "I've been living alone for a while."

The Prospector and the Gambler

"820," ARTY SAYS. HE'S UNDER ORDERS TO CALL OUT THE THX PRICE EVERY TIME IT changes.

It's an hour into the game of chicken: the Prospector and the Gambler versus everyone else in the reputation market. The Gambler's in the chair, watching the big screen, hands gripping the armrests. No way he's going to touch the keypad early. The Prospector sits in the mental passenger seat, covering his eyes.

"819."

The Prospector's sure something is wrong. The price has dropped thirty-four dollars since they sold, but most of that change was in the first twenty minutes. The last forty have been creeping down, sometimes by pennies. The video, it's clear, is not going to make a difference. Who cares about viral videos anymore?

Arty says, "The county has issued an evacuation order for this area."

"Never mind that," the Gambler says. There was an evac order twice a year. "Is the fire more than five miles away?"

"Yes, just barely. However, wind speeds and shearing have increased significantly. Also, the latest THX price has moved up to 825."

The Prospector yelps. It's going back up! We hit bottom. Buy back!

Calm down, the Gambler thinks. If they unwound their position now, bought back all the stock they'd sold and returned it to the owners, they'd only keep about $500K of the 12.8 million. The Gambler didn't make this move to make a lousy 4 percent ROI.

The Gambler asks Arty about the spread of the video, and they're relieved to hear that it still hasn't hit the public venues. All this price movement is just the rumor mill getting cranked up to speed. Word's spreading there's something up with Tom Hanks, but nobody's sure what it is. Nobody but the folks in the Chateau Marmont, and they're not telling the commoners.

"Hold steady," the Gambler says aloud.

But the Prospector can't stop worrying. What if Hanks or his handlers know about the video, and take steps to get ahead of it? A preemptive press conference would wipe out all their gains.

These constant interrogations and arguments were exhausting, but it was the only way the Prospector and Gambler had found to manage doubt and anxiety. They'd always had trouble in that department, and the emotional responses of other people were a constant source of confusion. Unfortunately they'd passed this deficit to their daughter. They didn't necessarily want the girl to go plural, however, so they'd assembled several of Arty's subsystems and installed them into a pair of glasses—a kind of emotional support AI. Did she still wear them? Did she think of the Mods when she wore them?

"815," Arty says.

The Gambler's attention snaps back to the task at hand.

"I just found the video on two public social networks," the AI says. "And the price just dropped to 792."

The Gambler whoops. They'd just made another $300K.

"Also," Arty says, "the nearest fire line is now four miles away."

"What? You just said it was five!"

"There's been a sudden increase in—"

The walls beep. The house has just switched from the grid to battery power.

"—wind speed."

What the hell. They lean back in the chair and look at the ceiling. Come to think of it, there'd been noise leaking into the work wing for the past hour or so. That was unusual, because the room had been aggressively soundproofed. The design goal was to make the world outside their work become invisible and unheard.

And how well has that been working out for us? the Prospector asks snarkily.

"We're leaving the wing," the Gambler tells the AI. "Keep giving us updates. We're not unwinding yet."

Arty doesn't answer. The Gambler and the Prospector hurry down a short hallway lined with foam baffles and push through the padded door, into the kitchen. It sounds as if the house is coming apart. The cabin timbers are creaking and moaning. The copper-bottomed tops hanging above the stove clang as if sounding the alarm. The kitchen's south-facing windows rattle in their frames.

Beyond the windows, the backyard is remarkably clear of smoke, though everything has taken on a yellowish cast. The trees, some of them over thirty feet tall, seesaw violently in the wind. The sky above them is gray with smoke, but tinged red.

The Gambler and the Prospector walk to the living room, and stop in shock before the bay window. The tree line is a wall of flame. The sky above has been transformed in a way that's difficult to process: the colors and the scale of what they're seeing seem deeply wrong. They go to the front door and touch the handle. They think: This isn't smart. But we have to see.

A new mountain has appeared. An inverted mountain, half a mile wide at the top. A thick, churning cone of fire and smoke. The fire seems to be thrashing itself into a frenzy. It's capped by a huge, dark cumulous cloud that cuts off all the light behind it. Lightning flashes inside it.

They hear a rending sound, and jerk back. The roof of their garage suddenly rips free. It's hauled into the air, flapping, shedding pieces of itself. Then it's sucked away over the burning trees, into the whirling, fiery mass.

The Country Doctor

THE DOOR TO COLLEEN'S APARTMENT IS UNLOCKED—NOT A GOOD SIGN. THE DOCTOR calls the woman's name several times, gets no answer. She steps inside, and her daughter follows her.

The living room is a warm space the Doctor's appreciated in the virtual visits. The bookshelves, she can see now, are filled with biophysics textbooks, Colleen's former profession. A foldable table is set up in front of an armchair, on a plate are the remains of breakfast sandwich. She's still feeding herself, so that's good.

The Doctor tells her daughter to wait here. The girl's staring at her feet—which means she's really staring at the inside of her glasses. Her hands are clenching and unclenching, a sign of anxiety.

"Don't worry," the Doctor says. "This will just take a minute."

The Doctor walks to the bedroom, still calling out Colleen's name. She doesn't want to spook her. The bed's unmade. The attached bathroom is empty. She spots Colleen's blue wristband in the sheets. It's designed to be very hard to remove. She pictures Colleen outside, in the smoke, trying to make it to the university in time for her class.

She hears a splash. "Colleen?"

She walks into the bathroom, pulls aside the shower curtain. Colleen's sitting in the tub, water up to her chest, watching a video on a tablet. The old woman looks up. "Did you see this thing with Tom Hanks?"

The Doctor kneels beside the tub. The water's cold. "How long you been in here, honey?" She helps the woman up, dries her off. Then she finds clothes and underwear in the dresser.

Colleen smiles apologetically. "I'm sorry, I can't quite recall your name."

"We talk on screen every week. You call me Doc."

"Oh! MD or PhD?"

As the Doctor helps her into her clothes, they chat about Colleen's "current" research, which concerns fusion proteins and something called onco-condensates. The Doctor wonders why Colleen left Indiana and decided to retire out west. Why is she living alone? Who's going to take care of her? The progression of dementia is not linear, and Lewy body dementia attacks both the mind and body. She could be fine one week, and three days later be unable to feed herself. The collapse—and there was always a collapse—never failed to surprise the family.

The Doctor is pulling socks over one of Colleen's blue-veined feet when the woman says, "Oh, hello there. Are you all right?"

The Doctor's daughter is standing in the doorway, glasses and mask still on. Her hands are fists. Tears run down her cheeks.

The Doctor goes to her. "What is it? Tell me what happened."

"I'm too late," the girl wails. "I'm too late."

"What are you talking about? Too late for what?"

The girl takes off her glasses. Her eyes are filled with tears. She shows her mother the insides of the glasses.

The Doctor stares. "What is that?"

"A tornado," the girl says. "A fire tornado."

The Last Cowboy

AS THEY ENTER THE OLD MAN'S HOUSE, A TELEPHONE IS RINGING. IT SOUNDS LIKE the phone in the Cowboy's granddad's house, the metal clanging of a real bell. The old man ignores it, says they'll call back if it's important. The ringing stops and the Cowboy's grateful. He's feeling woozy.

The old man moves some books from a long couch and tells him to take a load off, don't worry about bleeding on the cushions. A joke. Then he walks through a doorway at the end of the room and pulls shut a pocket door. The door's painted a lustrous red.

The Cowboy's head falls back. It's a big room, with a high, peaked ceiling and exposed timbers. Shelves line every wall, and many of them hold typewriters. There must be thirty in the room. Small electrics in pastel colors. Big clunky manuals with round keys. One of the machines sits in a wooden box, hinged open; it looks like some kind of mechanical computer, with exposed gears and dials. The air is cool. He wonders how rich this old man is.

The red door slides open. The old man walks out holding a tray. He sets it on a table, closes the door, and picks it up again. An awkward, slow dance. Then he carries it to the coffee table beside the couch.

The tray holds a pitcher of iced water, a glass, and white plastic first aid kit. The old man pours the glass full. The Cowboy downs it, though the cold makes his skull ache. The old man laughs and refills the glass.

The Cowboy asks if the man has a dog.

"Pardon?"

The Cowboy nods at the red door. "I used to have to do that. Keep the door closed to keep the dog in."

"No." The old man frowns. "That's just . . . habit."

The phone starts ringing again, in some far room. "Only a couple people have this number," the old man says. "I suppose I better take it. You sit tight, okay? I'll be right back." The Cowboy realizes that the old man must have an actual landline, with a receiver that sits in the same place all the time.

The old man takes his time. It's another five rings until the Cowboy hears him pick up the receiver. There's a pause, and then the old man says something, his tone disbelieving. The Cowboy can't catch the words. Then the old man's voice turns angry. It's the first hint of grit in his affable demeanor. A moment later a door shuts, cutting off the sound of the conversation.

The Cowboy gets to his feet. Steadies himself. He's still light-headed, but the water has helped. He looks at the red door. Glances back. There's no sign of the old man.

He walks to the door and slides it open.

It's a spacious, old-fashioned kitchen. The air smells of something dank, and fruity. The only light coming from the window over the sink. There's something large lying on the countertop, under a tablecloth. It's long and thick as a quarter of beef. But the shape is all wrong.

The Cowboy bunches the tablecloth in his fist and pulls it off.

It's a human body, carved apart. The Cowboy's not a squeamish man. He's worked a slaughterhouse, and walked the floors of meat processors.

But he's never seen this. His stomach threatens to expel his lunch and he puts an arm across his mouth.

The chest has been sliced open, and the flesh has fallen away from the ribs, exposing white bones of the ribcage. Most of the organs have been removed.

The Cowboy hears a sound behind him. He reaches for his holster, then remembers that the gun is outside.

"Well," the old man says. "This is awkward."

The Prospector and the Gambler

THE PROSPECTOR AND THE GAMBLER STARE OUT THEIR FRONT DOOR, PARALYZED BY the undeniable fact of the firestorm. Then push the door closed. The wind tries to shove it back open.

The house isn't built to withstand a tornado. Certainly not one burning at 2,000 degrees and spinning at 150 miles per hour. There's no basement. No Aunty Em cellar. And the shallow crawlspace is crammed with house batteries and cables.

They need to run, but there's also no car—that left with their wife and daughter months ago. It was on the to-do list to buy a new vehicle, but they hadn't felt the need for one. Groceries were delivered weekly. Every other material need was brought to them by FedEx and UPS.

The Prospector and the Gambler shout, "Arty, call 911!" There's no answer. "Arty?"

They run to the nearest screen, which is built into the armchair. The screen is live, so the electricity is still on, but there's no connection to the internet. What the hell? Their fiber line runs underground. Did the firefighters cut it while making a firebreak? Or did the entire hub go up in flames?

It's the Gambler who remembers that they haven't unwound their position. They're still on the hook with fifteen thousand borrowed shares.

The Prospector tells them to shut the fuck up. They're in this mess because they weren't paying attention to the right things. Have you never heard of Maslow's hierarchy? The Prospector grabs control of the screen and tries to switch over to wideband cell coverage. There are towers on the other side of the ridge, so surely one of them has survived being incinerated . . .

But no. No bars.

Reception has always been shitty here in the hills, but with the fiber line there was never any need to rely on wideband—or satellite backup, or microwaves, whatever carrier pigeon technology the locals used to rely on.

This no time to panic, the Gambler thinks.

There's no better time! the Prospector answers. We're going to die here!

Something heavy crashes through the bay window. Glass explodes across the room. They throw up their arms, too late, and when they bring them down their wrought-iron patio table is in the room with them.

Maybe if we can get to the road, the Gambler thinks, we can pick up some bars and call for help.

The tornado is heading straight for us. We can't outrun that.

Do you hear . . . a beeping?

The Prospector and the Gambler look around. Is it the smoke alarm? No. It's coming from outside. The sound is very insistent.

They walk hesitantly to the front door, which is shaking in its frame. Amazingly, the doorbell cam is still working. On the small screen, they see that a white car has pulled up onto the lawn. It's only six feet from the front door, and its headlights are flashing on and off. The horn blares for three, maybe four seconds. Then three quick beeps. It's as if it's talking in Morse code.

The Prospector and the Gambler think, Is that Audi Murphy?

The Last Cowboy

THE OLD MAN PUTS UP HIS HANDS AND TAKES A STEP FORWARD. "EASY THERE, BIG fella. It's not what you think."

"Stay where you are," the Cowboy says. He's pretty sure he can take the old man. Unless he's hiding a weapon.

"Take a close look at that thing," the old man says. "Remind you of anybody?"

The Cowboy doesn't want to turn his back on the old man. But he steps to the side so he can see the corpse's face. The young man does look familiar. Even dead, there's something about those eyes, that curly black hair.

"Holy shit," the Cowboy says. "It's the guy from Bosom Buddies."

The old man winces. "*That's* what you remember? Never mind. You can see it's me, right? Somebody sent it as a joke."

"Why's he holding a statue?"

"That's an Oscar. It's not real. The whole thing's not real. Look—" The old man steps toward the counter and the Cowboy makes a fist.

"I'm going to move slowly," the old man says. "Which means pretty much my usual speed." He reaches for the hand of the corpse, pulls up one of its fingers, and bends it back. It breaks free with a snap.

"Stop that!" the Cowboy says.

"Watch." The old man puts the finger in his mouth and bites down.

The Cowboy shoves the old man against the wall, and grabs the corpse finger from him. It's cold.

The old man's in pain but trying to speak. The Cowboy takes out his phone and says, "I'm calling the police."

"It's vegetables," the old man says.

"What?"

"Take a bite. It's supposed to taste like meat, but you can tell the difference."

The Cowboy looks at the finger. The end, where it was snapped off, is pink with a white bone protruding. He sniffs it. It doesn't smell like any kind of meat he knows of.

The old man nods. "Go on."

The Cowboy bites down. Chews. "God damn," he says. "Tastes like ribeye. Ribeye and . . . celery."

"I know, right?"

And then the Cowboy bursts out laughing. "I thought you—I thought you was a—!"

And now the old man's laughing too. "You aren't the only one. It's all over the internet."

The Cowboy reaches into the body cavity. "May I?"

"I can't finish this all this myself." And that starts them laughing again.

A bit later the old man asks for a favor. His publicists are mad, and really want him to address the so-called controversy ASAP. Would the Cowboy mind using that phone there to take a video? He really needs to address the public.

The Cowboy says, "It would be my honor."

The Country Doctor

THE DOCTOR'S DAUGHTER IS PACING COLLEEN'S BEDROOM. THINGS HAVE BEEN happening fast for the last half hour. Finally the girl lets out a long "Yesssss," which is her version of her other parent's we-just-scored whoop.

"Are they okay?" the Doctor asks.

"The Mods just got into cell range. They're calling. Hold on." The girl's wearing her Miss Motes.

Colleen says, "I don't know what's going on." She's said this several times.

"My daughter hacked my car," the Doctor says. "And sent it to rescue my ex." The Doctor doesn't try to explain the plural pronouns.

Her daughter says, "Don't worry, Mods, I already put in the route. It stays clear of the fire." A pause. "Well, *here*. Where else would you go?" Another pause. "That's okay. Mom has a job. She's good at it."

"Who are the Mods again?" Colleen asks.

The girl looks over the top of her glasses at her mother. "Okay, they'll be here in a couple hours. They're broke now."

"What the what?"

The Doctor's daughter continues to talk to the Mods while the Doctor makes some faux chicken salad for Colleen to eat for supper. Then they put on their masks, and Colleen insists on shaking hands with the daughter. "Thank you for visiting," the woman says. "Come back any time."

The smoke is just as thick on the way home, but the day seems to be cooling off. Still, they'll both be sweaty messes. And the Doctor has a dozen VHVs to get through before the guests arrive.

Her daughter says, "You still love the Mods, don't you?"

The Doctor sighs through her mask. "I'll always love them, I suppose."

"Will you get back together?"

"No! Definitely not."

The girl stops walking. She adjusts her glasses and says, "Look at me. And take down your mask."

The Doctor rolls her eyes, but does it.

The girl says, "Definitely not? Or almost definitely not?"

The Doctor thinks, if there's one thing she's learned from her ex, it's that there's no such thing as definitely. Definite is for chalk players and outright suckers.

"Very close to almost definitely not," the Doctor says.

The girl listens to a murmur in her glasses, and tilts her head. "I'll take it."

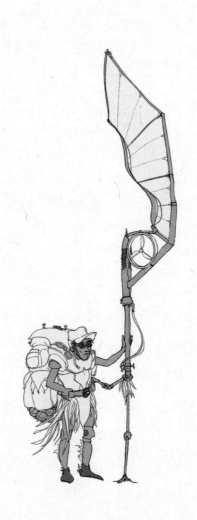

5 CRISIS ACTORS

Greg Egan

1

"EVERY YEAR THAT YOU DELAY YOUR MIDLIFE CRISIS ADDS ANOTHER TWO YEARS TO your lifespan. That's just simple arithmetic."

Carl laughed, but his father's demeanor remained entirely sincere. He hadn't meant the remark as a joke.

"I'm long past the halfway point," his father added stoically. "But there are higher harmonics where I still have the chance to intervene. There are peaks and troughs that represent every fraction of the human lifespan, and quantum mechanics teaches us that we can modify the shape of those waves, nudging their phase and changing all kinds of outcomes that used to be seen as inevitable."

Carl's first impulse was to bite his tongue and try to steer the conversation back toward reality without starting any arguments, but then he noticed the jar, as big as an ice cream tub, sitting on top of the bookshelf behind his father's armchair.

"It doesn't teach anything of the kind," he said bluntly. "How much did you pay for that crap?"

His father turned and followed his gaze to the jar of Harmonic Advantage Supplement. "None of your business. And when did a degree in geology make you an expert in quantum mechanics?"

"It doesn't," Carl replied, "but I did enough undergraduate physics to know the basics. You didn't specialize in the history of England, but if some con man on the internet told me that the order of succession to the British throne was decided by a series of MMA cage matches, I'd be willing to defer to your own education when you assured me that that really wasn't true."

His father groaned. "So you think Fourier analysis is as much of a joke as mixed martial arts in the Palace?"

Carl walked over to the shelf and picked up the jar. He'd been looking for a price tag, but he found himself morbidly skimming the spiel on the side. "I studied Fourier analysis, too," he said. "You need it for seismology, among other things. And I can tell you with the utmost confidence that it does *not* say that your life is 'built from harmonic waves' or that you can 'postpone the final node' by taking pills full of 'microcrystalline quartz.' Now, there's something I'm qualified to talk about. This is sand. You've bought a big tub of sand."

"Yeah, yeah, like that's nothing special!" his father retorted. "Except that *this sand* has been kept out of the light for thousands of years, building up energy in its crystalline defects. If you don't believe that, maybe you should hand back your degree, because it's precisely the science behind the most sophisticated methods for dating ancient artefacts."

Carl was flummoxed for a moment; he reread the side of the jar, and found a line describing, more or less correctly, the principles behind luminescence dating.

"That's not the point," he said. "Yes, you can find the age of some sediments by seeing how much light buried grains of quartz give off. So what? All it proves is that these people can look up something on Wikipedia, and then pretend it makes their sand pills more credible."

"Oh, so nothing ever counts in their favor!" his father replied heatedly. "They can be right about absolutely everything else, but you don't want to believe in the health benefits, so you get to that point and then slam your mind shut."

"Everything else?" Carl protested. "There are a thousand true things that can be said about sand! Listing them all on a jar of sand pills won't make the sand into a cure for . . ." He looked at the label again. ". . . arthritis, hypertension, irritable bowel syndrome . . ."

His father raised his hands. "Can we just drop the whole thing? You come into my house and I try to share some good news with you, and you treat me like a child. I should have known better than to tell you anything."

Carl felt chastened, even as his face burned with resentment. He wasn't going to apologize for speaking the truth, but he was willing to change the subject. He returned to the couch and sat gazing at the carpet, listening to the air conditioner laboring against the heat.

"It's Caroline's birthday next week," he said finally. "She'll be nine. Will you come to the party this Saturday?"

"Of course!" his father replied, all his anger melting away. "What should I get her? What's she into these days?"

Carl hadn't thought about that. All the children's books and toys came with their own hard-core agendas, and he didn't want to step into another minefield by offering a list of items least likely to infuriate one parent or the other, only to find that his father objected to them all.

"Buy her a gift voucher," Carl advised. "They grow up so fast," he joked, "that if you buy them the thing they asked for a week ago, they'll burst into tears because you should have known that, by now, it's strictly for babies."

2

WHEN CARL ARRIVED HOME FROM THE PARTY, HE TURNED ON HIS LAPTOP AND SAW that there was a new message on his RStance channel. He did the date-and-day calculation in his head, then pulled out the carved wooden chess set from the junk pile at the bottom of the bedroom closet and held up the white queen for the laptop's camera, turning the piece to expose the distinctive marbling.

Unlocked, the message appeared as a GIF, a crudely animated political cartoon that a casual onlooker could easily take to be the entire point of the communication—but the scribbled shading of a patch of the background included some wildly distorted text that few people or algorithms would notice. Carl placed a mirrored cylinder against the screen that reversed the distortion and let him read it; he memorized the details, writing nothing down, then quit the app, which zeroed every byte it had touched before exiting.

He sat for a while, pondering the assignment, wondering how many more minor tasks he'd need to complete before he'd proved he could be trusted with something bigger. His knees were aching from giving his daughter a shoulder ride for an hour while ducking down every few steps to avoid the decorations strung across his ex-wife's living room. He loved every minute he spent with Caroline, but it worried him when she became so desperate and clingy. Whenever he'd suggested putting her down for a while so she could talk to her friends, she'd looked as crestfallen as if he'd threatened to disown her.

The message had given an address in Penrith and a time window between three and four p.m. the next day. Carl checked that his uniform was clean and pressed, and that his tools and supplies were ready.

On Sunday afternoon, he set out early in case there were problems with the traffic, but the M4 flowed smoothly most of the way. Whenever a gap opened up in front of him, the air shimmered over the baking asphalt. He arrived with fifteen minutes to spare, so he circled the area, hoping to get a sense of the kind of bystanders he might have to contend with, but the streets, and the front yards of the houses, were mostly deserted. He'd chosen three possible parking spots in advance, and the first one he reached was empty.

He put on his C-Ture cap, changed to a different pair of sunglasses, and patted some adversarial facial hair onto his cheeks. When he opened the car door it was like stepping into a sauna. *Why were the tip-offs always in the hottest suburbs, at the hottest time of day?* After walking one block he was drenched in sweat, and he had five more to go, but he didn't want his own vehicle to be seen too close to the target.

The house was a two-story McMansion in off-white brick, the roof groaning under edge-to-edge PV. Carl didn't knock on the front door; he'd learned that that just attracted more attention from the neighbors than going about his business directly. The C-Ture unit was at the side of the building, and as the tip-off had promised there was no gate blocking his way, and no security cameras. When he slipped on his white cotton gloves it was hard not to feel self-conscious, like a burglar intent on concealing his fingerprints, but they were exactly what the real technicians wore to protect both themselves and the equipment.

He shut off the power, then unscrewed the metal cover and set it aside. The membrane took much longer to detach, with sixteen separate bolts. Carl lifted it away carefully, making sure not to touch anything but the support frame; a physical rupture would prove that someone had meddled with the device.

With the membrane removed, the exposed catalyst glinted in diffracted rainbow colors, like some strange artwork built from discarded DVDs. Carl couldn't help but marvel at the sheer technical accomplishment on display, however misdirected. Growing this kind of finely wrought fractal, with the surface area of a small forest's worth of leaves packed into a cubic meter, had sounded preposterous when he first heard it mooted, but they hadn't just made it possible, they'd made it affordable—at least to the sufficiently rich and vain.

He took the bottle out of his toolbox and dispensed a dozen drops, carefully spread out over the top surface of the iridescent block. The mixture of hydrocarbons and alcohols with branching side chains had been tailored to bind to the active sites in the catalyst, but unlike the products the catalyst forged itself from carbon dioxide and water vapor, they remained lodged firmly in place. Within forty-eight hours, the whole thing would be irredeemably poisoned: a very shiny, expensive brick.

The owners might not feel much financial pain from losing a trickle of carbon-neutral aviation fuel—which wouldn't have repaid the cost of the unit in their lifetime, anyway—but they'd be livid at having wasted their money on such a heap of junk, disinclined to fork out for a replacement once they realized that the warranty had expired, and more than willing to bad-mouth the technology to their friends. If the machine that was meant to buy them environmental prestige wouldn't deliver, the next best thing would be to take the high ground and denounce it as a greenwashing stunt that wouldn't even last long enough to recapture its own manufacturing footprint.

Carl reassembled everything and started toward the front of the house, then he heard a neighbor's car pull into their driveway, on the opposite side. He retreated, standing behind the wall, listening to car doors slamming and children yelling at each other. It had to be fifty degrees, but the kids kept fighting and dawdling, taking forever to get inside.

He felt acid rising in his throat. The tip had to have come from some-one in the neighborhood who knew the owner well enough to be apprised of their movements, so this irritating family might well include the anon-ymous informant. If that was the case, he could understand why they couldn't risk carrying out the job themselves; they'd be much more likely to be recognized by another local. But if it wasn't, and they noticed him, all it would take would be one conversation between the disgruntled owners and their neighbors to raise the possibility of sabotage.

He waited, sweat dripping down his arms, until the childish taunts became muffled and he heard the front door of the house finally close. He marched straight onto the street, not even glancing toward the adjoining house, turned in the other direction, and set off toward his car. If anyone had seen him, it would not have been memorable. And he couldn't let him-self be rattled by a tiny glitch in a minor prank like this, if he ever hoped to graduate to the big league.

Just give me some C4, he thought, willing it, like a prayer. *I've proved myself. I can hold my nerve. Let me take down something worth destroying.*

3

CARL SPENT THE EVENING UPDATING HIS BLOG, BLOCKING THE TROLLS AND catastrophists but replying at length to the merely unpersuaded.

"Even if the heating's part of a natural cycle, why should we stand by and fry to death?" asked CandourMan.

As host Epictetus, Carl responded with scrupulous courtesy. "We should not accept a single death, but what we're doing now is completely misguided. Carbon dioxide is plant food, and when its level rises in response to the heat, that's part of a natural feedback process that allows the forests to grow more rapidly, bringing the planet back toward its long-term equilibrium temperature. Cutting emissions, let alone pulling the gas out of the air, is precisely the wrong thing to do, both for the crop yields needed to keep us all fed, and for the climate itself. In hotter weather, plants narrow their stomates—the pores they breathe through—which means they need extra CO_2 just to maintain their normal metabolism, and still more to sustain the necessary growth spurt. We can plant as many trees as we like, but unless we fertilize them with sufficient CO_2, they won't bring the climate back under control."

CandourMan wasn't currently online, but Revellator chimed in. "If Earth recovered from the rise in heat before, without anyone burning fossil fuels to help it along, what's the big deal? It will recover again, won't it?"

"Even the natural cycle takes thousands of years," Epictetus replied. "Carbon capture will double that!"

Revellator went silent for a while, then came back with a Gish gallop of half-baked science, spurious references, and deliberate misinterpretation. Carl deleted the comment and blocked him.

When he checked the time, it was after eleven. He had an interview for a two-week consulting job in the morning; he needed to be sharp. His severance package from the university was dwindling, and he was starting to suspect that the lawyers advising him on the wrongful dismissal suit were just stringing him along.

He closed the blog, but sat unmoving. He was tired of squabbling with dilettantes and sneaking around the suburbs breaking rich people's toys. There was too much at stake for him to be wasting his time this way.

He fetched the mirrored cylinder and started up RStance, then began composing a message to his cell leader. "I'm ready for something more," he spelled out in awkward cursive with his fingertip on the trackpad, as it appeared in the mirror. "I'm smart, reliable, motivated." He winced and erased the embarrassing squiggle; this wasn't a corporate gig. "Give me the toughest job you have, and I'll do it. Whatever the risks, whatever it costs me." Short of mentioning dams or hydrogen plants by name, he could hardly make himself any clearer.

He sent the message. Going on past experience it was unlikely that he'd receive a reply for several days, but he was reluctant to shut down the laptop straight away. He went and brushed his teeth, thinking back over the words he'd used, hoping he hadn't sounded too desperate. If a cop had infiltrated the cell, wouldn't they keep pushing in the same direction, asking to be let in on ever-larger crimes?

When he returned to the laptop, there was a message waiting for him. Hairs rose on the back of his neck; he was so used to being ignored that this felt as eerie as getting a response from a Ouija board. He went to his minerals cabinet and took out the fragment of a chondrite he'd found in the Nullarbor, then held it up to the camera.

The GIF showed a cat fighting with a toy robot on someone's lawn, but the mottled shadows of foliage on the grass unwarped to spell out the reply: "Are you willing to go undercover to expose the Big Lie? Knowing you'll be putting yourself in danger?"

Carl's stomach clenched with anxiety, but his heart soared. All the menial tasks had finally paid off; they were going to let him tear the whole farce wide open.

He paced the living room, struggling to compose his answer. It needed to be an enthusiastic yes, but it also needed to elicit more information—without disclosing the fact that he had no idea which particular Big Lie they meant, or exactly what they wanted him to do about it.

4

THE TRAINING COURSE FOR THE CYCLONE EMERGENCY RESPONSE VOLUNTEERS started with a first aid certificate. Carl had kept his own certificate up to date, as he'd sometimes needed it for fieldwork, but he went along to the session anyway, to ensure that he didn't miss out on any of the networking opportunities.

In a hall in Leichhardt that had once been a church, twenty people gathered around the instructor and her mannequin. The volunteers ranged in age from their twenties to their fifties, he guessed. Carl tried not to judge them by their appearance, as if he could sort everyone into fanatics and followers by a few simple cues, but he was disappointed that there wasn't a single Extinction Rebellion tattoo on display.

The echoey acoustics of the wooden-floored hall gave the whole thing an earnest, amateurish feel, like a community theater group. None of the first aid protocols seemed to have changed since his last refresher course, but he kept his attention scrupulously focused on the instructor as she spoke; he needed to be perceived as absolutely serious about every aspect of his induction.

In the tea break, he stood a few paces from the urn and let people initiate contact, telling them the truth if they asked: he was a semiretired geologist, hoping to make better use of his free time. Eventually, a small group crystallized around him, chatting, merely by virtue of the location he'd chosen.

"It was Cyclone Odette that really got to me," Andrea said. She was a high school physical education teacher in her thirties, with an intense demeanor and a tightly wound ponytail. "When I saw what that did to Townsville, I just wanted to punch someone. We could have nipped this in the bud fifty years ago, if a few more politicians had grown a spine."

Carl nodded sadly, but kept his mouth shut; if he started trying to mimic the true believers and parrot all their talking points, he was afraid it might sound as much like a parody to them as it did to him.

"It's just a lack of scientific literacy," Vinay, the dental student, opined. "People have had the evidence in front of them for decades, but every parliament is full of lawyers who believe there's no problem you can't talk your way around."

"I think it runs deeper than that," Bruno suggested. "I could list half a dozen Nobel laureates who bent over backward to minimize the problem, or pretend it wasn't anthropogenic. People can convince themselves of anything, if they set their minds to it." Bruno was a retired civil engineer, a balding man with a weathered face who made Carl feel slightly anxious, as if their similarities might render his own insincerity more visible.

The instructor called out, "Can we reassemble, please?"

"Time to stanch those robot hemorrhages!" Carl enthused, slapping his hands together with glee.

As they took turns learning to stop poor Resusci Annie from bleeding to death after a wind-borne branch had impaled her thigh, Carl tried to imagine how each of these students would respond when they realized that their mission on the ground would be every bit as staged. Maybe a few of them knew already, and were going into the charade with their eyes open, but CERV recruited from the general public, and he'd had no problem enrolling after nothing more than standard medical and police checks. Among these twenty people, he could hardly be the only one who'd be appalled at the cynical deceit they were being roped into.

Then again, if it was for a higher cause—and they were surrounded by peers who would encourage and enable them—hadn't all the psychological research shown that most people would rationalize away their qualms?

5

CARL WAS ASLEEP WHEN THE CERV APP STARTED WAILING LIKE AN AMBULANCE siren. He picked up his phone from his bedside table and stared groggily at the alert, his finger hovering above the DECLINE button; the best thing about being a volunteer was that no one could compel him to go through with this. But then his news app chimed in with its own portentous claims about the impending tragedy, and he knew he'd never forgive himself if he ended up having to stare impotently at the same kind of nonsense for the next four weeks.

He called a ride share to the airport, and ended up in the same car as Andrea. "This is it!" she said, as she climbed in beside him. Carl smiled and nodded, trying not to let her twitchy body language rattle him.

She pulled out her phone and summoned up a map showing a mix of satellite imagery and computer projections. Cyclone Uriah had formed midway between the Solomon Islands and Tuvalu six days before, and was tracking south-southwest toward Vanuatu. Carl didn't doubt that it would be a significant nuisance, but everyone in its path would have had plenty of time to prepare and take shelter. The only real role for CERV would be to help orchestrate the disaster theater.

When they reached the airport, Carl spotted the remainder of the group, gathered around a snack kiosk while they waited for clearance to go further. He and Andrea checked in their luggage, then joined the others.

"I swear it was faster when you could just queue up and walk through a security gate," Andrea grumbled. Carl couldn't argue with that; the whole foyer was scanning its occupants in real time, but dealing with weaker signals and moving targets made the process more protracted.

"No stage fright, you two?" Vinay asked. He was smiling, but Carl could see how restless he was, screwing and unscrewing the cap of his water bottle.

"After all those rehearsals?" Carl replied. "We could do this in our sleep."

Bruno glanced at his phone. "Oh, I've been green-lit," he said. "See you in the cabin."

Carl took out his own phone, and watched the red silhouette acquiring random blobs of green.

"At least they're sure there's nothing sharp in my hypothalamus," Vinay joked.

Carl said, "I'm more worried about what they might find in my liver."

The group trickled through into the terminal; by the time Carl joined them, the flight to Port Vila was boarding. CERV hadn't needed to charter a plane, but the commercial jet, which would normally have been full of tourists, was returning almost empty. Watching the flight attendants go through the emergency procedures, Carl could see the worry on their faces. These beat-ups really were cruel to everyone.

With so much room, every passenger had been given a window seat, but once the lights of Sydney were behind them there was nothing outside but dark ocean and an overcast sky. Carl had purged his phone of anything incriminating, leaving him with none of his usual means of passing the time, so he picked an action movie from the in-flight entertainment system and let the screen and earbuds feed him enough color and motion to keep him from dozing off.

The credits rolled just as dawn reached into the cabin. Carl looked out to see Efate Island emerging from choppy gray water, a blotch of impossibly lush green. People had lived and thrived here for millennia, and the forests had been around since the chain of volcanic islands first acquired enough soil to sustain them. There had been cyclones for all that time; one more was just a blip in the archipelago's history.

"Thanks for coming," the flight attendant said, as Carl disembarked. "We appreciate your help."

"My pleasure," Carl mumbled awkwardly, but as he walked out onto the airbridge he pushed aside the pang of shame the words had evoked. He had every right to be proud of his intentions; exposing the forces seeking to exploit the Vanuatuan people for their own agenda was as honorable a goal as any visitor could aspire to.

6

A MINIBUS TOOK THE NEW ARRIVALS TO THE CERV OPERATIONS CENTER, A SCHOOL gymnasium where the local chapter, as well as those from Fiji, New Caledonia, and New Zealand were already encamped. People were drifting in and out of the building, or lying on their sleeping bags talking on their phones. Carl caught Bruno glancing up at the ceiling, and asked jokingly, "You think it will hold?"

Bruno said, "As long as the walls stay up I'll be happy."

The next briefing was almost an hour away, so after placing their belongings in their allotted spaces on the floor the group walked out into the town in search of breakfast. A steady wind was blowing in from the ocean, but Carl was soon dripping with perspiration as he followed the others toward a café someone had picked from a map.

The owner of the café had already boarded up the windows, but it remained open for business, and there was some portable plastic furniture on the pavement outside. Carl ordered scrambled eggs and croissants, and sat gazing down at the water. Twice protected from the open ocean, a small bay facing the side of a larger one, it was still exhibiting a relentless swell, with wave after wave crashing against the mangrove-lined shore. On the gently sloping street before him, the colorfully painted buildings he could see looked like a mixture of timber and brick, far from shoddy but not exactly bunker-like either.

Back at the gymnasium, the CERV coordinator, Anton Seule, welcomed the new arrivals and explained the plans for the morning: basically, sandbagging. Everyone had been allocated a portion of a low-lying street that had been chosen as the site of a barricade against the possibility of rising water.

"They should build more sea walls," Carl suggested as his team of five lined up to collect their shovels and a stack of empty woven bags.

"It's complicated," Bruno replied. "A hard barrier in the wrong place can accelerate erosion—reflecting back the waves so they carry sand away, undermining its own foundations. You can use a more porous structure, which traps sand like the roots in a mangrove swamp, but there's a limit to how much protection that will give from a storm surge."

Carl was sure there were ways around all of these quibbles, but he didn't want to get bogged down in an argument, pitting his expertise against Bruno's.

When they reached the street they'd been assigned, there was already a large pile of sand, presumably left by a dump truck. One of the team, Barbara, a quiet woman Carl hadn't spoken with much, had brought a frame they could hang the bags from while shoveling in the sand, and they soon settled into a rhythm of filling and stacking.

It was a simple enough job, but in the training drills they'd never had to keep up the routine for more than half an hour. A couple of young kids appeared, watching them, shy at first then laughing and joking. When they addressed the group in Bislama, the local English creole, Carl struggled to grasp their meaning, but Bruno seemed to have no trouble. "It's a little bit like Tok Pisin," he explained. "I worked in PNG for a while."

Carl stopped taking swigs from his water bottle; it just seemed to make him sweat more, and thanks to the humidity that did nothing to cool him. The sky was full of gray clouds, with the sun barely showing through as a pale white disk. He tried taking off his broad-brimmed hat, just to let more of the breeze reach his face, but then it felt as if the whole hemisphere above was raining heat down on him, and he quickly replaced it.

When they took a break, Andrea brought out her phone and checked the forecast. "Uriah is category four now," she announced. "Expected to cross the northern islands by nightfall."

"Most of them have concrete shelters," Carl said.

"Sure," she replied. "But what will be left outside? What will people be emerging to?"

Carl resisted the urge to respond that the pious note of concern in her voice would do nothing to improve the outcome. It was a cyclone, not a picnic; no one had been promised a good time. People would do their best, and get through it as they had before.

It took the whole morning for the five of them to use up all the sand—with the wind stealing a portion—but when Carl stood back and looked at the result it was impossible not to feel a sense of accomplishment. The barrier stood in a natural channel that any ascending water would be forced to take, and though it blocked the street, people could still detour onto the sloping ground on either side to get around it.

As they trudged back through the town, they found that all the shops and cafés along the way had shut their doors, and the streets were deserted. The clouds had darkened, all but blotting out the sun; battling the wind to make progress was comical at first, but then wearying, and the gusts were almost enough to knock an adult off their feet.

In the gymnasium, people returning from the various work parties were queuing up for a communal lunch, ladled out from a huge steaming pot with a fragrant odor that reached all the way to the door. With a virtuous ache in his limbs from the morning's labor, Carl was tempted to surrender to the air of camaraderie and just celebrate a job well done. But he quashed the nascent Stockholm syndrome and gathered his thoughts.

He excused himself and left his companions, heading in the direction of the bathrooms. With everyone intent on getting fed, it was easy to slip unseen into the passageway that led behind the stage. The building doubled as an auditorium, and not just for school assemblies; a quick search revealed a list of past musical performances and plays. It was hard to navigate in the gloom, but eventually he found a pair of rooms that seemed well placed for costume changes and other theatrical business. Once he was out of the passageway, he risked using the light from his phone, and the second room turned out to be exactly what he'd been seeking. Apart from a couple of filing cabinets and a wobbly table, there were three tall wooden cupboards, and one of them bore a hand-written label that read *Accessoire de scène*.

Inside were five plastic swords in metallic gray, a crumbling box full of stage make-up, wigs and beards, and something that might have been a royal scepter. He rummaged through the box, sure that a bottle of fake blood would be in there somewhere, but then it dawned on him that whoever had been charged with enacting the scenes of carnage must have taken it already. The props cupboard would be an innocent-seeming place to stash it, but it would be no use if it was still here at the height of the storm.

He leaned against the cupboard, disappointed; a geotagged picture of the bottle would have been the perfect start to his exposé. There were too many witnesses on the ground, and too many phones ready to capture every event from multiple angles, to try to manufacture casualties with deep fakes, however sophisticated the technology. It had to be done the old-fashioned way. The only question now was, *by whom*?

"What are you doing?"

Carl turned to see a woman standing in the doorway. Her lanyard read CERV Fiji, but he couldn't make out her name.

"I was looking for the bathroom, then I got side-tracked." He picked up one of the swords and brandished it. "Reliving my youth. I was Banquo in my high school *Macbeth*. I should have been the lead; I learned all the lines."

The woman stared at him, entirely unmollified. "Would you put that back? We're all guests here! You can't rummage around in school property!"

"I'm sorry." Carl replaced the sword and closed the cupboard.

"The bathroom is that way." She pointed down the passage.

"Thank you."

As he walked away, he tried to recall if there had been anything in the cupboard that could have served alongside the missing blood—something the catastrophe's props master might have forgotten, and would need to return for. But any bandages used would be the real thing, taken from the first aid kits, and there'd been nothing like fake glass shards, or blocks of rubber masonry. In a Hollywood production, with scrupulous health and safety standards, no one would risk placing an actual piece of broken windowpane within a hundred meters of an actor. But this performance would be far edgier, more improvised, with all manner of ad hoc practical effects. He just had to keep his eyes open, and be prepared to question everything he saw.

7

IN THE AFTERNOON, AT A NEW LOCATION, THE WORK PARTY TOOK THEIR SAND straight from the back of a truck, with a tarpaulin helping to shelter the load from the wind. Even so, a constant stream of grit whipped out through the opening, stinging Carl's arms and face, and each shovelful on its way into the bags seemed to be dissolving before his eyes, like sugar in hot water. They should have found an indoor space for this part of the job, but it was too late to try to organize anything.

It was barely four when they returned to the gym, but the sky had grown dark and it was spitting rain. The satellite images showed Uriah's swirl impinging on all of the islands to the north, and bearing down fast on Efate.

Carl found his sleeping bag and lay down. There was more food on offer, but he was too tired to eat. Heavy rain began clattering on the metal roof, so loud that it took him a while to discern the separate groan and rattle of the building's frame shuddering in the wind.

The lights in the hall went out. The gas flame warming the volunteers' dinner revealed a small group of anxious faces, and then a swarm of phone screens lit up and faded in waves, as their owners checked something then decided to conserve their batteries. Carl joined in, and saw that there was no signal.

A few minutes later the lights came back on, and everyone cheered. Bruno sat down nearby, holding a plate of stew.

"You're not hungry?" he asked Carl, yelling to be heard over the drumming on the roof.

"No."

The rain quietened abruptly, but then the wind rose up to fill the silence, playing howling bass notes on the gymnasium. Carl was a long way from any entrance, but he could feel a powerful draft of cool air flowing through the hall.

The roof began making a new sound: sheet metal banging against the rafters, which meant a few of the fasteners had come loose. A faint mist of water began to fall from the ceiling, the droplets making a pallid rainbow before the lights went out again.

"If the building collapses," Carl shouted, "wouldn't we be safer outside?"

"It's not going to collapse!" Bruno yelled back. "And if you go outside, there'll be pieces of flying tin just waiting to decapitate you."

Carl rose to his feet; he had no intention of fleeing, but he couldn't stay still. The cooking flame had been snuffed out, but the rectangular fireflies winked on and off in the darkness as the spray grew heavier.

The roof screeched and peeled halfway open; rain pelted the floor, and Carl could dimly perceive people scrambling to move or protect their possessions. He picked up his sleeping bag and slung it over his shoulder with the opening pointing down; the exterior was waterproof, so this ought to be enough to keep it dry inside. With the rain soaking his clothes, he shuffled in the dark toward the side of the hall that was still partly sheltered.

He stood, huddled beside a stranger, his teeth chattering, telling himself there was nothing to fear. Even if the roof was stripped away completely, any airborne debris was more likely to sail right over the walls than to land a perfect shot between them.

8

AROUND FOUR IN THE MORNING, THE WIND BEGAN TO DIE DOWN. THERE WAS STILL no phone signal, so it was impossible to be sure what Uriah was doing, but when Carl looked up and saw a patch of clear, star-filled sky through the gap in the ceiling, it seemed likely that the worst was over.

Someone found half a dozen battery-operated lamps, and Carl joined in mopping the water off the floor, while another group ascended the side of the building on ladders and managed to sling a series of tarpaulins over the hole.

By dawn, the command center was more or less habitable again, and a head count of the volunteers confirmed that no one was missing. But when he stepped outside, what Carl could see of the town from the school's high ground made his heart sink. Hundreds of roofs had been torn away, dozens of buildings had collapsed, and those streets that weren't inundated were strewn with debris. All the vivid blue and pink walls he recalled from the day before had vanished, the colors buried in water, splashed with mud, abraded away, or reduced to splinters.

The volunteers assembled for a briefing. "Uriah has left Vanuatu," Seule assured them, solemn but resolute. "We have reports of mudslides from Espiritu Santo, and many roads are damaged there, but so far no casualties. Our first job now is to make a sweep of the town, identify problems, and give assistance. Every team will be assigned an area to check."

Carl's phone still had no signal, but the GPS and peer-to-peer were working, so he was able to receive his instructions. He'd become separated from his team, but as he walked out of the school grounds carrying a first aid kit, he saw Bruno, Vinay, Andrea, and Barbara ahead of him, and he ran to catch up with them.

They barely spoke as they entered the town. On the first street, the houses were mostly intact, and the one collapsed building had been empty when it fell, with the owners, just returned, surveying the ruins. Bruno offered help clearing up the site, but they insisted that they and their neighbors could manage.

On the second street, Carl saw a small crowd gathered, and he could hear frantic shouts and wailing. The five of them ran toward the hubbub; a house of wood and tin lay in ruins, and it was clear that the onlookers believed there was someone trapped beneath.

Half a dozen people were already moving through the wreckage, searching, though no one seemed sure where to look. Bruno approached and spoke with them, and out of the exchange a system emerged, with the searchers passing pieces of the walls and roof back along a chain of volunteers, clearing away the debris instead of lifting and replacing each piece where it had fallen.

Carl and Vinay took the splintered beams and scraps of tin from two of the searchers and handed them on to Bruno and Barbara. The crowd had grown quiet; one elderly woman, who Carl supposed was a relative of the missing occupants, was being comforted by friends, and everyone else had found a place in the chain.

One of the searchers shouted, and his friend helped him lift away a beam, exposing a woman lying motionless on the floor. Her eyes were closed, but the only wound Carl could see was a deep gash in her lower leg that was still bleeding.

The man who had found her squatted down and examined her, then called out excitedly. Carl didn't understand what he'd said, but from the man's tone it was clear that she had to be breathing.

Carl picked up the first aid kit and approached. He knelt down beside her, cleaned and disinfected the wound, then quickly bandaged it. It would need stitches at some point, but he was more afraid that the woman might have a spinal injury. He was about to raise the possibility that the neighbors could improvise some kind of stretcher when she stirred and sat up, agitated.

She spoke to the searchers, directing them as much with gestures as with words. Carl watched as they moved a short distance away and began stepping gingerly through the broken wood. Everyone was distressed now, but they kept to the system, passing each object they lifted down along the chain so it wouldn't hamper their efforts.

When the child lying in the rubble started crying, his mother wailed, but the man who'd found him broke into a smile, then reached down and scooped him up into his arms. Carl looked around at the neighbors, some yelling in triumph, some weeping with joy.

Vinay put a hand on Carl's shoulder, struggling to stay composed. Carl nodded to him in a kind of affirmation, afraid to speak lest he lose control himself.

Bruno called to them, "OK, well done! I've logged this for the medics, and they'll be here when they can. Let's get on to the next street!"

9

IT WAS EARLY AFTERNOON WHEN THE FLIGHT LANDED IN SYDNEY. AFTER SIX WEEKS away, Carl's apartment looked strange to him—all the shapes familiar, but the surfaces dull, like an imperfect attempt to recreate the place from memory.

He threw his clothes in the washing machine, took a long, hot shower, then microwaved a frozen lasagna.

His laptop lay in front of him on the table as he ate. When he was finished, he sat for a while, dreading what was coming. Then he booted it up and started the RStance app.

"I found no evidence of fake casualties," he admitted. "Though I didn't get to Espiritu Santo myself."

He washed the plate and fork he'd used, then sat by the laptop, waiting.

After fifteen minutes, there was a reply. He unlocked it with an old bottle-opener, then dewarped the GIF of trolleys running back and forth over bodies on a tramline. "Good job," the message read. "Your scrutiny must have scared off the crisis actors. Can you stay with CERV, to help keep them in check?"

Carl had been expecting to be upbraided and demoted: he'd failed in his mission, and let the Resistance down. For the last six weeks he'd been growing ever surer that when he'd been caught searching the props cupboard, that had blown his cover and guaranteed that he wouldn't be allowed to see anything suspicious.

But even if they *had* guessed who he was and why he was there, if it had stopped the catastrophists lying to the world, faking deaths to milk people's emotions, wasn't that a kind of success, regardless?

He'd dreamed of rising to the highest level and being picked for a bombing or assassination—but if he was honest with himself, he had never been sure that when the time came he really would have been willing to risk his freedom. To risk never seeing his daughter again.

If he stayed with CERV, holding them to account, keeping them honest, that would not be a small thing. He couldn't force them to accept the truth and acknowledge the real causes and solutions of the problems they claimed to care so much about—but in the end, the truth would assert itself. In the meantime, he could play a modest part, reining in their excesses and thwarting their attempts at disinformation.

He placed the mirrored cylinder against the screen again and scrawled his reply. "Understood. Remaining with CERV until further instructions."

Then he picked up the phone. Caroline would be home from school now, and he'd promised that as soon as he was back he'd come and tell her about the cyclone, and everything he'd seen and done on the islands.

6 WHEN THE TIDE RISES

Sarah Gailey

THERE IS A GOBY IN MY CUPPED HANDS. I DON'T HAVE TO WORK VERY HARD TO keep it there, even though it probably wants to be back with its school. I just lifted up my hands around it in a bowl of latex-covered fingers and it committed itself to its new home, swimming in steady, unpanicked ellipses, lipping at the heels of my palms.

It is bright red and bright orange and vivid electric blue, the same colors as the Octarius Industries logo that repeats over and over across the entire surface of my wetsuit. The company is the only thing that stands between me and the ocean and these colors are the symbol of that protection. Maybe, I think, the goby feels safe in my cupped hands because it can see those colors. Maybe it thinks I'm part of the school. Maybe it sees that logo and says to itself *here is the place where my friends and I stand together against things with mouths.*

Or maybe it just doesn't have the kind of brain that runs from things. I don't know. I don't really know how fish think. Or if they think at all. It isn't my job to know that kind of stuff.

I spread my hands and the goby swims away fast, moving unerringly toward its school, faster than I could ever move in my dive equipment. As the school vanishes into the kelp forest, I flush hot with envy. Octarius gives us good gear—the vests and regulators are top-of-the-line, the tanks are always filled with the right mix for the depths we're working at. I have my own mask and wetsuit, I don't have to share with anyone, not like some other working farms I've heard of where you have to wrestle your way into someone else's soaked suit the minute they're done with it.

It's not that I don't like the gear. It's not that I don't appreciate it. Of course I appreciate it.

It's just not the same.

My body isn't made for this. In fairness my body isn't really made for anything. It wasn't made for topside, where my already-weak lungs couldn't cope with the dust storms and wildfire smoke, and my swollen joints locked up every time there was weather, which was always. I'm better down here, where the temperature's predictable and the air is cycled and processed. Still, I'm acutely aware that this place wasn't ever supposed to be a place for humans to live. Even with state-of-the-art equipment I'm nowhere near as agile as a creature that was born for this environment.

There are solutions for that, but I can't afford them. Yet.

Speaking of Yrene. She passes by me too close, swimming just as fast and agile as the goby did. She's doing it to be an asshole. I know this because it's Yrene and her primary occupation, besides defense at the Eastern perimeter of the kelp forest, is being an asshole. Also because I'm at the Western perimeter right now and it's not like Rising Tide ever comes this close to the dome to steal kelp anyway so her patrol shouldn't bring her over here. There's no reason for her to be near me right now other than to be an asshole. The evidence stacks up is all I'm saying.

Yrene got comprehensive mods a few months ago, along with a promotion to the Eastern perimeter because you can only work that far from the dome if you can stay in the water for more than an hour at a time, and with the mods she can stay in the water for the rest of her *life* at a time. The mods are beside the point, she was an asshole before she got mods. But they're also not beside the point because I am bone-deep achingly jealous of her and being jealous of someone is bad enough by itself but it's just so much *worse* when that person is also an asshole.

Mods don't make you psychic but Yrene can hear my thoughts somehow because she flips around and looks right at me. Her top exposes the lush frills of flesh that sit just below her collarbone. They flutter in the water as she breathes. Gills cost 750 credits at the Octarius surgical center in the East Dome, ₵500 if you've got a signed affidavit promising that you'll get a promotion to the interior zone after you recover. So to her that's ₵500 worth of fuck-you she's fluttering at me, and to me it's ₵750 worth of fuck-you, and that ₵250 difference is another thing I can throw on the pile of reasons I resent Yrene.

It's a big pile. Other things in the pile include:

- Her spleen (₵400 to sextuple red blood cell production, so she can hang onto oxygen and thermoregulate without a wetsuit)
- Her Octarius-issued harpoon gun (I don't need one but I don't like that she has one and I don't)

- Her relationship with my shift manager, formerly *our* shift manager, Eustace (chummy with lots of inside jokes including probably some that are about me)
- Her lungs and ribcage (₡900, collapsible so she can surface and dive without anything crumpling or exploding)
- Her uniform (free and supplied by the company; now that she's modded, all she has to wear is a stretchy top, and it's flattering and that's not fair)
- Her legs (gone)

That last one is the most prominent grievance in my mind right now, because she's showing off her speed and maneuverability by turning upside down to flip me the double-bird. The tail is in company colors but it doesn't look tacky and loud the way my wetsuit does, it looks natural and kind of flashy like a goby or maybe one of the prettier sheepshead. It's ₡1,700 without an affidavit, ₡850 with an affidavit, ₡600 if you have an affidavit *and* combine it with two other procedures so you can rehab faster and get back to work sooner.

Yrene was gone for six weeks. When she came back she was ₡2,400 in debt to Octarius, which sounds like a lot until you realize that between the promotion and the extra shifts she can work at depth, she's quadrupled her salary. She's going to work off that debt within two years, faster if she picks up extra shifts, which she can do without getting hassled by the company doctors because nitrogen's not a problem for her anymore. Just two years and then her whole new body will belong to her along with all that perimeter defense money she'll be making.

Me? I can't even take out a loan from the company bank because if you want to take out a loan from the company bank you need a fucking affidavit and I don't have a fucking affidavit because I don't have whatever it is that Yrene has that makes Octarius look at her and see potential that mustn't be wasted. So I can't even try for a job in the interior sector until I've finally saved up enough money to get my mods (₡3,750, all of which I have to pay in cash up front).

It's taken me nine years to get almost-there. In six more months I'll have enough to get it all done, one fell swoop. And then I have to recover and train and interview for a defense job like the one that Yrene got handed to her for no good reason.

It's not that I care all that much about defending Octarius Industries' property. It's just that working on the defense team is the only way I can

97

100

WHEN THE TIDE RISES

be in the water full-time. Octarius is strict as hell about how much time we spend outside the dome on account of Rising Tide trying to recruit Octarius employees. The company line is that Octarius invests a lot of capital in members of the OI family and it's not right for some thieving Tides to benefit from that investment just because they can't be bothered to commit to stable and productive futures in the kelp-farming industry like we do.

I mean I'm calling that "the company line" but it actually sounds pretty honest when you take out the part about stable and productive futures.

So anyway even if OI gives you a tail, you have to account for the time you spend outside the dome. If you're on defense you can straight-up *live* outside the dome if you want and just call it "extracurricular observation." If I save enough money and recover well enough from the mod procedure and excel in my training and ace the interview, I can give up dome life for good.

But for now I'm stuck out here, on the outskirts of the central branch of Octarius Industries' Pacific coast kelp forest, on urchin duty.

I kick my feet up behind me and reach down to snatch yet another urchin—fist-sized, covered in purple spines, headed for the holdfast of the nearest towering kelp. If he was headed for the huge leaflike blades of the kelp, or even the stipes they grow off of, maybe he would have a different fate. Those are renewable and grow back faster than fast, which is the whole point of the kelp farm. I mean Octarius probably wouldn't be *delighted* at a pest animal eating up their profits, but it would probably be okay to take a slightly less scorched-earth approach to getting rid of them.

But this urchin doesn't want to eat the best parts of the kelp, the parts on the thallus. This urchin has never even heard of konbu. He wants to eat holdfasts, the ropy fists the kelp uses to grasp the seafloor. Because of that, he has to die at the hands of the OI canteen cooks.

He wanted to *eat* dinner, but instead he's going to *be* dinner.

He's on sand, headed from one rock to another, so I can just pick him up with my hands instead of prying him loose with a dive knife. I toss him into the stiff-sided bag at my waist then return to scanning the sand and rocks at the edge of the kelp forest. I've got forty-six urchins in this bag. I need four more before the end of my shift, which is in—I check my dive watch—three minutes.

Shit.

I find one nestled between two rocks and jimmy it loose with the dull edge of my Octarius Industries–issued dive knife and I have two minutes left. There are two more a little closer to the Western Dome, not too far off from a sunflower star that I'm sure is planning to eat them for dinner. Too bad for him. I've got a quota to meet. They go into the bag and that leaves me with fifty-five seconds, plenty of time to find one last urchin before shift is over.

Except that there are none in sight.

I turn in as quick a circle as I can, looking for a spiky silhouette, a purple shadow like a bruise on the seafloor, a patch of rock that looks a little too perfectly round. Nothing.

I signal Artie, who looks like he's just waiting for the shift to be over—he's faster than I am because he doesn't spend as much time hating Yrene—and point to my eyes, then wave a flat palm at the seafloor, our abbreviated sign for *help me look*.

He swims over to help me search. That's Artie for you, always helpful, always reliable. I met him on my first day in the dome twelve years ago now and he hasn't let me down once.

There are only fifteen seconds left when we spot it. The last urchin from this swarm. I don't know how it got past me, but it did.

Artie gives me a push as I start swimming toward it. He sends me rocketing toward the kelp and I kick hard to try to make it in time because that last urchin has gotten all the way up to the holdfast it craves and it's probably chewing on that ropy root right this very minute.

I grab for it with clumsy fingers that immediately get clumsier because my dive watch lights up and buzzes sharply against my wrist. It's the end of my shift. I've been out here under a hundred feet of water, where the pressure is almost four times that of the inside of the dome, for twenty minutes. That's the max. That's my shift.

It's time to go inside.

I grab for the urchin again. This time when I miss my fist doesn't just close around water—it closes around the holdfast of the kelp, just above where the urchin sits. I let go reflexively. I doubt I'm strong enough to yank up a whole thallus off the seafloor on my own, but it's better not to risk it.

My wrist buzzes again, sharper this time, sharp enough to make me grunt. Octarius doesn't fuck around with shift limits unless you have a signed affidavit saying you're okay for overtime, and I don't have an affidavit so this watch is going to keep buzzing me harder and harder until I go inside.

But I can't go inside without this urchin.

I grab my dive knife. I don't want to risk grabbing the thallus again, but I should be able to use the dull side of the knife to pry the urchin off fast.

I wedge it under one edge of the creature and give a wriggle. I can feel it coming loose and I know that with just one hard jerk of the knife I'll have it and then I can go inside and there will be too much gravity but at least I'll be another few credits closer to what Yrene has.

My watch buzzes again and this time it sends an electric jolt up my arm. It's not supposed to send a shock like this, not until the fifth warning, but I don't know, maybe I missed a couple of warnings or maybe I didn't put enough contact gel between my skin and the electrode or maybe it's malfunctioning, or maybe this is just more of my shitty luck because the current that it sends through me rattles my bones and makes my vision blur and my jaw clench and my knees and elbows lock out straight.

It only lasts for a second.

But that's long enough. Once it's over, I look to where the urchin is and see that my knife has gone right through the holdfast of the kelp. Clean fucking through. I'm not usually strong enough to do that in one stroke, not at this pressure and definitely not at the end of a shift, but that shock locked my joints out hard and fast and now this kelp is hanging on by just the thinnest fiber.

As I watch, my muscles twitching in the aftermath of the shock, that fiber pulls taut, stretches, and snaps.

An entire hundred-foot-tall thallus of kelp begins to drift toward the surface. I grab for it but I'm weak on account of being fucking electrocuted and before I can even get close to catching the kelp, a bare hand closes around my wrist.

The next thing I know I'm being tossed across the threshold of the decompression airlock.

The watch lets out a soft chime as it registers that I'm inside. The airlock doors close behind me, and as they do, I catch a glimpse of Yrene's retreating form, the yellow underside of her tail flashing as she vanishes back into the kelp forest.

She threw me inside like it was nothing.

The decompression airlock is my least favorite place. It's about to become my second-least favorite place because as soon as this thing is finished cycling I know I'm going to get called into Eustace's office.

I hate this part of the dome because it slowly brings me back to the environment where humans are supposed to be happiest—one atmosphere of pressure, air instead of water. But it's trying to replicate ideal surface conditions, which is a problem for me. The gravity is too much and it's bright and noisy and while being at pressure in a human body isn't great, I miss the way the water presses in all around me, hugging my body and holding it together. Sometimes, in the dome, when I feel like I'm going to fly apart if just one more person talks to me, I imagine the water keeping me in one piece.

Right now I savor that embrace for just one more minute as I swim to the benches at the far end of the chamber and clip in. Artie is already waiting for me there. I kept us at pressure for a few minutes longer than the maximum recommended amount of time, so we have to stay in this little tube for eight minutes instead of the usual three, which means that he's going to be kind of pissed at me because he's hungry and doesn't want to have to wait for dinner.

There's a heavy *thunk* as the magnets in my station release the gear from my back, then a soft chime as the chamber, recognizing that both of us are seated, starts to drain. Gravity creeps in around me and pain settles into my joints as it does. Once the water is below chin level the same magnets release us from our vests. Artie stands up to strip, but I stay where I am, trying to keep myself in the water as long as possible.

"Damn it," Artie says once his mask is off. He doesn't add "I'm starving" or "why did you do that" or even "what happened out there," probably less to be gentle with me and more because he can't choose between them.

"Sorry," I say reflexively. The joint of my jaw crackles as I flex it.

He starts to strip, unzipping his wetsuit and peeling it off with impatient, jerky motions. "Damn it," he mutters again. He gives up with the top half of his wetsuit hanging loose around his waist like a partially shed exoskeleton, runs his hands through his wet hair. He closes his eyes, working his jaw to try to get his ears to pop even though the water isn't even drained yet so there's no way the pressure will be low enough for that. "Did you get that last one? Did you make quota?"

I shake my head before realizing he can't see me with his eyes shut. "No. I almost had it but then my watch got me."

"Good thing it did. You were four minutes over."

That can't be right. Four minutes? It felt like two at the most. "Are you sure?"

"Sure, I'm sure. I was fucking stuck in here the whole time because I'd clipped into the bench already. The mags had my vest and wouldn't let me go. What kept you so long?"

I shake my head. "I don't know. I thought . . . I thought I had more time than that." No wonder the watch shocked me.

"Well, you didn't." Artie's voice is sharp but not angry. "You want a hand?"

The water is around my knees now, so gravity more or less has me. I do this every shift and it's senseless—waiting for the water to drain before I stand up, so I can stay in it longer. It just makes it harder to get up, in the end, because I have to fight full grav instead of letting the water lift me to a standing position. "No," I say, because I'm stubborn, ask anyone and they'll tell you. Artie frowns like he knows I'm just being stubborn, but he doesn't help me because he knows better.

We spend some time not talking. Artie and I are great at not talking. Fresh water rains down from the ceiling in a comprehensive waterfall, stripping the salt from our bodies and our equipment. Once the deluge ends, the drylock compartment in the wall pops open so we can towel off and put on domewear. We're stuck here for so fucking long that we have ages left after we're dressed. We let our ears pop and we let the air get lighter a little at a time and we breathe out nitrogen and breathe in oxygen and there's not even a hiss as the mix changes but the little lights along the wall of the chamber slowly shift from red to orange to yellow to green, and after a whole ten minutes (I can hear Artie's stomach bellowing) there's a friendly little chime and the door at the far end of the chamber lets out a pneumatic *crack-hssssss*.

Eustace is waiting for me outside the door, just like I predicted. That chamber used to be my least favorite place, but once I see Eustace's grimacing face, it slips down in the rankings.

We walk to his office in silence. Artie takes both of our urchin bags to the weigh station, and I know he'll get me a plate at the commissary so I don't have to worry about showing up so late that there's nothing but wakame and room-temperature oysters left.

"So," Eustace says, settling into the chair behind his desk. There isn't a chair on my side of the desk. I have to stand there, my hair sending little drops of water slithering down the back of my neck to soak the collar of my Octarius-yellow sweatshirt, marinating in the silence that follows that "so." It's not a pleasant silence.

I like Eustace more than Eustace likes me so I'm careful with how I answer. "What do I need to do to make things right?"

Eustace leans forward on his elbows. "This is pretty serious." He's still not saying which thing I'm in trouble for—losing the kelp or staying at pressure past the end of my shift. Probably both.

"I know," I say, because I do, and then I add "I'm sorry," which I know won't be enough but maybe it will.

"I like you a lot," he lies. "But this isn't up to me."

Fuck. Shit. Fuck. I take a halting half step toward his desk, lifting my hands in a gesture that could mean anything but in this case means *please don't fire me*. "I'll do whatever I have to do. Please, I really need this job, I love this job, I love Octarius and I'll do whatever it takes to fix this, please, Eustace—"

He holds up a hand to silence me. "I'm not firing you." I start to thank him but he points at me and I shut up quick. "But you're on probation. And I've gotta take the next couple of shifts off your schedule. That's company policy for anyone who ends up having to spend more than eight minutes decompressing." He sees my skepticism and adds, "*Without* prior authorization. You know what I mean. It's dangerous. You could have gotten really hurt."

I only sort of know what he means. Lots of people spend extra time in the decompression chamber after they work overtime. Lots of people go back in the water the next day and the day after that too without taking recovery time or seeing the company doctor for a sign-off, and they don't get lectures about how it's *dangerous*.

But Eustace never approves me for overtime or extra shifts. Maybe it's because my joints and bones are messed up enough as it is and he thinks he's doing me a favor by keeping them from getting worse. Or maybe it's because he's friends with Yrene and has to prove his loyalty to her by dicking me over. I don't know. The part of this that matters is the part where I'm already earning the absolute bare minimum and now I'm losing shifts.

I try to negotiate. "What if I go see Stan?" I hate visiting the company doctor but I'll do it if it means I don't have to stop working. I can afford to wear a paper gown while a hack doctor pretends to examine me. I *can't* afford to stop working, not when I'm this close to getting my mods.

"Oh, you'll go see Stan," he says. "You got zapped pretty good. He's going to want to check out your heart, make sure you can still dive."

I stifle panic, trying not to lose my shit in front of Eustace. "Of course I can still dive," I say, my voice cracking halfway through the sentence.

"We'll see," he says, frowning.

I nod, biting the inside of my cheek hard to try to keep from crying. "Okay. Thanks, Eustace." I don't know what I'm thanking him for but it seems like the thing to say. I turn to go, eager to be out of sight so I can freak out.

But before I can go, Eustace says "Hang on." I'm hoping it's the kind of *hang on* that means *I've reconsidered and actually we can make this all go away*, but when I look back at him I know it's the other kind of *hang on*, the kind that means *this is about to get worse*. "We have to talk about the damage you did to company property."

It knocks the wind out of me. Doing damage to company property is bad. It's really bad. "Right," I breathe. "I'm really sorry about that. It won't happen again."

"It had better not. And . . . look, I'm sorry, but I have to ask. It's company policy. Let's just get it out of the way: Do you have any relationship with Rising Tide?"

The question is so startling that I can't answer right away. "Do I what?"

He says it again, slower this time. "Do you have any relationship with the terrorist organization Rising Tide? Is there any reason *at all* for me to go through the immense headache of reporting you to the defense team for possible sabotage and collusion?"

I laugh and then I stop laughing fast because maybe laughing will make me look guilty instead of incredulous. "No! No, I can't—I don't even know how I would—terrorist organization?" He gives me the kind of patient stare that communicates restraint. "I thought they were just . . . I don't know. A nuisance, taking kelp and stuff. Fucking around with experimental surgical mods. Not anything serious."

The weariness drops from his voice for a moment and he grows stern. "You don't think stealing from the company is serious? They sabotaged a defense monitoring system along the Southern Perimeter last week. You don't think that's serious?"

I am suddenly aware that there was a right answer to give him a minute ago and I didn't give it. "No. I mean yes, of course it's serious, and no, I'm not involved with them. Not at all. What happened, what I did, it wasn't sabotage. It was an accident."

Just like that, he's back to the Eustace I know how to navigate: tired, overwhelmed, eager to have me out of the way. "Good. That lines up with what Yrene had to say."

"When did you talk to Yrene?" It's not important but the words just kind of fall out of me.

"During your ten-minute decompression cycle," he says pointedly. His gaze is steady and not all that sympathetic. "Look, I'm supposed to write you up for this . . . but if I do, and the defense team finds out that you stayed out past the end of your shift *and* uprooted an entire thallus of kelp, they're going to bring you in for questioning. I don't think you'd enjoy that."

"No," I agree. I don't know exactly what *questioning* involves and I don't want to find out.

"So here's what I'm going to do instead." He activates a keyboard in the surface of his desk and types something, his eyes flickering as he reads something on his private display. "I'm going to tell the company you bought the thallus for personal recreational use."

"Bought? A whole thallus? Do people do that?"

"All the time," he replies distractedly, still typing. "For parties or whatever. Usually C-level execs, not fieldworkers, but whatever, maybe you won a sweepstakes and wanted to celebrate. They don't need to know and it's not like they'll investigate. As long as it looks like you compensated them for the thing instead of just losing them income, they'll be happy."

I run my fingers through my still-dripping hair. "Wow. Thanks, Eustace, I—I don't know how to thank you. This really means a lot to me." I mean it. Maybe I've been wrong about him. Maybe he likes me as much as I like him, after all.

"Don't mention it. Ever. To anyone." He finishes typing and his eyes focus on me again. "Okay. You're all set."

"That's it?"

"That's it. I transferred the funds out of your Octarius account. You're lucky you're such a tightwad. You had enough to buy the thallus and still have enough credits left for your appointment with Stan." He points at me, a dismissal and a warning put together. "Don't let this happen again."

Something in what he's saying buzzes at me like the end of a shift. "Wait. Wait, how much did this cost?"

He lets out a humorless laugh. "A lot. Don't worry," he adds, seeing my face fall. "Your savings covered it, easy. And hey, at least you made your quota today, right? It's not like all that was for nothing."

I drift out of the room, almost numb but not quite. That warning buzz starts to rise in my chest and fill my throat. He transferred the funds out of my Octarius account. My Octarius account, which I've been slowly (*so* slowly) filling over the course of nearly a decade. When I looked this morning, it had an even ₵3,400 in it. I have no idea how much a thallus costs. I try to do worst-case scenario math in my head before looking at my account, hoping that I'll come up with something worse than what it turns out to be, so I can be relieved.

The most expensive thing I've ever paid for is my hips. All my joints are bad but for a while there my hips were the worst and it was getting to the point that I couldn't stand up off the bench in the decompression chamber without Artie's help, stubbornness be damned. So I went to Stan and he injected some kind of goo in there, something with a steroid to bring down the inflammation and a genetically modified coral synthate to restructure the places where my bones were trying to fuse. *I usually only have to give this to old-timers*, he said as he slid the needle in, and I clenched my teeth and said something about my arthritis being ambitious, and he laughed and then he charged me ₡75. That's a little over two months' pay, before what Octarius takes out to charge for food and rent and equipment.

That injection pushed my plan to get mods back by six months.

I squeeze my eyes shut and tell myself that the thallus probably costs twice that. It's ₡150. Four months wages before expenses. Between the shifts I'm losing and that amount coming out of my account to pay for my fuckup today, my plan will get pushed back by a year. That means a whole extra year of working tiny shifts, scraping together a little money at a time, watching Yrene swim circles around me.

Another year of gravity. Another year feeling the creaking of my knees and hips with every step I take. Another year in the dome.

I wait for the crush of it to fade, like waiting for my ears to pop when I'm in the decompression chamber. It only takes a few minutes. Once my heartbeat stops pounding in my temples and I stop feeling like I'll die if I have to spend a whole extra year down here, I open my eyes. I'm ready to look at my balance.

I tap the face of my dive watch three times to pull up my Octarius account. The facial recognition is old and slow, but after a few seconds it flashes green, and then my account summary comes up.

My heart sinks. This can't be right. I must be misreading, missing a zero somewhere. It was just one thallus of kelp out of the entire forest. One thallus out of a forest that's big enough to change the oxygen levels in the ocean, big enough to reduce the carbon levels in the atmosphere, big enough to save the world. It was just one thallus.

But no matter how long I stare, the number doesn't change.

Of the ₡3,400 I had when I woke up this morning, ₡567 is left.

I MOVE INTO ARTIE'S PLACE BECAUSE I CAN'T AFFORD MY OWN ANYMORE AND HE feels sorry enough for me that he doesn't say *no* even though he probably wants to. His place is spacious—tall enough to stand up in, wide enough that both of us can stand next to our hammocks without needing to be inside each other. I hang my hammock just below his. My ass brushes the ground when I lie down but that's okay.

The ventilation system in the dome is no joke—it keeps us from suffocating on our own carbon dioxide and also it does a great job mitigating the more fragrant concerns that arise when you're in an airtight dome full of people. It's also noisy as hell, which is to my benefit right now. I try to cry as quietly as I can so I don't keep Artie up all night but I'm not that quiet and I'm counting on the ventilation system to cover for me.

I think I'm doing an okay job until Artie's hand drops off the edge of his hammock. His fingers flex in the air until I grab them.

"Sorry," I say, my voice thick and wobbly and miserable. "I didn't mean to keep you up."

He doesn't say anything for a long time and I figure he's probably either mad or falling back asleep until he makes a disgusted noise. "Fuck's sake." I'm about to get indignant because hey, I don't think I'm being that bad of a roommate already—but then he squeezes my hand hard. "We gotta quit this rig."

It startles me enough that I stop crying. "What?"

"We have to get out of here," he says. "This place is gonna kill us both."

I don't really know what to say to that. Artie was born here and I've always assumed we would both die here and that means working for Octarius. You can't exactly live in the company town if you don't work for the company. This is our best option: stay in the water, away from the surface, away from the weather, and work until we stop breathing. "What would we possibly do if we quit?" I ask. "What, you wanna go live topside?"

He lets out a breathy, angry laugh. "Come on. I'm serious."

"So am I. Where would we go?"

"It's not like Octarius is the only place in the water where people can live."

I hesitate. "You're talking about Rising Tide."

"They're not what you think they are."

"I know. Eustace told me today. They're not just biohackers," I whisper. "They sabotage company equipment too. He made it sound like they're dangerous. And they're thieves."

He answers fast enough that I know he's been thinking about this a lot and I wonder how much he's been thinking about it and why he hasn't said anything sooner. "How can it be theft if it's something that should belong to everyone anyway? The international subsidies that got Octarius off the ground were intended to fund projects that would benefit *everyone*. Rising Tide is just taking what they're owed."

"The kelp forest *does* benefit everyone," I whisper. "It's a sustainable—"

"Come on," he interrupts. "Food and fuel being *sustainable* doesn't matter if you get shot with a harpoon gun for trying to get your hands on some of it."

"Don't be naive," I snap. "It's not like OI can just give kelp away. The company has to make money *somehow*."

His reply is so soft that I almost don't catch it. "Why?"

". . . Why what?"

"Why do they have to make money?"

I don't have a response to that. It's like he's asking why we need air in our dive tanks or why I have to lie down to sleep. I know there has to be an answer, but the harder I try to figure it out the more lost I feel.

I have a sinking feeling that he's already made up his mind about some things.

"We could get out of here. They have their own dome and we could go live there. They could give you mods that you wouldn't have to work a decade to save up for, and I could do something more interesting than collecting sea urchins," he insists. "We could go together."

Longing gnaws at me like an empty belly when he mentions the mods. "The mods they do can't be safe," I say, and even to my own ears I sound unconvincing.

"They're exactly as safe as the ones you'd get here."

"How do you know?" He doesn't answer me, which makes me think the answer is probably not one I'd like anyway. I try to keep my voice measured but of course I can't keep it measured because Artie is my best friend. "It sounds like you've been planning this for a while." More silence from the hammock above me. "When were you going to tell me?"

He sighs. "I wasn't."

I feel like my lungs are collapsing. "You were just going to leave me?"

His reply is painfully gentle. "Well, no. You were gonna get your mods and apply for Defense and go live in the water. I figured . . ." he trails off.

"Figured what?" It comes out in a whisper because I can't reach full volume, not with this much shame crushing the air out of me.

"I figured this was always just temporary anyway. Me and you. But now you won't be able to get your mods here for a long time." The last part of that sentence comes out reluctantly. Artie isn't great at being delicate but I can appreciate that this is his best effort. "So instead of waiting for you to leave me behind, I thought we could leave together." He squeezes my hand hard. "You can get the things you need now. Come with me. Please."

Here's the part where I'm supposed to say something that proves that I had thought this through. Something that will let Artie know that I had considered the fact that I'd be leaving him behind when I got my mods. But the truth is, I was only focused on the fact that I'd get to be in the water full-time.

I haven't been thinking about who I'd be leaving behind.

And now he's trying to take me with him into a new life, and instead of saying yes, I'm frozen. I feel like that little goby, cupped in the big, gloved hands of Octarius. If those hands fall away, will there be a school waiting for me to swim with it?

Or will I just be on my own in an ocean that's big enough to make me disappear?

I'm quiet for much too long, longer than indecision alone would merit. "Artie, I'm—"

"Forget it," he says, letting go of my hand. "It was a stupid idea anyway. I didn't think it through." He shifts above me. "Let's just go to sleep."

I wrap my arms around myself tight, imagining the water holding me together. "Okay," I whisper. "Goodnight."

He doesn't say anything back. I lie there in the dark, waiting to hear his breath get slow and even and steady as he falls asleep. But it never does.

I GO TO THE DOCTOR AND PAY HIM TO GIVE ME AN AFFIDAVIT SAYING I CAN STILL DIVE. I attend a probationary training in which I am handed a packet about the dangers of staying at depth for too long and told to read it. I eat breakfast and dinner with Artie when he's not working and it's no more or less awkward than usual.

He doesn't bring up Rising Tide again until the end of my first week of probation. We're eating dinner—miyuk guk with chunks of preserved mackerel—and he's sweating a little because he overdid the chili oil again.

"You gonna survive?" I ask as he mops his brow with the hem of his shirt.

He grins at me. "Never felt more alive."

"Say what you will about Octarius," I say, shucking an oyster from yesterday's harvest with clumsy fingers, "they know how to feed us." It's the kind of thing we always say, the kind of thing that should land easy, but it doesn't land easy at all. It lands hard and sits on the table between us panting and writhing while we both try to figure out what to do with it. I shoot my oyster in one awkward swallow, then wipe my mouth on the back of my wrist. "I didn't mean—"

"I know you didn't," he says, putting his spoon down and frowning at the beads of red oil that shimmer on top of his soup. "But you did, though."

"That was careless of me." I reach for his hand and he doesn't reach back but he doesn't pull away either. "I'm sorry."

His eyes are the saddest eyes in the whole world. "Them feeding us shouldn't be a compliment," he whispers. "We shouldn't have to be grateful that we get to eat every day. Not when it's food that we harvest *and* pay for."

I feel sour all over. I'm not mad at Artie but I don't know who I'm mad at so I point it at him. "Spoken like someone who never went hungry on the surface," I say, and I mean it to come out clever and world-weary but it comes out bitter and spiteful. "You were born down here," I add. "You don't know what it's like up there."

His eyes stop being sad. They stop being anything. "Okay," he says mildly, picking up his spoon again.

"Artie. Come on."

"No," he says, not meeting my eyes. "You're right. I don't know what it's like up there. It makes sense why you'd be satisfied with how things are down here, after all you saw when you were topside. I get it."

He says it like I've settled an argument—he says it like I've won—but I can't help feeling like I'm losing something.

MY TWO WEEKS OF PROBATION END AND I GET A SHIFT ASSIGNMENT AND I CAN barely zip up my wetsuit, I'm so excited. I get to go back in the water. It's been two weeks in the dome, two weeks of gravity, two weeks of pain. My joints are swollen and it's hard for me to grip anything well enough to suit up but I manage. It's worth it.

Before we clip in to our vests, Artie catches me by the shoulder. "Hey," he says, "I'm really glad you're going back in the water." And then he grips me in a tight hug, just for a second. "I missed you."

"I missed you too." I'm relieved that he's not holding our weird fight against me, that he's still my friend. I don't know what I'd do without Artie. I decide to talk to him about Rising Tide again tonight, to really listen this time. I want to be a better friend to him. He deserves that from me.

The pool fills slowly with water and then the airlock opens and we swim out. I'm giddy at the feel of it—the way the water holds me and supports me and lets me move freely. Together, we head toward our assigned sector for the day, where a fresh urchin herd has started to move in on the forest.

We're ten minutes into the shift when they arrive.

It happens just like anything happens in the water: they're not there until suddenly they are. I startle and drop the two urchins I'm holding, then swim backward and away from the strangers. Two of them, in dark green gear that keeps them invisible right up until the moment they melt out of the kelp. One is in a diving rig like mine. The other has a long, slender tail that's covered in the same dark green pigment as their skin.

They look back and forth between me and Artie. My heart is pounding because they're in camouflage, which means they're probably from Rising Tide and they don't look dangerous but Eustace's voice echoes in my skull saying *collusion and sabotage*. Defense is probably already on the way. I need to be anywhere but here and that needs to happen fast.

I reach for Artie to pull him close to me so we can get out of this together.

Only, when I reach for him, he isn't there.

He's swimming away from me. He's swimming into the kelp. And that's when I know the thing I didn't want to know. That's when I know I've run out of time to talk, to listen, to be a better friend.

He's leaving with them. He's leaving me here. He's given up on me.

Only he hasn't, because he turns around and gestures to me, a gesture that isn't a sign but that transparently says *Come on. Come with me. Don't stay here without me, come with me and these strangers and let's lead a different life.*

I hesitate. I hesitate because in that moment when I thought he was abandoning me I wanted to go with him, I wanted it bitterly, I wanted to leave this place and find what else there might be in this ocean I've lived in for over half my life but barely seen. And now it turns out I can have that. I can go with him.

And it freezes me, just for an instant. The sudden flush of enormous, terrifying possibility.

It freezes me just long enough for something to flash through the water, past the left side of my head and toward Artie. One of his new companions—the one with the tail—shoots through the water and grabs him, yanking him out of the way of the thing. I twist to look behind me and see Yrene coming toward us, bullet-fast, her harpoon gun drawn.

The Tides tug at Artie, pulling him into the kelp. He thrashes, fighting them, and they let him go and start to swim away, the one with the tail glancing back to see if Artie's following.

He isn't. Not yet. He's staring at me. He's waiting.

And then Yrene is next to me, her spent harpoon gun holstered at her hip, her hand on my wrist gentler than it was when she shoved me into the decompression chamber. I look at her and because of her mods I can see her whole face, unobscured by a diving mask or goggles. Her eyes are bright and urgent and sadder than I've ever seen her.

She lets go of my wrist and signs to me, fast in spite of the drag of the water. *Are you leaving?*

I sign back with both of my hands, slow and clumsy. *I don't know.*

She stares at me for a moment longer, nodding slowly even though I haven't given her anything to agree with. Then she draws her harpoon gun, presses it into my hands, and swims past me. She doesn't look back. She just vanishes into the kelp forest, after my best friend and the people he's decided to follow. The weight of the harpoon gun in my hands makes me certain neither of them are planning to come back.

The ocean presses in around me on all sides, holding me together.

112

7   I GIVE YOU THE MOON

Justina Robson

THE APOCALYPSE WAS A TERRIBLE DISAPPOINTMENT.

There was no great flood. Fire did not fall from the sky, not even a meteorite. You couldn't even write the line, "Death stalked slowly in her cloak of many viruses, because Terminators always walk," because although that was true it gave the event a lot more color and interest than it deserved. Even displayed in graphs and comparative charts with numbers and pulsating animated globs and fire-crisping maps it took thirty years to complete. It progressed by boring increments of boom and bust before fizzling out to inconvenient embers in the cities, where for ages its only sign was the sudden hacking cough of passersby to startle the occasional cat from its nap on the hot pavements. Millions died, several times, and nobody since had stopped banging on about it in case it wasn't really over, though what their anxiety was going to do to fix it was anybody's guess.

Jack took off his hat. The lesson that had filled his hearing and vision vanished. He set the hat down on the sand beside him and sat in the sudden quiet of the calm sea and the empty sky, not even a gull to see. The breeze boxed his ears with a random blather. A hundred meters to his left the old man who had been fishing when he started his lecture, was still fishing in exactly the same spot. As far as the eye could see in all directions, they were alone.

Behind them Jack felt the continental bulk of Africa sitting quietly, satisfied with whatever was going on. It had a cozy quality this afternoon, not so much at their backs as having their backs in a way that seemed to say that they were free to do what they wanted about whatever they thought important, silly little creatures, it would still be there regardless, no worries, until something happened to it far in the future that changed it into something new. But Jack wouldn't see that, it was a problem for future Africa, though as Africa had no problem with it there was no problem at all. Continents were lucky that way.

Right now Jack's problem was that he had to complete his history course before he could qualify for Viking Adventure. Jack had lived his whole life on this coastline and Viking Adventure would take him far away from it, through strange lands to the white North where the last ice still capped the planet. He longed to feel it, to taste it, to see how cold it was. Here on the beach the temperature was about 30°C and the idea of a glacier, a frozen river, a snowfield—felt like the most amazing thing there could be. Almost unbelievable that it existed. And the Vikings themselves, creatures of legend: he felt a kinship of a strange kind to them, savage travelers wandering their own coasts, fearless upon the sea in ships made by hand, out of wood—forests! Ah, to walk in a thick forest of trees, hunting deer, fending off wolves, spear in hand, and a helmet with horns on it, and a sword and shield, and big fur boots . . .

He bent down to pick up a shell half buried in the sand and studied it for a second. Chamber after chamber went spiraling away, around the bend, old fossil houses turned by a living lathe. That's what Dad had said about them. He peered in, tried to see further, further into the past. If only the stupid lecture was as fascinating as a shell. If he put on his hat he could know all about it, maybe see through the shell itself into its secret vaults.

But it was nicer with the secret in it.

He dropped it back where he found it and walked up to the fisherman, taller than he was, thin like him, wearing a nearly identical blue cotton fishing hat in a size too big with the brim pulled low over his eyes. At his feet the rod was rooted in the sand, its curve moving idly; nothing on the line.

DARIUS WATCHED THE TIDE ROLLING SLOWLY IN. IN ANOTHER HALF AN HOUR IT would reach his feet and then it would be time to pack up for the day.

With the extra vision granted by his hat he was monitoring the levels of flow in the Eastern Atlantic Reactor. The huge machine lay at modest depth, sieving plastic from the Benguela Current as it bore northward up the coast; a scrubbing brush for seawater. The ominous name fitted its appearance, not its function. It was an old beast, a cage of steel and—ironically—plastic, holding a sequence of membrane filters and ferrofluid resonance chambers out into the flow. Its aquaplaned sides and solar-powered motors kept it positioned at the fastest run of water. It sat as one of a series, number twenty-one out of forty of its bony kind, strung down toward the Cape from Gabon. Far above, almost invisible in the sky, albatross gliders monitored his little patch and the whole of the Atlantic Sea Farm, guiding the cleaners away from pods of whales and other cetaceans, sending them to depth when storms threatened to disturb their balances. But a human was required to check, verify, and interpret their findings. Darius kept his line out, his eye on the inner workings of the filters during his shift. He cued a maintenance crew to make ready for a resupply and cleanup. Good old Twenty-One, another billion tons of water cleaned, another, better day for everyone. He felt fond of all his machines.

The line bobbed as the weights—packed instruments working to read all the sea's secrets—rode the waves. There was no hook, no catch for fish. He'd caught dinner an hour ago and now he was only fishing for information.

Closer to home his cast of drone crabs were busy on the seabed, picking up man-made pollutants and logging notes of other debris they encountered as they patrolled. They periodically constructed buoyant cubes of garbage and floated them to the surface. The albatrosses noted the positions on their ever-changing charts and deployed pickup craft to return the casks for reprocessing at the nearest shore facility. It was automated. But some jobs were hard to automate and they popped up frequently, usually when crabs got stuck in and around wreckage. Then Darius would have to personally intervene and drive them out by hand—well, by hat, but everyone still said by hand like it was the days of controllers that you had to wiggle and press instead of hats that picked up your intentions and transformed them directly into processes elsewhere.

Darius had come to the coast for the wrecks thirty years ago, before hats, in the days of hand controls. There had been no crabs then, only human workers and their various tools, on shore and boat, living a leisurely lifestyle on the fringes of the Blue Wild where they were tasked with policing, maintenance, cleanup, and reporting. This was during the slow buildup toward the international accords that finally came together to reclassify the globe's seawater habitats into Blue Farm and Blue Wild. This piece of the Namibian coast, where desert met sea, was a part of the Wild now. Its beauty was reserved for what wildlife might come, and for small and regulated numbers of human visitors who paid in reward tokens or immense amounts of money for the privilege of spending a few days in one of the hotels. From there they fished and walked, or rode camels or robot hobbyhorses up and down the surf line, painted pictures, tried yoga, all the usual things people did when they wanted to feel they'd become closer to nature.

Darius had been a cleaner, then a builder, as they renovated some of the more stable shipwrecks into living quarters and luxury restaurants.

After they were done he became a tour guide, both on shore and undersea, until he left that life for something that felt more like giving back. He had joined Blue Wild as a crab master when Hyundai had started up their part of the shore operations here, and now he fished the coast and monitored the drones. He lived in a little hut of his own during the week, where his son could visit him every few months, and come and ask questions, and stare impatiently at the sea, and not do his classes.

There he was now, coming up after just half an hour of study, hangdog expression, nearly as tall as Darius already and easy to recognize by his ungainly assortment of elbows, knees, hands, and feet. He was newly awkward in gait, hesitant in a way he'd never been a few years ago, even though he was the only other human on the beach for miles.

Darius missed that little boy. Always so happy. Free of care. The program for kindergarten was gentle like a soft breeze, full of the wonders of the world, none of the difficulties. Then the inescapable courses about the past had come and a serious, pondering heaviness had set in like bad weather. Could be his age a bit. It came and went.

At his age Darius had been in a very different world, a bricks-and-mortar school with papers and exams. He'd not liked it, had skipped as much as he dared to wander the street instead, despite the threat of capture and punishment. It was strange to think back on it, because now he couldn't get enough of staying in touch with his interests, far and wide. The possibilities were endless in the connected world of daily lives, where you could dip in and out of someone's experience a world away, see things through their hat, be in their moment. It was a time made for dreamers and drifters.

It was a miracle Jack had got this far really with that kind of background, but Darius was proud of him, because years ago Jack had got it into his head that he wanted to be a Viking and damned if the kid hadn't stuck to it, limpet to its rock, clinging to that strange dream. He'd saved his tokens, taking extra learning credits, doing all he could to earn his place, and nobody could say no to it because he was going to buy the reward all by himself. It belonged to him and him alone.

Not like Darius hadn't endorsed it. Because it was still education when you looked at it. It was history and learning how to live without modern conveniences, like humans did before the industrial age had wrecked the biosphere. And Jack's mother, when she was alive, always said study and work for what you want. Never listen to other people. The world isn't like it used to be. We've got the Accord that says anyone can learn, can't be stopped, and tokens to buy things we'd never have thought of, and nobody can say no to us now for any reason. Stay at home, travel the world, be here, be this, that, the other. Do what you want to do. All you have to do is contribute and save. She'd been the Accord's biggest fan, Marta, proud that her own mother had worked hard to see these new methods brought in, and that she was alive on the day it was signed up to, a global dedication. Yes, of course, at first it was hard going, took forty years to get it anything like functional, had to be frequently saved from ditching into various ideological and aggressive pits, but in spite of all the nationalisms and setbacks it was still alive. It gave a sense of possibility that hadn't existed before and it delivered. Mostly.

He wanted so badly that it would deliver for Jack. *Things must get better*, he said to the Marta in his mind, *they must. We have to make sure they do.*

Darius thought Jack would have wanted the usual—days out, sports, extra tech—but Jack had come home one day from school with the Vikings book and that was that. What about something closer to home? Marta had said. What about Kaokoland? Beautiful animals to see. Heritage of our own to treasure. Even if it doesn't seem as exotic as Europe, it's still good.

But Jack sighed. He liked Kaokoland well enough, but these ferocious ancients had stolen his imagination right away with their wooden dragon-ships and their romance of conquest and discovery, their bravery in the face of sea and ice. Somehow they felt more wild and full of possibility.

While Jack dreamed of ice Darius felt uneasy about the trip, no denying that. He'd never been to Europe, and he felt an old anger about the past, couldn't help it; not a personal one that is, for living folk who weren't involved, but for all them that were, far away and invisible to him, hidden by history. They were in Europe, surely, still. And in the world of his anxieties he saw Jack would go there, idealistic, full of ideas about Vikings, and there would be some kind of unpleasant thing that was bubbling around inside that society, rising to the surface like crab-garbage. A face that didn't fit, a strange voice, a wrong move in a place where you couldn't know the customs enough and trouble would start. Well, he couldn't know that for sure, but he felt worried about it. And instead of being useful Darius'd be on his beach, sifting for news of whales and dolphins, sharks and shoals, telling them all about his fears, wondering if they'd carry them to the cold waters of the North Sea and ask the seals how it was going these days in that place that was a home to all the old invaders.

Seals had no problems with nationality. Only with orcas. And the whims of fish. And humans of course.

Darius thinks of these things because he knows Jack has reached modern history and is covering the twentieth century and its various tides and reckonings. The weight of this knowledge is a burden in the body, not just the mind. It has heft to it, as if genes are a chain back through the ages, dragging the past and its unfinished business. Children shouldn't have burdens. It irks him that he had to learn and his son had to learn about this. It might be better if Jack was protected from it. What you don't know can't hurt you. They said history must be known so it wasn't repeated, but what was there to fight about without it?

The past was another world from which this one was born. An inadequate parent, but the only one. Some kind of shame makes Darius want to slither off into the sea.

He's keenly aware that he keeps telling Jack to finish the history course. But he wishes the history course didn't exist. He doesn't want to be the witness to crushing disappointment, doesn't want to have to feel that himself, again.

A crab is stuck. It has been cycling through its disengagement protocols for over an hour and now it has reached the point where it signals him for help. Its battery is a bit low. If he can't get it out quickly he'll have to bring up the others to recover it. It's a long job and the sun has started to go down. And here's Jack, silent and watchful because he's not able to go on with his lesson.

Darius takes off his hat, holds it out. A boy should learn to do something useful.

"Want to drive this crab out of trouble for me?"

Jack's eyes light up immediately. He thought he was going to get a telling off for failing. "Yeah!"

They switch hats.

JACK LOVES TO DRIVE THE CRABS, EVEN THOUGH THEY DON'T DO ANYTHING OTHER than grub along for waste material and even though they're nothing like a game. They require a knowledge of the sand, the silt, the strange configurations of legs they can get into and how those things conspire to free you from a terrible trap. You free the machine from something it can't figure out, just because you're human and you'll try all kinds of things until you win.

They're a puzzle and sometimes you discover things that you didn't know about too, because by accident you shiver and shake, try the legs in new patterns, dig with the claws and some miracle happens and you have a new move in your repertoire that you'd never have thought of without the accident. Plus, the crabs are important, very valuable, doing great work, and helping them makes him happy, like a good deed for the day. He's good with the crabs, they're a happy place.

This one is rammed nose down against some piece of steel from the wreck of a hulk, long scuppered. It's too rusted and decayed for it to be worth stripping for steel. Instead it's part of the diving school's monthly advanced skills trips to deep waters. Jack's been there. You can go into the rooms inside it. It is mostly buried in the thick silt of the continental shelf and even though the chances are incredibly thin, more thin than the lottery, Jack always hopes he's going to find a diamond. You never know.

He sometimes looks for a hint of bronze or silver, a chunk of wood that might be from a Drakkar ship that came long ago, bearing Vikings. It's silly. They didn't come this far south. But they could have. If they'd wanted to. Nothing to stop them but the distance from home. He felt their urge to find, to discover, to get for themselves some piece of the world. But his world was pieced out.

The crab has only 15 percent battery left, and after a test of each possible operation there's some fault with the left-side front legs too. The balloon of garbage attached to it has wedged hard between one of the skeleton's ribs and a section of its skin. First thing is to seal that off, label it, tag it, and detach it. Even with that done it remains stuck, but at least it isn't an anchor on the crab now.

Jack moves his arms and the crab, mapped into his nervous system by the hat, copies him gingerly, a little left, a little right, forward, back. There is no leverage that will move him backward he discovers. The efforts of the ordinary systems to get themselves out of trouble have, thanks to the garbage balloon, actually dug it deeper in.

A bloom of silt, pale clouds, covers the cameras, swirls and shuts him into a tiny world of fog and guesswork. He can feel, through his own muscles, just how the little robot is held fast by the weight of the ship, the thick density of the mud, its own peculiar shape. On the beach he can still feel sun on his skin as he weaves and dances, searching for a clue that his brain will find without him thinking about it, just because he's an animal who understands how to deal with these things. It's fun and today, boy, it's difficult. Sweat runs down his brow and, without a hand to use, he shakes his head.

The crab twists itself deeper. Uh oh.

DARIUS WENT BACK TO THE SUNSHADE OF THE SOLAR TENT AND SAT DOWN TO MAKE a brew. Just out of interest and not because he was prying, he put on Jack's hat and glanced at the last lesson. Apocalyptic Times, 2020–2030. Yeah, that was a long course, long and the subject of a lot of argument and opinion, so much so that any effort to make a cohesive grab at the whole picture was exhausting. No wonder Jack was struggling. But you have to struggle or you don't get through it and the big picture is important, the one they all lived by now.

He figured his way through the menus of the lesser hat until he was able to send a personal call out to Windhoek. He was put on a timer and spent the wait fixing the teabags and the mugs, a place for Jack to sit when he was done, a snack from the cooler.

Then Esther answers. "Hi, Darius!" She beams. They say that—someone's smile beams—but it had just been a figure of speech to him until he saw her smile and then he understood. It had beams, like joyful lasers that cut straight through everything to a simpler world in which all things are right. It puts him right, straight away. Everything is all right. Although he suspects she's like this with everyone, he's delighted, though it's a guilty pleasure. Even though Jack's mother is long gone always the guilty twinge. Well, you live with these things.

"Hey, Esther." An awkward moment, will he say anything? "How's everything?" He won't. A disappointed feeling, but there's still hope, of a kind, they do have reason to chat. Esther is the lead local coordinator of Special Cleaning, which tracks the prevalence of biohostile chemicals in their precinct. Darius files reports for her department. There's a perfectly good channel that doesn't require personal contact, but they had met at a dinner hosted for a few award winners when he had won a Blue Wild Commendation and she had been at the same table and he'd had some wine and forgotten to ask what she did until the end of the night, by which time they'd already been talking for hours. So he hadn't been scared off in time, and now there was a thing he had to deal with here, a dance he had to do, without knowing the steps.

If she detected any awkwardness in him she showed no sign of it.

"Ah, you know, I think soon I'll be out of a job. The clean up on the southern coast is so good now we're getting numbers that are almost neutral." She beamed, and he smiled back. It was a good feeling, and not just because of the feedback in the hat, subtly beavering away to reinforce the appeal of otherwise mundane tasks, but because every success against the desecration was a step forward on his own personal sense of value. "But it also means I have less points," she said. "Do you know, I think I'll never reach my goal. A few years ago when things were still bad I was doing really well, but now unless I move on to some other position—I did a few sums and it could be another ten years before I have enough credit." She sighed and did a dramatic shrug.

Darius felt a pang of concern. Would she really go? It had been—lord, it had been nearly a year since the dinner and he was still pussyfooting around like a kid. But he'd done it for so long that he felt sure he was solid friendzone material. Nothing else.

"How are you doing out there? How's Jack?"

"Oh, he's great. Just digging a crab out for me. Doing really well. School's a bit of a struggle."

"Still the Vikings?"

"Just one credit short."

They both paused. One credit short of a major achievement was a huge deal. They'd bonded at their dinner party because they'd both been people with long term savings—the annotated fruits of a lifetime building up in their banks; Darius because he was happy out on the shore and had wasted no time explaining how wonderful it was to be out alone with nature, working on his favorite things. He wouldn't give it up for the world. And Esther said she was saving for the moon. Not the whole thing. For the trip *to* the Moon, a walk on the surface, a two-day stay at the hotel, and then back again. In the grand scheme of all the things one could save for—and they were too many to scroll through in a day—this was the most expensive. For an average person it would take a saved credit lifetime of more than thirty years' human-advancing, world-tending achievement.

Esther had been on track for that, head down and full steam, she said at the dinner, but then, time began to tell. The years pass, not always as you expect, she said, looking into her wine glass. And then she'd laughed and made a joke and Darius had said well, he'd lost count because he never wanted to do anything but stay where he was, the coast was a perfect place, a liminal place, did she know what that was? Oh yes. Esther was up on liminal things, the in-between, the meeting place of one thing and another, a very Namibia thing. Oh, they had a wonderful night talking.

And now, Jack, of all of them, was going to make his grade and cash in. And Esther was short and Darius wasn't bothering, but Jack was going to make it and both of them felt how special it was, how rare. Most people settled for a series of little rewards.

"We must do something," Esther said from her office.

"Special. Yes." Darius was slower to react because it hadn't occurred to him that he should make it more special than it already was. How could it be even more? But now, in Esther's conviction, he realized that as a parent it was his business to mark it as such with a gesture. The ghost of Jack's mother waited in the background, wishing him on. But what? He'd given it no thought until now, and he felt ashamed suddenly, stupid, but also, and more importantly, at a loss.

"I know!" Esther said suddenly with a snap of her fingers, always bubbling and never more so than now. "Leave it to me. When will he finish?"

"I'm not sure exactly. Today. Maybe tomorrow."

"I need to go check the charts and call a friend. I had an idea. I can't tell you now in case it doesn't work out but keep me posted! Oh . . . was there something you wanted to say? I mean, you called me."

"Ah. Um. Nothing special. Just checking in." What an idiot. He was still blundering about in the mire of finding a gift. Years of sun, sea, sand, and wreckage had addled his mind. He was more place than person. He had a distinct sense of groping about, trying to put bits of himself back together, weave a self from the flotsam to make something that could sail.

"Well if you think of anything," she said and then she blinked away before he had a chance to reply.

He was left sitting in the hut, looking at Jack do the comical, awkward dance of the sand crab tango, feeling alone and foolish. God save us from old men, he thought. He should help Jack.

He tuned into the pole and line, to catch the feed.

BY USING THE CRAB'S SIPHON TO PUMP WATER AROUND IT AT HIGH SPEED AND THEN working the legs and pinchers together Jack had figured out that he could get the silt to loosen into a thick soup. Any pauses had it quickly solidifying again but he felt sure that if he could just keep going long enough he could dig down, flip over, and get out facing the other way. The contortions he had to figure out, recorded for other crab operators to laugh over later, made him feel like those yogis who could get both legs behind their heads and then stand on their hands. He was nowhere near that, but it felt like it, and he was trying not to laugh and blush at the same time as sweat ran down his nose and into his eyes. Butt in the air, his mind kept trying to frighten him off with dire warnings of complete humiliation and the distant seal colony started honking at the same time, which completed the circus just as the battery warning started to pump out its red alert.

Hot on the beach Jack danced like a crazed beetle.

Deep in the chill of the silt the crab spasmed and wrenched itself about, siphon spraying wildly at top volume. Muck and murk ballooned into vast fallout and there, on the camera for a moment he saw something shiny, with a gleam of wan light from the crab's headers reflecting off something that looked like the rim of an embossed treasure. Then it was lost in the whirl and darkness as the crab reached a depth that gave it space to turn beneath the old stanchion. With smooth agility, it flipped and swiftly worked itself upward, outgassing spare air from its lift canisters in jets to either side.

The battery red filled his vision but it was fine. As the power died the emergency buoy deployed in a burst of bubbles and the old drone was safe on its spidery line, towed to the surface to await repair.

Jack took off his father's hat and found himself sitting on the burning hot sand, breathing heavily. A few meters away the rod and line bent caringly toward the tide. He got to his hands and knees and then to his feet and staggered forward into the oncoming surf. The cold water iced his feet and shot straight to his brain. It was bliss.

"That," said his Dad's voice from behind him, full of amusement, "was epic."

Jack groaned and then laughed. He'd be the stock instaclip all week, all year maybe. But it couldn't spoil the feeling of victory and the sudden lurch of surprise at that silver metal edge buried so deep. "Did you see the treasure?"

"Treasure?"

"There was something under the ship. About two meters down. Metal. Old."

He turned and saw his Dad picking up his hat, holding Jack's out toward him. "I'll take another look. But first, what about this history course?"

"Man . . ." There was nothing like a parent to remind you that things sucked.

"I thought maybe since you were so good at fixing my problem I could help you with yours. Do it together?"

"And I get to say what I think and you don't try to fix it?"

His Dad took a breath and then shut his mouth, lips firmly closed for a second. "Okay."

"Okay then." Jack sighed heavily and took his hat back. They had their tea first, then walked along the shore together toward the black seal splodges massed to the north, the soft roaring ocean to their left and the gentle roll of the beach dunes to the right. The hats said there were no visiting lions near enough to cause any trouble, the prides that had come thanks to the drought were at the desalination rig to their south, taking advantage of its free fresh water and the shade of the palms that had been planted around it. Later they'd be moving north too, looking for a seal dining opportunity, but history wouldn't take that long, hopefully.

The AR feed began, a formal rectangle of TV in the top right of their vision, a voice in the mind, a narrator who somehow managed to make it sound as though they were both familiar with these old ideas but still thrilled by them: "Humans have evolved to adapt because we are constantly fighting ourselves through the huge systems of ideas that we generate about everything we touch. We are our own arms race. The pandemics of the early twenty-second century brought exterior focus on our planet to the fore at a critical point in time, when the internet and machine learning tools were capable of creating new environments, making old methods of governance and trade obsolete. Today's massively gamified system of logistics that covers the globe emerged from the shopping habits and trends of that period in time. And from there we can trace those roots right back through to the very earliest periods of human endeavor . . ."

At last they'd stopped doing war, genocide, religious stupidity, greed and tragedy and all the things about human behavior that made you want to bury your head.

". . . although it wasn't until the repeated decimation of the population and the loss of almost all recognizable civilized institutions in economics and infrastructure caused by a combination of disease and climate change that corporate delivery systems and data analytics ended previous forms of party political representation . . ."

Oh no, right. Before the rising, the fall to the bottom.

Jack found himself gazing out to sea, across the huge expanse of the Atlantic, breakers whitecapping far offshore and rolling to paw at his ankles. The wind whipped around his head, tugging the hat as if suggesting he throw it away. The voice and the other images might as well not have been there.

He felt his dad nudge him, the prompt at the thought level, connecting one dot to another just enough for Jack to see what it was that the old man was getting at.

Before you learn to turn over, you have to really get stuck.

His ideas took shape.

Things were impossible and awful, and then, bit by bit, you did things until you got free of the past. He grinned as he combined that thought with his afternoon of crab wrangling, and put that down as part of his final essay. He thought of the metal shine. You never knew what you might find.

ESTHER PUT A CALL IN TO JULIA. THE LOCAL TIMES WERE CLOSE ENOUGH SHE DIDN'T have to give it a second thought, even though Julia was thousands of miles north in England. Julia was busy but she'd left her feed on Browse. For Esther it was almost time to finish for the day, so she put her feet up and allowed herself a surf in Julia's afternoon as she waited.

Julia lived at the top of a high-rise, one of a few in the city center, and it had great views but Esther most enjoyed the fact that instead of the old city palette of concrete, glass, and steel here nearly everything was greened over, and if it wasn't green, it was some interesting Victorian brick and stone arcade or frontage, with only a few strategically left long lines of modern architecture.

The recovery strategy for Northern Europe post loss had been to withdraw to the cities, using them as much tighter hubs than in the past: heat was effectively conserved and distribution of supplies better managed. Those buildings that were basically large glasshouses had been converted to vegetable factories, planters on a massive scale, while older structures were remodeled into contemporary housing. Even with fairly generous portions offered, this still meant that the remaining population had abandoned almost all suburban structures and those areas were being reclaimed and rewilded. Julia was part of an aquatic group that specialized in the restoration of natural waterways and the decontamination of groundwaters, and she and Esther had been in many of the same circles for years.

Esther was able to view what she wanted through Julia's hat, although in this case it wasn't a hat, it was a headset shaped like a hairband, the one with the glitter disco boppers on the head if she wasn't mistaken. She could see the tiny colored reflections of the sunlight glancing off the boppers onto the rich leafy surrounds of Julia's balcony where figs and grapes twined in trained profusion over whatever lay beneath. As Julia worked she was idly nipping the tips out of her tomatoes and feeling the mulch for moisture. Across the road on another tall building, which Esther thought had been a bank, she could see small birds fighting and darting in and out through a temperate rainforest that clung to the wall, watered by misters concealed by the leaves.

Data from Julia's headset showed Esther what everything was, how it had got there, what it was for. She glimpsed the river, boats upon it, low and long, and the canal, and then beyond them the brickwork of mills and the yards by the railway where all the dismantled buildings were sorted for scrap. There was a green run that crossed the human landscape, cutting through the city, where people rode horses in the daytime. Somewhere south of here there was a park for driving cars and riding bikes, racing and all kinds of things. What used to be in a preserve and what had been every-where had reversed their positions.

Whatever Julia had been preoccupied with finished and her line cleared. She noticed Esther's arrival with a quick straighten up and an "Ow!" as her lower back twinged. "Hello. What brings you in today? Did you figure out if we owe you a water credit?"

"Ah no, that's still pending a review. You're good for it at least for another month and if you do get called for it then it's only going to be some rig sup-plies. The Chinese covered us for a year in exchange for extra solar. This is more a personal call. You used to be in with the Venturers set, Julia. Were there Black Vikings? Did they get to Africa?"

Julia looked out over the city center. Cloud was coming in from the west but the white stone of the old hotel near the station was glowing with oncoming sunset and there wouldn't be rain today. A mercy. The river was at bursting point. She swung her mind around toward the piece of her that used to deal with the Northern Britain retreats when she was an apprentice. She'd managed their resources and immigration as they took on and left off people who were touring. The British base for the perma-nent "Viking" population was at Lindisfarne, but they had places all along the coasts. "Black Vikings. Why are you asking me?"

"I thought you were the expert." Esther had a cheeky voice on, one that Julia always felt was the audio equivalent of having someone pinch your bottom.

"Not like entire groups of African Vikings," she said after a moment's pause for reference in the Venturer's Database. "But there were colored Vikings. So definitely possible. Even if there weren't any we've got about thirty Black Vikings now on the Northward rotation so you won't feel out of place, and . . . why are you asking? Are you trading in your Moon Ticket?"

"Ah, I . . ." Esther explained about Jack. She may have dwelled a bit on Darius, more than strictly necessary. She ended with, ". . . and you worked on admin for the Venturers, didn't you?"

"It was ages ago," Julia said.

"But I have this idea," Esther went on, getting what she really wanted with good-natured determination, "because I heard him talking about it . . ."

"Esther, have you been spying on Darius?"

"Only for research purposes. He's always in Browse anyway. It's an open channel. Mostly just the sea to be honest, and sometimes some sand. He thinks about a lot. This morning he caught a . . . No, no. Anyway, listen to me. Going on The Ventures at Jack's level will only give him a week with them. I was thinking a whole summer would be good but it's a long way from home . . ."

Julia listened, twirling a tomato leaf, and at the end of Esther's plan she said, "That is some package of extras right there, Esther. Long haul. I mean. It's a lovely thought. But I can't authorize that kind of excess. Even if I was the admin. Which I'm not. I . . ."

"I can give you the extra. I've got my eye on a new job."

"I thought you were short of credits. This would be—I don't know. Some massive amount."

"I am. I was. No, I've thought about this a lot, Julia. I want to do this. I did want to go to the moon . . . but it's more important to give something special to someone whose life will really be helped by it, rather than spend it all on yourself, isn't it? And I've got so many saved up, there's loads I can still do."

Julia, friendship radar now tuned in to its very sharpest setting, reviewed the information that Esther was sending her. There were strict rules about credit trading, particularly when it involved large amounts, but it was possible to make gifts sometimes, for certain things. "Are you sure, Ess? You'll never make up that much in any job I can think of."

"It's cool," Esther said. "There's a position managing the solar panel farms in the desert. They grow a lot of crops in the shade there now. We've started a vineyard. There'll be wine. You can come and taste it. And it's too late for me to have a child now. This is like having one. You know? Lots of people sponsor. This is just me doing that. I mean I could die tomorrow and then I'd just have left it all to the national pool, so this way at least I get to do what I want."

Ten years of savings, she was talking about. And Julia knew about the sudden leap of age coming at you because she was ahead of Esther by ten years and yes, priorities do change. Dreams become other. She'd rather liked the idea of Esther on the moon, goddess of all she surveyed. But lately there was news of war again in the Middle East, as people never did let go of their grievances that easily. The idea of more conflicts had tired her out. Tired everyone out in her social world, as if all they had done in laying the ground for mass cooperation was to be wasted again. A few attacks in the right place often disrupted communications, made the heart race with fear that a piece of the world was going to be lost, or all of it, in some reversion to older ways. It had a way of sharpening the mind.

"I'll sort out the forms," Julia said. "He'll need vaccinations. Up to date . . ."

"Thanks," Esther said quietly, cutting off Julia's dedicated and accurate information dump. "Thank you. I owe you one."

"It's not going to be instant."

"That's OK. Better do it right."

"And Esther."

"Hm?"

"If you've waited this long for a date and you're trying this hard maybe you should take the initiative, you know? Call when it's *not* about work."

Airy, happy, dismissive—"This isn't me trying. I don't have to try. This is for Jack."

"Right. As you say. I mean, we're all Browsing. No special reasons. Just on random. You could get anyone, anywhere in the world. Skydivers, rocket scientists, tennis stars, models, geniuses . . ."

Esther hung up on her with the air of a proudly pleased/displeased fairy queen.

Well, she deserved it for the butt-pinching tone, Julia thought, taking up her feed spray and moving slowly along, one plant at a time, through her personal jungle. She felt a moment's sadness for the loss of Esther's dream. How her eyes used to light up and her voice would shine as she spoke of the moon: she'd reach its silver sands (never cheese dust for Esther, silver sands, like a fantasy novel) and stand there in the footprints of the first ones, and look down to see the Earth at last entire.

She had a way with words, Esther, and a way with dreams. It seemed wrong to let her give it away, but then again, it was just like her to do that, because she knew what it felt like to have such a thing in the first place.

Julia's own ambitions had been far more parochial and she'd achieved them early, netting her position at the top of this garden tower and a comfortable pastime that made her feel she did good. She could take part vicariously in space travel and the derring-do going on about the globe at any time, thanks to people leaving their lives up for Browsing. She'd never felt the need to actually go in person. And the Viking Venture—that was hard off-grid living for someone used to a cozy life. She'd tried it for a few days and hated it with a passion. So much mud, and rain, and wind, and no thermal underwear.

"I hope you like it," she said aloud to Jack, shaking her head. People didn't know what they were in for. But you could always bail out. It was for fun after all.

THE COLD CURRENTS OF THE SOUTHERN ATLANTIC DRIVE NORTH UP THE COAST OF Namibia. Their bitter temperatures keep the water rich with nutrients and provide a home for fish that are as long-lived as people, and as slow to mature. They also bring thick fog all along the sea and the shore, cutting out light, tamping down sound, turning everything into a softer form of itself.

It's been weeks since Jack turned in his painstaking essay, forming unwanted and exam-friendly opinions on information equity, stakeholder education, and all the reward and response systems that now dominate the connected human world as if they are rats in an endless maze, pressing levers for food, learning special tricks for the hell of it. Day after day he waits for news of when he can go, patiently, helping Darius with the fish counts and the water samples and the management of the crabs. His dad's life is boring. But it's peaceful. And he did pass. He got his credit. He's on his way. Eventually. But all this waiting is hard.

The fog burns off by midmorning, usually, but today it's lingered, keeping the temperature chilly. Darius has an early start—and Jack is with him, yawning, and complaining, because they've searched that wreck every day and found nothing and he thinks he imagined that metal, or that it was some Coke can or other worthless nonsense. The sea is always doing strange things with its belongings when you're not looking.

But today he's looking at the fog and it's rolling in lightly off the sea, propelled by the wave action. It's thinning, and here and there patches of clear air appear and among them suddenly, offshore, a silhouette.

It has a smooth upward curve, like the bold sweep of an axe, and a triangular, proud head, bent at the neck, and a long, long body that rides just clear of the waves and he can see and then not see the unmistakable red and white of a huge single sail across its back.

It's a Drakkar longship. Only five thousand miles off course. Give or take. But it's definitely there. The oars are creaking and their dip-splash is cautious as they creep in, closer, closer. He's not sure he's awake. Maybe someone is messing with his hat. He takes it off. But the ship is still there. Dip. Splash.

"Dad! Dad!"

"I see it." Dad seems less surprised than he ought to.

Jack realizes suddenly it's real, not a dream. It's actually there. It's come for him.

"But it's not on the itinerary," he says, knowing the route of their journey by heart. (It goes Greenland, England, Finland, Sweden, Germany, France, Spain, and then back again in a constant tour stopped only by weather and acts of cosmic disaster such as satellite failure.)

The Drakkar moves closer. Oars feather it about. In the prow stands a tall man mantled in grey fur. His long dreadlocks are bound in silver and bronze. He has an axe in his belt. He raises his arm.

Jack stands like an idiot, a fish gasping for air, until Denzel Ironsides gets out of the ship with a leap that owes a lot to faith and drama, and only a bit to hat-advice. But he lands it, thigh-deep, with the Drakkar dicing with death behind him as it checks its draft against the sands. He has to yomp through the shallows for quite a while before he reaches the beach; six feet and six inches of solid warrior. He doesn't have a helmet with horns on, of course, because those aren't authentic. But he does have a horn and as he grins and stamps his way up to Jack he stops and puts it to his lips and it sounds out a strong, lonely braying that shoos away the last of the fog.

Half a mile north the seals begin honking.

Jack turns to Darius at the sound of the call and his face is transformed completely into absolute joy.

The Vikings have come. All of them.

In a ship.

For him.

For this moment Darius would have spent everything. But he didn't. He doesn't know how it happened.

Then, after a minute's thought, he does.

"HERE WE ARE," DARIUS SAID, GESTURING AT THE SMALL SHACK THAT SERVED AS HIS major outpost.

Esther, dressed in her best, still cool from the car ride out, held her scarf firmly against the wind, and stepped indoors out of the brilliant sunlight. "This is very bijou," she said after a moment. "More bijou than I imagined." She sat down in the best chair at the box table where it was set with the finest wooden tableware, and Darius fetched tonic water out of the cooler. The fish was on the barbecue. The bread was sliced. They had an excellent view of the sea, which was calm, and only the odd whiff from the seal colony.

"I want to thank you," he said, "for what you did."

"Oh, it was nothing," she waved her hand, surveying the beach as if it was paradise. If it hadn't been a minute ago, it now rearranged itself that way in her presence.

He took out the shell that Jack had found a few days before and set it in front of her. "For you."

It was a worn conch, rather white and scrubbed by the sea to the point of losing its projections, but as she picked it up it was cued to his AR memory feed. As he looked at the shell she would see the video postcards Jack had sent from his travels northward, and the brave (and sometimes hair-raising) voyage of *The Sea Stallion II*, which, after its dramatic entrance, had taken a blimp cargo-lifter long-haul flight to Algiers, before resuming its usual route for this time of year, plowing steadily up the European coast, pausing often to "raid" scenic places.

They enjoyed looking over them together for a few minutes and then she saw what else he had put in the shell.

She blinked, looked at him. "So much time," she said.

"I'm not using them and I probably never will," he said, suddenly shy. "There's enough for you to buy your ticket."

She paused, blinking. She put her hand on his hand. "But there's not enough for two."

He smiled. "I can wait down here."

Her face, normally so cheerful, was teary and upset, so much so he wondered if he'd made some kind of mistake.

"It's too much!" she said, blotting her face with her scarf.

"Not enough," he said decisively, raised his chipped cup to her, and they clinked. They sipped. The tension broke.

"Thank God I wasn't saving for Mars!" she said. "You could die before I got back."

"Are they even going to Mars yet?" he asked.

"Yes, later this year . . ." and the conversation was off again, easy as the rollers moving away down the beach.

8 DO YOU HEAR THE FUNGI SING?

Chen Qiufan

translated by Emily Jin

ACCORDING TO THE LORE OF BAENL, SUMMER DOWNPOURS WOULD ALWAYS FOLLOW the annual Rain-Praying Festival, where the people came together and chanted their prayers to the gods.

This year was a little different. Together with the first rainfall came a minor hailstorm and two mysterious guests, and the news of their arrival sent a ripple of curiosity through the quiet, remote village. The elders said that the weather was taking stranger and stranger turns. The messages that the singers sent to the gods received no response. "If the trend continues," they said, worried, "harvesting rice will soon become impossible. Our livestock will die."

The first time Ah-Muih saw Su Su was during the grand feast to welcome the village's honored guests. The feast, held in traditional potluck style, was the amalgamation of the best cuisine from every household: fish pickled with chili peppers, sour radish and duck stew, air-dried pork ribs, crunchy algae: of course, a feast would never be complete without an assortment of fat, juicy local mushrooms—summer was the prime season for wild mushrooms.

After a few rounds of toasts, the villagers began to sing a song in the Baenl language. The song was a magnificent tapestry woven from varicolored threads: though with varying timbre and pitch, the singers sang in synchrony, their voices resonating in the air. Ah-Muih, the youngest and least experienced singer at the table, was the last one to join the chorus. Her voice, crisp and high, was a skylark that glided between earth and heaven freely, building the song to a soul-shattering climax.

The villagers chorused a long and shrill whistle, marking the end of the song. They raised their cups and invited their guests to join them together in another ceremonial toasting song.

Su Su, the younger one of the pair, was the first to be chosen.

Ah-Muih could not take her eyes off the new girl, who looked to be about her age. From what she heard, the girl was from the Bay Area, somewhere far, far away from Baenl. Her skin was as pale and smooth as porcelain, and she wore her hair in a pixie cut, bangs cleanly tucked behind her ears. However, throughout the dinner and the ceremony, her face remained as calm and cold as a winter lake, never showing as much as a frown or a smile. The delicious food on her plate was barely touched; her cup was full, too.

"I don't drink. I can't sing, either," responded Su Su flatly, not even bothering standing up. The glasses she wore fogged up, veiling her eyes behind a thin coat of white mist. Ah-Muih caught a glimpse of a fluorescent blue glow from the edge of her frames, flickering like fireflies in the night.

"Su Su!" The girl's companion, a plump middle-aged man, raised his voice warningly. Ah-Muih remembered him as Su Su's direct boss, Li Xiang.

Su Su did not budge.

"Please forgive her bad manners—she only just graduated from college. Let me take this for her," said Li Xiang, squeezing out an awkward smile. In one gulp he finished the rice wine in his cup and his face turned beet-red immediately; even his oily forehead glowed with pinkness. Showing the crowd his empty cup, he cried out, *"Oh—Lo!"* imitating the way that the villagers drank with one another.

A roar of cheers broke out. Su Su, however, remained silent, as unmoving as a wood-carved statue.

The way that the girl seemed—tense, out of place, kept to herself—made Ah-Muih feel bad for her. Leaving her seat, she went over to where Su Su was sitting and placed a hand on the girl's shoulder.

Su Su's body jolted at her touch, then stiffened. The fog on her glasses dissipated at once, revealing a pair of eyes wide with shock and anger.

"What the hell are you doing?" snapped Su Su.

Ah-Muih pulled her hand back instantaneously as if she had been burnt by fire. "I'm just . . ." she stuttered. "Well . . . I saw that you weren't eating much. You didn't like the wine or the songs either. You seemed . . . unhappy. Like a black buffalo."

What kind of a weird simile is this supposed to be? Su Su rolled her eyes. When her gaze landed on Li Xiang—who was enthusiastically singing along to the villagers' chorus—she couldn't help but roll her eyes again.

I guess I shouldn't upset my boss, she reminded herself. Then she pursed her lips and forced out a small, reluctant smile. "I'm doing fine. I mean, the reason we're here is to help you folks connect to the hypercortex, right? We can save the drinking and singing till later."

Ah-Muih frowned, unsure whether she had fully understood what the city girl meant. *Oh well*, she thought, *she came all the way to Baenl. I should do my best to be a good host.*

"If you need anything, just let me know," said Ah-Muih, showing the girl a toothy grin.

"Really?" Su Su's eyes lit up at once. "I haven't introduced myself—my name is Su Su. What's your name?"

HALF A MONTH AGO, WHEN THE CITY DUO FIRST ARRIVED IN BAENL, LI XIANG HAD told Su Su that this village, tucked away in the folds of the mountains of southwest China, was the only blind spot in the hypercortex network in their area. As long as this spot existed, the entire grid area that Baenl was a part of would be flagged incomplete. The ramifications would directly impact their department's interdepartmental ranking, employees' promotional opportunities, and the company's future.

China's carbon emissions had peaked in 2030. It had then adopted the even more ambitious goal of nationwide carbon neutrality by 2060. However, the climate, a hypercomplex system, was slow to respond to these changes. The probability of extreme weather had skyrocketed: summer became longer and forty-five million people were exposed to fatal heat waves. Extreme rainfall events became more common, leading to flooding rivers that harmed the lives of over a billion people. Drought, on the other hand, was long and drawn-out where it happened, and various regions were at the risk of severe crop yield reduction.

The hypercortex network was born out of the dire need to confront these climate challenges. A next-generation network, it mapped the digital world onto the physical world with maximum precision and resorted to artificial intelligence to dynamically adjust parameters such as resource deployment, energy consumption, pollution emission, population flow, and vegetation enhancement, in order to counteract the loss induced by climate change.

Nine point six million square kilometers of land were in the process of being covered by an enormous, invisible web of AI governance. It split the earth into grids, securing control over even the smallest pair of coordinates. Yet if blind spots—places that were not connected to the network—were left in any grid areas, it meant that the entire grid would be unable to reach its optimal effect.

There were no public highways that connected Baenl to the outside world. To reach the village, an off-road vehicle took them to the nearest accessible entrance, then they climbed through the mountains on foot.

"Why can't they build their village at the bottom of the mountain?" complained Su Su, already out of breath. In her field of vision, there was no ending to the serpentine, rugged mountain road.

"They don't trust outsiders," said Li Xiang, who was panting so heavily that he could barely squeeze out words. "Especially men. That's the reason why we need you here . . ."

"You mean they live in a matriarchal society?"

"Something along those lines. Their social structure is . . . very premodern. It's up to you to win their trust."

"Then what are you here for?"

"For support!" The forced smile on Li Xiang's face, which glistened with sweat and grease, looked so awful that Su Su would rather he stopped trying altogether. "I'm here to take care of your supplies, and . . . your safety!"

"Bullshit," Su Su muttered under her breath.

The narrow forest path was muddy, forcing her to focus on what was happening beneath her feet. After meeting Ah-Muih at the reception feast, Su Su had asked her to show her the way to the village's signal transmitter, which she needed to successfully activate the smart dust—smart sensors about the size of snail shells—that teams from her company had previously cast into the grid area.

Su Su was from a coastal city in the prosperous, bustling Guangdong-Hong Kong-Macau Greater Bay Area, where she woke up every day to the shimmering ocean outside her bedroom window. The ink-blue water stretched into the horizon as if it was boundless. For the week that she had been in Baenl, wherever her eyes landed, there was nothing but dull mountains, blocking her line of vision. On foggy mornings, mist as thick and heavy as cream would slowly stream down the peaks, cloaking every inch of the forest in vast whiteness, threatening to swallow up the village. Her head buzzed and her chest tightened at the sight of the impending fog-tide, as if the sticky-looking substance could clog her brain and heart as well.

"Hang on!" She called out to Ah-Muih, who was speedily leading the way. "I think we're on the wrong path."

According to the work logs, the last team sent by the company had installed the transmitter at the top of a wooden tower—the optimal node that guaranteed the signal would cover the entire village. Yet the wooden tower, now barely in view, was clearly falling farther and farther behind as the villagers moved further into the mountains.

"Just hurry up! You're slower than a duck," Ah-Muih shouted back, picking up the pace.

They were now deep in a swath of verdant forest. Meager sunlight, cut into tiny, diamond-shaped fragments by the dense canopy of leaves that hung above their heads, flickered on Su Su's face. To Su Su, the forest was full of dangers: round, heavy beads of dew fell from above, splashing their faces and shoulders with stinging chilliness. Strange chirps, barks, and howls surrounded them like a chorus, as if to warn human intruders to stay away from their territory. Milk-white mist, moist and cold, gathered at their ankles, veiling the moss on the ground like the cover on a beast trap, luring her into slipping and falling.

"Where are we going?" asked Su Su as she gasped for air, her face damp with sweat.

Ah-Muih did not respond. Arching her back, she nimbly dived into a tunnel formed from a tangle of tree roots and veins.

"Wait up!" Su Su cried.

With both her hands and legs on the ground, she clumsily crawled forward in the tunnel. She couldn't tell where the tunnel led; only the pull of gravity tugging her downward reminded her that she was on a steep, descending slope. Her thin fingers sank into the thick heap of rotten leaves on the ground, which felt oddly mushy. Occasionally a tingling sensation on her ear would remind her that she was not alone—lines of ants and dangling spiders never failed to send her into a screaming fit.

The leaves beneath her body gradually dissolved into reddish-brown spongelike flakes. Their putrid odor permeated the tunnel. Ah-Muih, on the other hand, had disappeared. She had led Su Su into this labyrinth made out of roots and humus and trapped her in here. A sharp tinge of panic washed over Su Su. *What if the Baenl girl's friendliness and enthusiasm were disguises to fool her? What if she was up to something?*

An ominous rustle came from above her. Struggling, with her chest close to the ground, she craned her neck to look up. It was a giant centipede about the size of an infant's arm, red and shiny, waving hundreds of antennae and legs menacingly. Su Su went pale. Stifling a cry, she pushed forward, getting away from the creature as fast as she could. Slipping on the rotten debris, she lost her balance and tumbled down the tunnel. In a flash of light, she saw that the tunnel she was sliding down led to a cliff.

In despair, she stretched out her arms in an attempt to grab onto something—anything—that could save her from the fall. Her fingertips caught onto a tangling ball of thready substance that felt like silk, covered in pungent slime. *Are they tree roots?* She had no time to be sure. Gripping the silk tightly in her fist and yanking with all her might, she wrapped them around her arm like a lifeline, hoping that they would slow her down.

The silk seemed to have read her mind. Soon she couldn't tell whether she was pulling the silk, or the silk was coiling around her. The soft substance was surprisingly firm, vigorously holding her in place the same way thin roots supported a sturdy tree. A mere inch away from the cliff, the tumbling came to a halt. The silk, now a velvety harness bound to her upper body, dangled her in midair a foot above ground. She was a flying insect caught in a shiny spider web. Before she could even catch her breath, she broke out into a fit of incontrollable hysterical laughter, as if it could vent out all the terror and stress from moments ago.

Ah-Muih reappeared, beaming as she looked at Su Su. "Finally! You're smiling," she exclaimed cheerfully.

"Are you out of your mind? Get me down . . ." pleaded Su Su, croaking, so exhausted that her voice was now nearly a whisper.

Ah-Muih stepped forward and began to help Su Su untangle her body from the web. "Looks like *she* likes you," she muttered. "She has given you her blessing."

"What? Who?" asked Su Su, even more flustered as she struggled to shake off the mysterious sticky substance.

Instead of responding in words, Ah-Muih pointed to a hill steps away from where they were standing. In the crevice of mountain rocks, a metallic installation glinting with silver stood erect, its shape resembling an enormous corkscrew.

HISTORY SHOWED THAT EVERY TIME BAENL CAME INTO CONTACT WITH OUTSIDERS, the villagers ended up moving even deeper into the mountains.

The elders said that the people of Baenl had the spirit of wild grass: firm, stubborn, with unyielding faith. Unable to resist the astronomical relocation subsidies and the constant pestering of government workers, other neighboring villages had moved to the plains where the local government established new towns and infrastructure to accommodate them, and readily welcomed what they called "modern life."

Ah-Muih had been to a few of those new towns. They looked no different from the kind of cities that she saw in videos. Villagers soon adjusted to their new lives with tap water, electrical appliances, and the internet. Abandoning hand-dyed cotton clothes, they bought trendy dresses manufactured from chemical fiber off the web, delivered to their doors. Parents gave their young children "city" names so they would fit in better with the outsiders who rushed to the towns via recently constructed highways.

Gradually, people forgot the language they used to speak and the songs they used to sing; they no longer worshipped ancestors or spirits of nature, the once-unbreakable bond between the people and their deities fading until they were little more than colorless fables. Then, a series of strange illnesses descended upon them: insomnia, headaches, allergies, weakened muscles, and a disturbed heart . . . the doctors of the outsiders were unable to diagnose the cause of these ailments, nor could they prescribe effective medication. "Change your diet and living habits" was their bleak suggestion.

The elders told Ah-Muih that the mountains had summoned back the souls of her lost children. As they grew farther and farther apart from the roots of their ancestry and nature, they became soulless bodies walking the earth, no better than zombies or robots. Taking the stern warning, Baenl was extra cautious about outsiders. *Treat them with grace but keep your distance*—Ah-Muih had learned the Baenl rule by heart ever since she was a child. There was no need for hostility, yet she certainly shouldn't allow outsiders to get their way too easily, either.

Su Su, though, was different.

The outsiders that Ah-Muih had met always carried themselves with a certain kind of calculated composedness, as if their gestures and emotions were performances already rehearsed to perfection. Compared to them, Su Su exuded a peculiar child-like innocence. It almost seemed as if she has never been socialized into the orthodox order of outsiders. Her thoughts and feelings were not only untamed like the wild grass that Baenl people honored, but also utterly exposed, even when she knew for sure that she would upset her boss. The way that Su Su did not fit in—or rather, did not even try to fit in—made Ah-Muih feel that she was genuine. An honest person who never pretended. A clear stream, a refreshing mountain breeze.

"Why is it that Baenl has to connect to the . . . hypercortex thing that you were talking about?" asked Ah-Muih.

Su Su, bubbling with eagerness, threw out a series of responses that made Ah-Muih's head spin. She brought up "cloud" and "earth," but the way she referred to them led Ah-Muih to believe that those terms did not exactly correspond to the kind of cloud and earth that she was familiar with. She also asserted that the world was multilayered, with layers overlapping with one another horizontally and vertically, and that the hypercortex was the supernode that connected all the layers.

"I know!" exclaimed Ah-Muih, excited that something finally hit the right chord. "Just like how hot pot works, first you prepare the soup base, then you put different ingredients in, and add more soup. A layer of oil floats on the surface of the soup, and the pepper and the chili float on the surface of the oil. If you scoop with a ladle, you'll get a taste of everything!"

Su Su, with her mouth hanging open, was stupefied by Ah-Muih's remark. After a moment of hesitation, she took off her glasses and put them on the Baenl girl's face.

"Hey, I don't need glasses to see! Why are you giving me this—*wow*."

White mist gathered and shrouded the lenses at once. A completely outlandish world appeared before Ah-Muih's eyes, an overlay of mountains and rivers that were no longer mountains and rivers. *Baenl was no longer Baenl.* Deep underground were fiber-optic cables, winding, undulating, and intertwining like the bodies of gigantic dragons, and above the clouds were communication satellites that rotated steadily. Between earth and heaven, layer after layer of translucent webs of varying texture overlaid every inch of land, engulfing rocks, trees, and houses in a dazzling rainbow glow. The silk that comprised the webs seemed to have come alive. Some rapid and some slow, they flowed in all directions like thousands of millions of interlacing streams.

When Ah-Muih cast her eyes down, she saw that the edges of her palms had grown translucent too, shimmering with gold. *No.* A wave of raw fear rushed through her veins. Her breath quickened.

"Don't be scared. This is only a simulation to show you how matter, energy, and information interacts."

Whipping off the glasses, Ah-Muih rubbed her eyes with the back of her hand, already sore from the high-intensity animation. "Is this what Baenl is going to become in the future?" she whispered.

"Baenl's future is not something you can even begin to imagine," said Su Su shaking her head. She spoke with such brutal honesty that Ah-Muih wasn't sure whether Su Su cared what she thought or not. "You'll see what it's like when the day comes."

Ah-Muih fell silent. The elders were right. In the hands of outsiders, Baenl would march toward a future utterly beyond its own people's ability to judge or even comprehend. What was worse, it wasn't really their choice to accept or reject the overwhelming tide of change that loomed above the village. One day, they would run out of forests and valleys to escape into.

Ah-Muih's racing heart was a frenzied moth trapped in the cage of her breastbone. *What can I do? I am the youngest singer of the entire village, who has never even led a single ceremony . . . I am nobody.*

A hand waved rapidly before Ah-Muih's dazed eyes, dragging her back into reality. "Are you alright?" It was Su Su's voice. "I mean . . . I just don't understand why you people want to get rid of the transmitter."

"Because she's angry."

"*Who?*" pressed Su Su, remembering that she had asked the same question moments ago.

Ah-Muih gazed into the eyes of the girl. A new idea flashed across her mind. She realized what she was supposed to do.

THE COMPANY'S NEW MESSAGE REMINDED SU SU AND LI XIANG THAT THEY WERE running out of time.

Three teams had been sent to Baenl before them, and each team had reported back with varying setbacks: the first never made it through the mountains. The second, having reached the village at last, was politely asked to leave after the reception feast as the villagers refused to accept their modernization program. The third, equipped with a government-issued permit after learning from the mistakes of their predecessors, finally planted the signal transmitter where they wanted in the village. However, within a month of their departure, problems surfaced. The transmitter sent back an empty databank, indicating that the sensors had not been put to use; the cloud server had also been disconnected. Without mechanical eyes watching over it, the blind spot remained blind after all. On the grid map, Baenl stood out as a bright red dot, alerting the higher-ups day and night that their mission of disseminating the hypercortex network was incomplete.

Su Su couldn't guarantee that the company would remain diplomatic and civil if they failed to convince the Baenl people again. She had heard rumors about "extra measures" that the company kept as a backup plan. When she asked Li Xiang what those measures were, the man fell silent. From the way he frowned, she could tell that it was probably best to avoid the worst-case scenario altogether.

Though maintaining a calm, indifferent facade, Su Su began to find herself more and more agitated as each day passed.

During Su Su's stay, Ah-Muih showed her around the village and introduced her to the multidimensional ecosystem of Baenl. The snow on mountain peaks melted into brooks that streamed downslope. The villagers cultivated terrace farmlands and established living compounds along the water. Through utilizing a set of delicately designed channels and storage units, every household shared the fresh, flowing water evenly. The villagers also stocked fry in their waterlogged paddy fields and hatched fish. When the fish were grown, they added free-range ducklings to the system. Fish and ducks, sharing the paddy fields, killed pests, rooted out excessive weeds, and loosened up the soil. Their manure, as organic fertilizer, was enough to nourish the entire expanse of paddy fields. This way, the villagers were able to harvest a cornucopia of rice, fish, and duck every year.

The most impressive feat to Su Su was the Baenl people's artful command of fungi: they used a rich assortment of fungi to ferment rice for wine, exterminate agricultural pests, improve the digestive system of buffalo, preserve mountain soil, secure the roots of vegetation, cultivate food (yes, mushrooms were the fruits of fungi) and medicine . . . but more incredible was the way the villagers applied fungi to architecture. Wooden boards, after fungi corrosion, took on a porous structure and increased greatly in elasticity. They were then used to make floors that used the piezoelectric properties of the fungus to generate electricity, lighting up overhead energy-saving lamps whenever people walked, skipped, or danced on it.

Where did all their knowledge come from? Throughout the tours, Su Su could not help but wonder. To the people of Baenl, handling fungi was as natural as acknowledging the laws of gravity.

The answer to her question was singers.

There were seven singers in Baenl, all female. In Baenl tradition, the honor and responsibility that singing carried was far more than mere entertainment. The singers passed down ancient wisdom to new generations through their songs. Singers were part of every major event in the village—holiday, ritual, childbirth, marriage, illness, funeral, moving house. They performed ceremonial songs and offered practical advice. According to Ah-Muih, sometimes the singers also presented prophecies, such as weather forecasts. Last year they successfully predicted that a great hailstorm would hit the village. The hailstorm only caused minimal damage—thanks to the forecast, villagers were able to reinforce their houses and fix animal shelters ahead of time.

Ah-Muih said that the singers were blessed with the power of gods and spirits. Gods and spirits resided in mountains, rivers, lakes, and swamps; in every bird, fish, rock, and tree.

Su Su could not bring herself to empathize with what seemed to her a kind of premodern, nature-worshipping pantheism, yet she was faced with a stark reality: the kind of language that Li Xiang and herself spoke, embellished with the jargon of technology and laden with promises of infinite energy, real-time information flow, more environmentally friendly and efficient agricultural methods, online education for the children on par with the opportunities offered in cities, boosted GDP per capita . . . it would never translate over to the Baenl people, who cared for rituals more than policies, and deities more than algorithms.

Eventually, she came to a conclusion: a ceremony must be held, so that the local people could ask their gods whether it was wise for Baenl to join the hypercortex network.

She was on the verge of a breakdown when she tried to write her report for the company. *How can I tell them that we need divine intervention? That a ceremony must take place? That we have no choice but to run the program through some gods that are beyond our control?*

Li Xiang came up with another idea. "Why don't you talk to Ah-Muih?" Eyeing her, he dropped a careful hint. "You know . . . perhaps the gods can respond in a way that would make everyone happy."

Meanwhile, Su Su's disappointment in her boss and her job grew stronger each day. She knew in her heart that she was not the most outstanding employee amongst the new graduates of Engineering Division VI. When Li Xiang recruited her for this mission, she thought with secret glee that perhaps her boss valued her potential or recognized her improvements. Only after she arrived in Baenl did she realize that the company had chosen her simply because she was the only woman in her department.

I want to leave, too, she thought. *I miss air conditioning and convenience stores, and I never want to see a single spider again in my life. But I don't want the mission to end in this way.*

She wasn't sure whether she had a choice.

"Bribe the gods? But you outsiders don't believe in gods, do you?" Ah-Muih was surprisingly calm upon hearing her proposal. "You mean . . . you want me to lie?"

Su Su saw the bitter disappointment in her eyes. She couldn't tell whether the disappointment really came from Ah-Muih, or if it was merely her own self-projection.

"I thought you were changing," continued Ah-Muih. "But you're more stubborn than a rock."

"I . . . I just wanted to . . ." Su Su opened her mouth, wanting to refute her, but she was at a loss for words.

Unwittingly, deep down inside, a small part of her wanted to agree with Ah-Muih. She knew exactly what the girl meant. She had been changed by the life she lived here in Baenl. No longer keeping up her stone-cold and distant front, she was more animated than ever before. Though she maintained her ground and firmly steered away from drinking and singing, she would occasionally find herself bursting into carefree laughter, then instinctively stifling it midway, utterly confused, like a computer that has frozen after detecting a piece of bad code.

The mist before her eyes cleared up. *You like it here*, said a tiny voice ringing in her heart. Everyone in the metropolises of the Bay Area were wound-up clocks that lived in the constant fear of falling behind. Every step she took was neatly calculated, with her true feelings concealed. The fresh, glistening greenness of Baenl was a stark contrast to the grey and dull world she came from. Everyone she met was relaxed and at peace with themselves; she could read the joy on their faces. It was genuine happiness, she knew, not the product of virtual simulations. The memory of air conditioning and convenience stores had already grown distant. *I guess I can try making friends with the giant spider spinning away in the bathroom corner*, she thought to herself with a tight, self-mocking smile. *If only I could stay.*

"I just wanted to help." Finally, Su Su buried her face deep in her palms and whispered, her voice barely audible.

A look of sympathy flashed across Ah-Muih's face. Gently, she set a hand on Su Su's shoulder and patted her comfortingly. This time, Su Su did not jump at her touch.

"Let me tell you a story," said Ah-Muih.

I sing of the lord of devils,
with horns and a black shawl.
Though with mighty power,
it is at once jealous, and in awe
of the family on the mountain,
that prospered with yield.
The youngest daughter raises the ducks,
the second daughter hatches the fish,
the eldest daughter plows the field.
Grandmother, mother, and father warn them,

"Beware of the devil!
Sing if it runs you down,
and our neighbors will arrive with their shovel."
One day an old woman passes by with a wide-brim hat,
a pair of trembling hands, and a bent back.
The youngest daughter holds her hand,
"How may I help?" she asks.
Responds the old woman, "I need an ingredient for my medicine,
a snow-white feather from a duck."
Says the youngest daughter, "For your health a feather I pluck."
Another old woman comes by the field the second day,
with aching feet, and a black veil across her face.
The second daughter takes her arm,
"Granny, what leads you stray?"
Responds the old woman, "I need an ingredient for my medicine,
A fish's coal-black scale."
Says the second daughter, "I pray for your health, please have the fish's tail."
The third day comes an old woman again,
gasping, wheezing, barely she stands.
The eldest daughter pats her shoulder,
"Can I lend you a hand?"
Responds the old woman, "I need an ingredient for my medicine,
a bunch of golden grain."
Says the eldest daughter, "Take it, and feel no more pain."
A storm roams the plains,
the old woman is indeed the devil, who gains
from conning the sisters into giving it three tokens
of magic, and now the spell restraining its power is broken.
Mushrooms ruined, forest on fire,
filth and muck in the streams, the situation is dire.
The enraged mountain gods discover
the three magical tokens, with them the devil conspires.
The gods then set out to find the cause,
the family on the mountain, punished for their fault.
The fungi spirit, hoping to bring them fear and fright,
destroys the ducks, the fish, the rice, leaving nothing alive in their sight.
Grandmother, mother, father, the three sisters,
hopeless, they cry day and night.
The village singers notice the muddle,
"What's the matter? Where's the trouble?"
The sisters weep, "The three tokens, the old woman, we are puzzled!"
By the altar a ceremony unfolds,
for Goddess Sax to help, her wisdom eons old,
for the mountain gods to see, the truth they behold.

147

Says Goddess Sax, "The three tokens of Baenl are magical,
worship nature, protect the mountains, stay kind and truthful."
Say the mountain gods, "The three tokens of Baenl are powerful,
to rid the village of the devil, be brave and be careful."

THE BAENL PEOPLE DECIDED TO LEAVE THE FUTURE OF THEIR VILLAGE IN THE hands of the gods and spirits. Ah-Muih, the youngest singer of the seven, was appointed to lead the ceremony. She convinced the others that Su Su should also be invited, as their honored guest.

"The outsiders brought the question to us, and it is only right that an outsider answers it with us," explained Ah-Muih. *Su Su was more than just an outsider,* she thought. *The girl had received the blessing of Goddess Sax.*

"Listen, you don't have to do it if you don't want to," said Li Xiang, reassuring Su Su. "We have already tried our best."

Su Su's heart raced with uneasiness. A part of her felt guilty, as if her insistence on the hypercortex project was a betrayal to whatever there was that came out of her delicate relationship with Ah-Muih, and that she would be the bringer of disaster to the village. The other part, however, was filled with anticipatory fear. What was going to happen to her at the ceremony? What did the gods want to do to her? What about the mysterious *she* whose shadow seemed to loom over these obscure, serene mountains? And yet she couldn't bring herself to utter the word *no* to Ah-Muih's invitation.

The ceremony took place beneath the wooden tower that was once home to the signal transmitter. A bonfire, encircled by ripples of duck feathers, fish scales, and grains, blazed in the center of the round altar. The seven singers lined up from youngest to eldest and gathered around the altar. They were dressed in splendid ceremonial robes fashioned from variegated brocade, decorated in gleaming silver ornaments from head to toe. Their faces were painted in yellow, white, and black, a collage of exquisite totems. Su Su, dressed exactly the same as the singers, now looked like a completely different person. She trembled with nervous energy as she trotted behind Ah-Muih, having never felt so helpless and out of place in her life.

"Now you know why we removed the transmitter," said Ah-Muih in a lowered voice.

"What am I supposed to do next?" stuttered Su Su.

"You do what you're most good at."

"And what is that?"

"Drinking, singing," responded Ah-Muih with a smirk. "Maybe dancing, too."

Su Su's eyes widened. "You might as well hold a knife to my throat!" She raised her voice in horror, then quickly suppressed her complaints into a mutter.

"Hey. Someone really did hold a knife to an outsider's throat and made them sing while peeing. Apparently, that worked," Ah-Muih's grin widened.

Su Su let out a heavy sigh and smiled back at Ah-Muih in response. She realized that the girl was only making a joke to help her relax. "I can't. This is . . . this is too much for me."

"Let loose! It's your only chance!"

Frowning, Su Su took the bowl of dark brown liquid from Ah-Muih's hands. With her eyes tightly shut, holding her breath, she drank the liquid in one long gulp, imitating the singers. Immediately she felt as if she had swallowed a ball of fire. She bent her head and broke into a coughing fit. It was a robust mixture of the rice wine's sweetness, the minerals' bitterness, the poignant taste of herbs, and a hint of the scent of earth.

Holding hands, the singers pranced around the bonfire clockwise. Ah-Muih was the one to sing the first note. Her voice, a clean, ethereal melody, was soon engulfed by a grand chorus as the other singers joined in one after another, varying vocals and timbres mingling into a symphony.

Su Su couldn't believe that the song was improvised. Never had she heard such a harmonious ensemble of sounds, unmatchable even by the most outstanding orchestra in the coastal metropolises. She was consumed by the raw fear of destroying the beauty and glory of the song if she dared open her mouth. A burning sensation emerged in her belly. Rising like a balloon, it pulsed between her ribcage and stung her lungs, scorching her windpipe on the way up. For a brief second, she felt as if she was about to spit fire.

"Sing!" Ah-Muih pinched her hand.

"I . . . I can't . . ."

"Stop thinking! Just open your mouth! You'll know what to do!"

Su Su parted her pursed lips. The first note soared like a bird set free at last. She couldn't tell whether it was the alcohol singing or it was really her own voice. At first, she could only follow the tune, slurring over the lyrics sung in the Baenl language that she didn't understand. Gradually, she no longer found herself struggling. As if a higher power had possessed her, she sang, in perfect synchrony with the sevenfold chorus. She couldn't believe her own ears. She was singing, just like the singers.

Ah-Muih's cheeks lit up in the rosy glow of the flames. The eight women began to dance. Spinning, turning, spinning again . . . they danced vibrantly to the song, every step right on the beat. The villagers witnessing the ceremony clapped and roared with cheers. Some joined in with the chorus. Li Xiang, standing in the crowd, frowned with worry—and yet he knew that it was already too late to call a stop.

Su Su was shrieking with laughter. Tears streamed down her face. She had never been as happy in her entire life. She no longer felt in control of her body, which merged with that of the other seven singers, making a perfect oneness that undulated to the soul-shattering rhythm, devoid of constraints and order. There was only happiness. Purity. Ecstasy.

"She likes you!" yelled Ah-Muih.

"Who?" asked Su Su with a dreamy smile.

"Goddess Sax! The Great Grandmother!"

"Whose grandmother?"

"Everyone's!"

"You're drunk!"

"You'll know what I mean in a moment."

"Wait—"

The fire before Su Su's eyes exploded with a radiating light, as if the parameters on her smart glasses had been adjusted. *But I'm not wearing glasses*, she realized in a daze. *It was the entire world that had lit up.* Consumed by flames. No, it wasn't just the brightness that had changed—the edges of every figure and object in her vision field were dissolving. Colors liquefied, vaporized, came alive, escaping from the bold-lined contours that bound them to their shapes, twirling and flickering and surging as if performing a frenzied dance.

"Ah-Muih . . . what did you feed me?" murmured Su Su.

Ah-Muih's face, beaming with joy, began to grow larger and larger in Su Su's blurry vision, infinitely distorting and expanding in all directions.

This must've been what the universe looked like when the gods first created it.

SU SU HEARD AH-MUIH'S SONG ON THE TIP OF HER OWN TONGUE. REVERBERATING IN her mind. The song was inside her. *Where is my own voice?* A microsecond after, the song split into two. A perfect duet, two voices endlessly entwining and synchronizing. A divine echo. A powerful frequency.

Riding the buzzing frequency, Su Su spiraled up toward the ceiling of the tower. The world, shimmering, was crystal clear before her eyes. Her gaze pierced through the darkness, sweeping across the mortise-tenon joints that held up the sturdy roof and the color paintings of legends and heroines, telling archaic stories that had persisted for thousands of years.

She continued to ascend, until she broke through the tip of the tower. Her physical body had ceased to exist. She was infinitely large, or infinitely small. Or both at once. She had become the frequency itself. The night sky, looking so sparse and dead silent from below, was in fact bustling with the signals of nature and the human world: turbulence stirred up by wings of soaring birds, pollutants and dust, negative ions generated from lightning, water vapor, infrared radiation that came from the surface of the earth, lights cast by nearby villages, calcium carbonate residues from artificial rainfall, oxygen, nitrogen, water molecules vibrating in the clouds, radio signals of varying frequency bands, cosmic rays . . .

These shapeless, formless, colorless beings transitioned between her consciousness and the exterior environment, exchanging information and energy along the way. Su Su's emotions ebbed and flowed to their trajectory. She realized in surprise that what she deemed as autonomous and subjective feelings were merely slaves of her surroundings. Melancholy, excitement, depression, zest . . . all of her emotions, no matter how trivial or subtle, were firmly connected to the macrocosm and the microcosm. Enmeshed with one another and with the rest of the cosmos, they were constantly convecting, radiating, conducting, volatilizing, disseminating from the surface of the Earth to the stratosphere, then all the way to the vast, deep space.

All of a sudden, she was struck with the epiphany that what appeared at first as strange and new had in fact been a part of her perception all along. Reassurance and disappointment surged in her heart at once. The wine Ah-Muih gave her must have contained some kind substance that had sensitized her senses and expanded her mind, endowing her with the ability to visualize previously abstract concepts. Other than that, there was no real mystery to dwell upon.

But she was wrong.

She had thought that those ubiquitous dark brown particles surrounding her were merely dust specks until her own frequency came into contact with theirs. A vibrant quiver hit her at once, indicating to her that the particles carried signals of life. *They're fungi spores.* Through one, she learned that spores equivalent to the weight of five hundred thousand blue whales were floating in the atmosphere. When trillions of them gathered together, they could affect the weather by triggering condensation nuclei, sending rain, snow, and hail to the ground.

Su Su, mesmerized by her new discovery, wanted to learn more. The frequency of the resonance pulled her toward the source of the fungi spores. She was a piece in a gigantic marble game that took place between earth and heaven. Gliding between spores, she plummeted down toward the ground. Her heart almost burst from the ecstasy of losing control. *This is what it feels like to let loose.*

The clouds parted as she fell. The black earth came crashing down. Making a dive, she plunged into the fresh, rich soil. Darkness. Moisture. Warmth. Her sense of touch replaced her vision. A new world a million times grander than the one before bloomed around her. She felt a gentle pat. A familiar stickiness. The silk that had saved her life in the tunnel. Back then she thought that those were the roots of plants, but now she knew better. Those were an entire network of fungi hyphae constructed from thin, tubular fungal cells that stemmed out, merged, and entangled.

She likes you. She remembered Ah-Muih's words.

Su Su was overwhelmed with awe. The fungi hyphae network, spreading over dozens of square kilometers deep in the earth, had already existed for tens of millions of years on this planet—no, perhaps for even longer. Arrogant *Homo sapiens* were mere infants in the face of their age and wisdom. To one another they transmitted water, nutrition, and electrical impulses that undulated like waves with an efficiency that surpassed self-proclaimed intelligent beings, coalescing forests, shrubs, and grasslands into a unity. They decomposed rocks, created new soil, and digested pollutants. They nourished and killed crops. They produced nectars and elixirs through inducing a peculiar kind of metabolism. By extending their reach to the greater ecosystem, they influenced the way that animals and humans think, feel, and act. *And yet humans were so oblivious to their presence.*

The vibrations coming from the fungi hyphae network explained the secret to Su Su. She saw her own body, which was filled with trillions of microbes that covered every inch of skin and every cavity. Those microbes outnumbered her body's cells by a large number, not unlike how the number of bacteria in human intestines outnumbered the stars in the galaxy. *They protect us and influence us,* she thought. *And they can kill us the same way fungi kill grain, if we can't live in symbiosis with them.*

Symbiosis was the way of life. Yet self-interested humans neglected the existence of a multitude of microscopic life, and turned their eyes and ears to nothing but their own reflections and echoes. She knew, however, that those life forms, like dark matter and dark energy that occupied more than 95 percent of the mass of the known universe, wouldn't cease to exist simply because of human ignorance. They have lived since long before the birth of *Homo sapiens*, and they would live on, operating with their own intricate algorithms, to witness a future distant and unknown that ventured far beyond the day humans went extinct.

Su Su was enveloped in a gentle vibration. A warm, ethereal, and expansive embrace that she melted into. Her heart was struck with a deep, tender love that was beyond words. Her mind delineated an archetype: a woman, as old and fathomless as the mountains and rivers, with infinite wisdom and grace. *The Great Grandmother. Goddess Sax.* Without her, the world would be devoid of the fresh scent of new leaves and the crisp chirps of birds; she could never have entered this realm of fantasy in the first place. The love from Goddess Sax sprouted countless infinitesimal hyphae that attached themselves to Su Su's consciousness. In a heartbeat, she could absorb the pulse and vibration and undulation of all life forms connected to this web of fungi. The divine gift from Goddess Sax.

She understood the reason behind the choice of Baenl. Ah-Muih was right.

Forget about the hypercortex. We are already immersed in a network. From the heart of the Earth to tens of thousands of meters up in the atmosphere, an immeasurable number of seemingly unrelated organisms lived connected to one another via the web of life. Together, they worked to regulate the delicate balance of our planet-wide ecosystem. Their computational power, a kind of superior, distributed intelligence, far exceeded the primitive and crude machine intelligence that humans were eager to offer as alternatives.

The thought of machines sent a shrilling wave of anxiety through Su Su's mind, sprouting and spreading like mold. Then, a new vibration took over, tuning her in to a vision consisting of a myriad of overlapping futures of Baenl. She saw that mountains and rivers were replaced by mechanical installations and artificial scenery. A semitransparent dome loaded with sensors hovered above the village, entrapping it. The bodies of the Baenl people were broken down into countless data nodes, and their eyes darted constantly between the reality and virtual interfaces large and small. She also saw . . .

You see it, don't you?

Su Su felt as if an eon had passed. Ah-Muih's song, previously hazy and distant, now sounded tangible again. She was landing, about to come to a halt against a solid, singular realm of reality. She collapsed into her physical body. As her being took on a definite shape and form, those indescribable feelings from the hallucination resurfaced as well. Her cheeks, wet with tears, tingled with a burning sensation and a stinging coldness at once.

Ah-Muih, I understand now. All of it . . .

What is it that you now understand?

I'm not here to help you. You're here to help me.

A smile, shimmering with an aura as old as nature itself, blossomed on Ah-Muih's youthful face.

"WHAT IS THE END OF THE STORY, THEN?"

It took Ah-Muih a while to realize that Su Su was talking about the Baenl legend that she never got to finish.

Then, with guidance from mountain gods and Goddess Sax, the family sets up a trap. The three sisters dress up in their best robes. They cook a feast of the devil's favorite foods and wine, and sing the devil's favorite song. The devil, unsuspecting, is lured into their home by the melodious song and the sweet scent of wine. The three sisters, pretending to be unaware of the true identity of the old woman, refill her cup again and again, until she is so drunk that she drops to the ground and falls asleep. The singers arrive and cast the spell of revelation. The devil's magic comes undone and beneath its human disguise is a massive black buffalo. It turns out that the black buffalo, exhausted from plowing the fields day and night, grew full of jealousy and resentment toward the family it works for. Possessed by the evil spirits of the mountains, it had turned into a devil seeking revenge. In the end, the family decides to resolve the strife with kindness. The three sisters promise to the black buffalo that they will take good care of its well-being. Together, the family and the black buffalo live a prosperous and happy life on the mountain.

"A happy ending," mused Su Su.

"Everyone likes happy endings," said Ah-Muih with a tinge of melancholy in her smile. She knew it was time to say goodbye.

"Hey, cheer up. Aren't Baenl people supposed to be the most optimistic of all? Even a hailstorm can be interpreted as an auspicious sign."

"That's true. We drink to hailstorms and sing songs of praise."

"There's one question that I want to ask you." Hesitantly, Su Su opened her mouth. "I . . . I don't know how to ask it."

"Say and ask whatever comes to mind. Be wind, be water."

"Who made the final decision? Was it Goddess Sax, or . . ." Su Su pursed her lips, her voice choking up. "Or you?"

After the ceremony, Ah-Muih announced to the entire village that Goddess Sax had blessed her with an oracle: Baenl would agree to connect to the outsiders' hypercortex network under one condition—that Su Su would spearhead the construction.

This meant two things for Su Su. She would have to obtain a direct authorization from the company, and she would have to return to Baenl and live here for some time. *Perhaps for quite a long time.*

When the decision was announced, Su Su saw conflicting emotions flash across Li Xiang's face, flickering like the shadows that the clouds cast on mountain peaks. At last, he smiled in relief.

Su Su gazed at Ah-Muih, who seemed to be deeply lost in a trance. *What is behind the pair of eyes that I am looking into?* A thought, out of nowhere, sprang up in her head. *Neurons, or a tangled mess of dark brown fungi hyphae?* Shivering, she shook her head to dispel the dark image that her mind had conjured up.

Though the execution of the project was laden with obstacles, Su Su was still thankful for what it offered her.

In her hallucination during the ceremony, she was able to see infinite overlapping alternative futures. In most of those futures, she saw herself stuck in the cracks and crevasses of mundanity, bounded and suffocating. It appeared as if her way was paved with a multitude of choices, but she knew that she had no freedom to choose for herself, after all. There was only one future in which she was really free. She was the supernode that connected the two different means of calculation, the two networks with paralleling magnitude of power. Like the duet in her dreams, she was meant to bring them all to perfect synchrony. In a future like that, humans would be endowed with the wisdom to restore and sustain the delicate balance between nature and technology, saving the fragile blue planet that they—alongside a multitude of other beings—cherished as home from destruction.

Goddess Sax's oracle pointed her to the future that she wanted. It was now up to her to pave her own way.

"She likes you. And I like you too," responded Ah-Muih, her tone nonchalant.

Su Su knew she should laugh, but controlled herself out of habit.

"Wait for me. When I come back, let's . . ." Su Su was stuck.

"Let's sing together," said Ah-Muih. A smile as radiant as the sun emerged on her face as she took Su Su's hands, their fingers entwining.

Finally, Su Su's lips curled into a smile. "Together," she said.

9 LEGION

Malka Older

BRAYSE PUSHES OPEN THE DOOR WITHOUT KNOCKING, AND THE TWO WOMEN INSIDE, who had been locked in quick conversation, turn on him, their eyebrows identically clenched above furious eyes. Unusual: his familiar face and aura of desirability are enough to make most people happy to see him, especially when they're sitting in his green room about to come on his talk show. He's only here, taking time out of his prep routine to try to make them feel more comfortable, get any of the celebrity-meeting jitters out off camera, for fuck's sake.

Brayse focuses his attention on the younger woman, dark braid naively long down her back. She's his guest; he recognizes her from about a week ago when she accepted the Nobel Peace Prize along with five others. They tried to remain nameless, which shows how innocent they are in this intrusive age; it didn't last long. She's still requested he avoid using her name, as if that mattered. "Welcome, we're so pleased to have you here. I'm Brayse Merittson," *And I'm not afraid to say my name.* "I'm looking forward to speaking with you on set shortly."

He holds his hand out and she evades it with the gesture that had become common during the pandemic, so she's one of those. Brayse puts his hand away and returns her nod, making sure to widen his smile as he turns slightly to include the older woman in the conversation (such as it is).

"Is there anything I can tell you before we start? Do you want to talk about what we'll discuss, or . . ."

"All of that was covered in the contract," the older woman says. "Go away."

Brayse smiles, though neither of the women is looking at him now. "Sure, sure. I'll go read the clause in the contract that someone else negotiated instead of"—neither of them is paying attention to him anymore, either; they are *talking* to each other in their own language, right over or maybe under him—"getting to know the person I'm about to interview on some kind of friendly basis," he pulls out of the doorway, closing the door behind him, probably totally unnoticed, "then maybe enjoying a cup of coffee and putting myself in a good mood for the show. Sure. Fantastic way to get the interviewer on your side." He shakes his head, walking back down the corridor. "Jer," he says to the air in front of him, tapping the part of his wrist screen that opened intercom to his assistant, "find me the contract provisions for this one for me to review, ta." He turns into his office, which is about half the size of the greenroom—the show sometimes booked bands or other groups—but he stocks much better alcohol than they offer the guests. He pours himself a shot of tequila and goes through the bullet points that legal prepped for him.

There aren't, actually, many provisions about topics he can't ask about; why didn't they just say that? Especially the lawyer or manager or whoever it was who dismissed him so brusquely. Wasn't that *her* job, to talk him through this? Protect her client so her client didn't have to protect herself?

Well, if they couldn't even bother to smile when he greeted them, fry 'em. This interview was supposed to be a score: the first given by anyone verifiably connected to Legion, the first since the Nobel Prize was announced. Now it looked like it was going to be a slog. Brayse's job, as he sees it, is to entertain his viewers while being both aspirationally witty and accessibly likable. He prefers to be on the same team with his interviewees, but it's not strictly necessary. And maybe Legion should face a little criticism, after all the adulation. He sips the remainder of his drink and heads to the studio, stretching his smile muscles and exercising his voice box as he goes.

The glass-walled streaming studio is a few feet underwater, allowing for natural light and cooling. For a long time Brayse had thought that was what the word *streaming* derived from, until he said so once and his producer, Lana, laughed at him and told him that it was much older than that design. But she's *old*, so of course she would know something like that.

Brayse settles into his chair, specially designed for him the way he likes it—if guests prefer more lumbar support they just have to lump it—adjusts his scarf, and settles into his on-air face. The countdown light flashes. He lets his mind run gently through what's coming up, but thinking of his guest he sees again that hard stare from her and her manager when he entered the room, as though they hated him. What the fuck did he ever do to them?

The show starts with a quick memetage of current events, different every day, although some would repeat over the course of a week or a month as stories developed, and there is always one related to the current guest. The meme team puts it together, along with the prefabs for Brayse's use throughout the show, and he mostly ignores it. With nothing happening in the studio the EYES, too, sit quiescent on their strategic perches, but Brayse knows that, despite their inert appearance, they are always recording. He's used to it, and keeps his face intent, alert, the man the audience would want to see unobserved.

That also means that when his wrist vibrates to let him know he's on he can ease into the figurative spotlight, rather than animating suddenly as though someone had flipped a switch. "Welcome," Brayse says, to millions of unseen watchers. He is intimate and alluring, he prides himself on it. He doesn't have to overemote, unlike his predecessors in the days of poor resolution and distant screens; he's as close as they want him to be, or closer. "In this hour"—day or night, depending on where people are watching from live or if they catch the recording—"we have quite an *important* matter to discuss, as we present the first interview with one of the architects of the *controversial* Legion app."

There's a snort in his ear from Lana. "You didn't like her, huh?"

Brayse hates it when she chitchats at him during the show, but she refuses to give up her access (as if he would ever, ever go off the rails; as if she could stop him if he did; as if she's in charge of him) and this time, instead of irritation, he represses a smirk. Lana might catch it, but fuck her. The audience might be influenced by it without noticing, which is all to the good for the dynamic he wants to set up.

Three of the EYES swoop down to hover by the doorway and offer multiple perspectives on the guest's entrance, but the rest stay on Brayse, where they belong, and he knows at least some of his viewers are watching his bright, even teeth smile instead of the small, dark woman who walks in and takes her seat.

"Welcome, welcome," he says. "We're so pleased to have you on and hear about Legion. Especially since the Nobel Peace Prize, I know you've had a lot of attention, and we're looking forward to the inside story of the innovation that has affected so many people." He shifts his gaze, just slightly, so that his smile will connect with the EYES, the viewers, instead of with her, since she doesn't seem to care about it anyway.

She doesn't know to do that, keeps her eyes fixed on him, and he calibrates her skill at engaging with the audience down another notch. *Don't overdo it*, Brayse reminds himself: winning plays well with the audience, bullying less so. Unless he can really convince them that it's deserved, but they didn't see that look in the greenroom, and Legion has been getting an awful lot of great press, even if some of his audience are probably (and rightly) suspicious of it.

"First," she says, with the precision of a nonnative speaker (And why doesn't she rely on an auto-interpreter? These people are so *precious*), "I must stress that our Legion is a collaborative project. No individual is responsible, certainly not myself."

Brayse hates this false modesty, so he goes hard sooner than he had planned, and he does it smiling and nodding. "I'm sure that being thought of as responsible for it could be a dangerous position, as it's still *very* controversial. There are a lot of people who aren't so pleased with the idea that—"

She interrupts him, which is annoying but probably worse for her than for him, in the eyes of the viewers. "Our Legion is not for pleasing people. In fact, it is so that we do not need to care whether people are pleased, ever again. And our Legion is why it is not dangerous for me to be known, just disingenuous, because we should all get the credit."

He chuckles, ready to respond with something, but she goes on. "At the beginning it was dangerous, yes. Very." She throws a prepared vid into the stream, or maybe her lawyer/manager does from offstage, because Brayse doesn't notice her fiddling with anything. "At first we were unknown, so our risk was the same as everyone else's. Which was of course very much higher than today." There are a few monitors shining in Brayse's peripheral vision, marked to be invisible to the EYES, so he can see what the viewers see, and without turning his gaze to watch directly he catches glimpses of what she's showing them. He expected gore, bruised faces, and other aftermath of violence, but it looks like dataviz instead, colored dots appearing, swirling, compounding. "But then, there was press, there were media attacks and bot rallies. People learned what we were doing, while our community was still too small to be effective. There were . . ." She pauses, swallows. It's masterfully done, in the midst of that calm discussion and the coolly parading dots representing abstract numbers; is it real, or is she better at this than he thought? "Gaps. Times when no one was watching, places no one could reach in time."

"How terrible," Brayse murmurs, because he has to, obviously. He shoots a quick look at the monitor, hoping the movement will be unnoticeable, but it is still showing impersonal dots, now diminishing to a sporadic line.

"Now, however, we are enough. We are always watching. We are protected and avenged."

The triumph in her voice won't play well. Brayse softens accordingly; he can be accommodating and helpful, garner admiration, and still win. "Tell us about the Nobel Peace Prize. Has it changed your life?"

She blinks at him. "No. What could it change?"

"Well, you're here," Brayse says, with his considerable charm, sweeping his arm around the glass bubble of a studio, the center point of attention for all those millions of watchers.

"But not because of the prize. You, and all the others, were asking us to talk to you long before that. If anything, the prize came because we were so popular. No, *Legion* changed my life."

Right, right, nobody cares about being famous, that's why they're all desperate for it. "Tell us about that. How did it change your life?"

Again, she looks at him as though the question makes no sense; then her face changes a little, as though understanding. "Maybe you've never been afraid? Felt unsafe?"

Brayse flushes on-screen for the first time in years. "I've gotten death threats," he says, chagrined at the edge to his voice, and forces himself to smile, look into the cameras of the nearest EYES. "Nothing to worry about, really, but I've been in a few ticklish situations."

Lana snorts in his ear, which is totally unfair: sure, she's seen all of the death threats and knows that show security has pronounced them all *extremely unlikely to be based in reality as we know it*, but she wasn't there that time at the bar when the big man had pushed against his chest, repeating, *I know who YOU are, I've seen you.* Or at the after party when he'd dumped out his drink, afraid one of his rivals had poisoned it.

"Hm," says the woman sitting beside him. "If it was nothing to worry about, it doesn't sound like you were really frightened. But, if you were, then you can easily imagine how it would change *everything* to not be afraid anymore."

He can't. "So was it this fear that led you to develop Legion? Perhaps a specific experience you had?"

She turns a look on him, the same severe look that she and the older woman pinned him with in the green room. "That sounds prurient, Brayse," she says, his name sounding overly familiar, or maybe that's condescension. "Almost as if you get some pleasure from imagining me being hurt." He's too stunned to answer her, and is grateful that most of the EYES are directed at her intent little face instead of his. Hopefully Lana has the sense to keep them there. "Will it make you feel better about our winning the Nobel Peace Prize if you believe we suffered for it? Or do you just enjoy seeing people get hurt?" *The EYES aren't the only streaming cameras in the room.* Brayse's gaze is sucked as if by a vacuum to the Legion pins on her shirt, all of them watching him.

She sits back. "Perhaps it is not that. Perhaps you just have the mediatic desire for cause and effect."

Brayse lets out his breath, wondering if all the Legionnaires watching are doing the same, releasing him from their unwavering crosshairs, deciding maybe he's not the enemy after all. "It just seemed logical," he says cautiously, and then pulls himself together. "What I mean is, we all want to know how this world-changing idea came about. If my guess was wrong, why don't you tell us?"

"Nothing happened to me," she says. "Nothing more than what happens to everyone. People called at me on the street, leaned into me when they were talking, touched my shoulder, my waist, my back, my leg, my cheek, when I didn't want them to, hugged for too long, complained when I didn't talk to them." Her eyes bore into him again. "Are you thinking that is nothing to change the world over?"

He thinks it's rhetorical at first but she waits. Lana is winding up her growl on his earphones and his own honed fear of dead air is screaming at him, but he doesn't want to fall into her trap, he's already struggling far more than he should be, so instead of comforting conversational noises he decides to go slow and snide. "I wouldn't say *thaaaat*," he drawls. "But surely, with all the critically urgent problems facing the world . . ."

"I was *supposed* to be solving critically urgent global problems," she spits, sounding angry for the first time. "Yes! I have degrees in engineering and marine biology. I was part of a special program working on aspects of climate change. I worked with social scientists and climatologists, we had a government grant. My time was supposed to go to that. All of the intellectual and organizing power that was put into Legion was supposed to do that. *I* was supposed to do that. But *you*"—he doesn't flinch this time, but it's because she's not talking to him, she's sweeping her gaze across all the EYES—"you just couldn't not hurt people, could you? Murder after murder after murder. Attack after attack. And so instead of quietly sitting in a lab, finding incremental and hard-won solutions to the *extremely* critical problem of saving our oceans, which is where I would rather be, I have to sit here and explain to you all not *why* killing people is wrong, because if you don't know by now there is no point," her eyes have come back to him, and he sweats beneath his tailored shirt, "but *how* we will prevent you from doing it again, or avenge ourselves if we are too late to prevent."

Fuck this. Peace prize or no peace prize, he's not going to let this half-grown girl push him around on his own set. "How very sad that you couldn't follow your dreams. These murders you mention. Did they happen to someone you knew?"

She meets his gaze but answers with a touch of irritation. "Does it have to be someone I know to change my life? Or do I only need to recognize that person as someone I could have been? Or do I only have to recognize that person as a person?"

"It's terrible, of course." Brayse is straining to keep his voice mellifluous, isn't sure if he's overdoing it. He reminds himself that most of the viewers will be on his side. "But when we speak of *global* problems, and surely the Nobel is intended to be a *global* prize, well, at the end of the day, doesn't Legion really only affect a certain segment of the population?" Some undefined shift in the quality of the silence in his earpiece makes him wonder if his producer might have a different view.

The young woman cocks her head at him. "Really? Doesn't the Nobel often go to people who barter a peace between two small groups of people? I suppose calling it *war* makes a difference. But that's not the more important point. Can you really believe that this change wrought by Legion doesn't affect everyone?" She throws another vid; this one at least has *faces*. Some of them are easily recognizable: Fenella Verity, Luisa Poirier, Özge Tayler, Norentina Pék. Others have identification halos: Chief Justice of the Albanian Supreme Court; Founding Executive, Gravaspeck Corporation; journalist; aid worker; caregiver; inventor; therapist; mother; programmer; chef. "All of these people," she says, "had an experience, which . . ." She keeps talking, but Brayse loses the thread a bit when he notices that these faces—yes, this vid is more appealing, it's still just a bunch of random faces, okay?—have replaced his own on *all* the playback screens, which means that Lana gave the vid override to every streaming channel. Ugh. Definitely on her side. But of course she is.

"Some of them had their careers, their goals, their lives, endangered by a specific person who found ways to threaten them with impunity. Until Legion. For some of them, their activities were circumscribed by unsafe commutes. Others had been attacked and were, quite rationally, too terrified to participate in life. Some were attacked *in* their homes, and could not work or study because they had been driven onto the street or into precarious living conditions. Without Legion, none of these people would be where they are. We, all of us would be missing their contributions." Brayse is somewhat skeptical of *that* counterfactual, because how could they know? But she's still talking as the vid switches back to—yep—dataviz. He manages not to roll his eyes. "If that's too anecdotal, we can see the correlation between Legion reaching critical mass in a country, and productivity and quality of life ratings both improving dramatically."

She's still talking, but Brayse is distracted by the sight of a diver outside the glass walls of the studio. That happens occasionally, but it's pretty rare. As usual, this one is staring inside, as if they had come down to look at him instead of at whatever ocean life is still surviving out there. He has to quell an urge to wave violently at them to move along, and schools his smile into place again. "All very admirab—"

She interrupts him, *again*. "But of course, Legion does not only affect people indirectly. It affects people very directly as well. It affects everyone who would have been attacked, bothered, annoyed, insulted, injured, or killed if Legion wasn't standing with them." Brayse wants to look at the Legion buttons on her blouse and won't let himself. "But it also affects the people who would have attacked, bothered, annoyed, insulted, or injured others if they weren't afraid of who might see and who might answer. Those people's lives are changed too. Surely you will agree with me that change is for the better?"

Her eyes are fixed on him with unseemly steadiness. That insanely intense look *can't* be playing well. "Of course, it's a wonderful thing, we all agree, and that's why the Nobel is so well deserved." He clears his throat, moving on to punch a few holes in this ridiculousness. "So if we put cameras everywhere, on everything, will we end all crime?"

"It's not about the cameras." *Isn't it though?* He wants to scream it. How did the Nobel committee fall for this? "It's about the community. The cameras just offer that community access."

He raises an eyebrow. "So they should give *me* the Nobel Prize next year?" That might have sounded a little sour, so he ups the charm. "After all, I have cameras here too, and"—gracious smile, aimed at the EYES—"an amazing community in my audience."

She doesn't even give that the reaction pause it deserves. "You have cameras, yes; but will your audience fight for you?"

Brayse turns to the EYES more openly this time, grin widening. "Well? Will you?" Will they? Are they out there punching the air, or maybe looking for Legionnaires to prove something to?

The woman is looking at him severely, as if she can see what he's imagining. "It's true that our Legion improved a bit on existing technology. We took a tool of the oppressor—surveillance—sometimes offered as a sop to justice, as in police cameras, and adjusted it to work for us. But when people focus on what we've done with technology, they miss the point. Most of the work we have done is in building our community and our anger. We support each other, help each other, we find outlets for our anger and teach each other how to use it. The cameras are, are, the medium that lets us connect," she is gesturing urgently with her hands as she talks, "lets us *translate* the power and need of our community in the fractured places where it interacts with violent, unfair, oppressive societies."

He can't remember his next talking point, which never happens to him. The diver has been joined by another, both peering into the well-lit studio. "So," Brayse tries. It's too early for this one, but he can always double back. "What's next for you? That is to say, for the whole team at Legion?"

"Perhaps I'll get back to saving our oceans," she says, and then, when he stares at her, she cracks a smile. "I jest. Legion has changed the world, yes, but it has changed some parts of the world more than others. There are still countries that block us"—*Of course they do*, he thinks, *what did you expect? And why shouldn't they?*—"and others that discourage our community in a myriad of ways, or attempt to minimize our communications. We are working on advocacy as well as legal challenges to make our Legion available and accessible to everyone. The Nobel Prize will of course be very helpful for that."

"And coming on shows like this, naturally." Brayse says it very smoothly. His earbud buzzes with silence. The woman across from him nods.

"Naturally," she agrees. "That's why I'm here. We are also working on a few extensions to, or specific applications, for the Legion model. For example, we are developing a function that will allow volunteers to watch your drink."

"Your drink."

"Can you imagine? Not having to watch your drink constantly when in a public place." She lifts the glass of water by her chair, turns it, puts it down again with a smile, and goes on before he can comment. "Not having to finish a drink before going to use the bathroom."

"I thought a colleague poisoned one of my drinks once," Brayse feels compelled to say. He gives it the tone of a humorous anecdote.

"Had they?"

"Had they what?"

"Poisoned your drink."

"I don't know, I tossed it out." He feels a bit silly, but flashes the charm at the EYES anyway.

"If you've been worried about the integrity of your drinks ever since then, you will find this upgrade useful," she says seriously, and his face heats again. She really imagines he uses Legion?

"It was a very specific circumstance," he says.

"Then you can imagine how much of a relief it would be for people among whom it is general. Really, I think it will be marvelous! We are also looking at options for dark places."

"Dark . . . places . . . ?"

She straightens in her chair, setting up for a serious talk. "As you know . . ." This is going to be boring. His eyes drift to the walls. The divers are gone, and he relaxes a little. ". . . works through our community *watching*. We see, in real time and in remotely held recordings, the perpetrators. We see exactly what they do." His eyes come back to hers, and she is doing that look again, the strong one, and he hates it. "Usually we see the full escalation. There is no hiding it, no argument. And with not one, or two, or three witnesses but thousands or tens of thousands, it is much harder to ignore, argue away, twist. It's a technique we learned from the civil rights movement, from iterations from in-person bystanders through digital technology." She pauses for breath. "But of course, if there is less visibility, our strength is diluted. If it is too dark to make out the attacker's face, for example, or to trace the precise unfolding of subtle aggressions into devastating ones." She tosses another vid. Brayse keeps his eyes resolutely on her face, but in his peripheral vision he gets a nauseating sense of undefined movement, pulse, obscured violence. It's far more disturbing than the gory vids he had expected, but, he tells himself, maybe that's just because he's not watching directly. "We're experimenting with high-powered lights on the buttons, with dye packs that can mark any attackers, and so on."

As if fucking watching people all the time weren't enough. "That seems like a significant step for you, doesn't it? It's one thing to watch, and another to stain someone's skin. You're moving from witnessing to acting." She opens her mouth and he beats her to it, with some satisfaction. "But then, members of Legion *do* act, don't they?" They are at the point in the interview where he can toughen a bit, it's strategic, a choice. "In fact, you've been accused of vigilantism, even of mob violence."

"The witnessing of our Legion doesn't stop," she says. Fuck, the divers are back, a small gaggle of them now, peering in. One of the EYES swoops around to take a look at them; some B-roll to remind people how fabulous the studio is, he supposes. "Any action taken by our community is likewise recorded and available. We hold ourselves accountable."

"And some of your members have been convicted of assault themselves, haven't they?"

"Some have," she agrees. "But in each of those cases, the convictions were reduced due to the element of defense involved—"

"It's not self-defense if you thump someone who's in a fight with someone else!" His outrage about that breaks through his calm, but Brayse hates that argument, that silly sneaking justification.

"I didn't say 'self-defense,'" she responds, calmly, and Brayse hears Lana snicker in his earpiece. "But it is community defense. When someone is attacked out of nowhere, for no reason, and you help them to fight off their attacker, that is defense. Wouldn't you help someone being attacked?" *Depends on the someone*, but saying that out loud won't help him, and he bites it back. "In a just world with just laws none of them would have been punished, and if you doubt that you can watch the vids for yourself."

"But this is why these other countries are blocking you, isn't it? Because you take the law into your own hands."

She is looking at him now as though she recognizes him, as though she knows him in some way beyond his public persona, which is impossible and a trick of her expression but he hates it anyway. She doesn't know him. She barely even sees him. "We take our defense into our own hands." Of course all those people in Legion are looking at him too, through her accoutrements. "If the State wants a monopoly on violence it's also required to defend its citizens, all of them." It's not impossible that someone in that massive group might recognize him: might have seen him off-screen somewhere, might have seen him do something personal, secret, might have . . . participated. "Yes, there are countries that oppose us. They don't want to be shown up for how they have failed, for years and decades and *centuries*, to protect their own. And of course there are always those who will fight any shift in power, decry any change. But since Legion began, not one person has been hurt by us who didn't hurt someone first."

"An eye for an eye then, is it?" Brayse asks. He can be cutting now, still time to pull everything into a feel-good package later. "Two wrongs making a right?"

"Legion," she says, putting her finger down on the table between them. "Does. Not. Make. It. Right. It makes it harder for people to do wrong, but only because they are afraid of what might happen to them, or ashamed when they see their evil reflected in a million staring eyes. Maybe with time this will become more ingrained, that is what we hope. But Legion cannot fix the wrongs that have been done."

She hasn't answered the *question*. "Are you saying it doesn't feel good when you see a mob beating up someone who—"

She cuts him off with a tut. "How I feel doesn't matter. You were speaking of the law; shouldn't laws be upheld? There is a long tradition of self-defense exceptions to laws against violence, and of people being allowed to defend their property and assets, sometimes to an extreme degree. This is communal self-defense, this is community enforcing the laws that most States have chosen to treat as secondary or unimportant. There is no incitement on Legion, no rallying speeches or instructions on how to make bombs or anything. Just witnesses. Witnesses who sometimes arrive to witness personally, to embody their presence. If they arrive to find the crime continuing, a person being attacked, of course they will try to stop that harm from being perpetrated."

"That all sounds very good, but you cannot deny that Legion has changed the way people act, how they relate."

"Of course it has! That's what it's meant to do. That's why we were awarded the prize."

Brayse inclines his head; it doesn't matter, his viewers will know what he meant, they will be just as angry about this unnecessary change as he is.

What more can he say? He's already done the *What are you doing next?*, which should have come more toward this end of the interview, but he got so muddled in the middle. "You say that you're not the only one responsible for Legion, that there are many of you. How does that work? How did it start?"

"We are many. If we could have had twenty, fifty people here to talk to you, that would have been more realistic, but we looked at past occasions when you have had small groups as guests and even two or three does not work as well as one." Brayse knows that criticism is of the format, not of him or of his show; he still doesn't like it. "How it started . . . it started quite literally, physically, you know. It started as a way not to have to walk alone, to have physical accompaniment, witnesses even if they weren't able to defend. And mostly they weren't." She looks down at her hands in her lap. Apparently she doesn't have a vid to illustrate this. "It turns out that two people is better than one, but not by much. Three is not very different from two. We tried adding more and more, but of course it is inconvenient, not feasible, to have such large groups always available whenever someone needs, or wants, to, perhaps, walk to their job or university. Or exercise outside. Or take a bus to an appointment or go out to dinner or visit a park." She takes a deep breath, as though the memory of those times oppresses her. "And we virtualized it. As I said, at the beginning, it was very bad. It did not make much difference, at the beginning. Because it is not enough for people to witness, it is not enough even to record the witnessing of crimes. The people with power have to care. And the people doing the crimes have to understand, accept, that the people with power care, and will eventually stop them." Another deep breath. "It took a long time for our witnessing to overflow to the extent that both those conditions were met. But we have finally gotten there."

It is the smugness when she says that, the utter complacency, that breaks him. Brayse leans forward, faux confidential. "You know," he says, "in my circles, women don't use Legion. Or if they do, they turn it off. And if they didn't, it wouldn't matter much. Famous people like us," he says, "we're used to being watched all the time. We're used to being criticized for things out of context, unfairly. And mostly, people forgive us. Because we're famous, and we're famous for a reason." He sits back. "But as I said, most women I meet don't use Legion anyway."

She looks at him steadily. "You think that. But we see you."

There is a loud cracking thunk, so sudden that at first Brayse thinks it's in his mind, a function of the surge of unfair fear he feels when she says that. He swings his head around in the direction it came from and sees one of the divers outside the studio raising their arm and swinging something heavy and metallic at the glass. The thunk this time has more cracking in it.

"Sir?" Someone is tugging at his arm. "Sir? We're evacuating, this way please." Brayse gets up, feeling detached from himself, swoopy and disembodied as though he were one of the EYES dancing around the jagged line in the glass. Is it sweating sea water? With a shudder Brayse snaps back into himself and turns to the access corridor. The woman he's been talking to, who just *threatened* him, for fuck's sake, is ahead of him, following someone from crew or security, he doesn't know.

Is the studio collapsing? What is wrong with those nutters out there? They should make it out, it's a short corridor to the surface, clearly they have procedures for emergencies, but his back itches with the thought of the ocean smashing through behind him. And what is going on? Are they anti-Legion activists, these divers? And if so, why the fuck couldn't they wait until she was done with his show to vent their rage? Or—a cold spike through his gut—are they Legion? Are they after him? Through the confusion, Brayse thinks he hears Lana laughing in his earpiece. Was it her? Is she a member of Legion? It had never occurred to him as a possibility. *Women in my circles don't join Legion.* And the woman from Legion had told him he was wrong about that. What has she seen? What do they know about him?

They are in the corridor now, dim and upward slanting, not running but hurrying at a quick jog. The woman from Legion is still just ahead of him, and in the faint light he can see her back, her tight ass, and he wants to brush his hand over it, just to show he can. Why not? It's right there in front of him, he could grab it, give him something to hold onto in this rushing disruption. Maybe she would jump and turn on him, angry, and he could smile like it doesn't matter, like he doesn't get scared or flustered even when his life's in danger. There's no one around but the security people who are urging him, even now, to hurry, *just a little bit further*, and they'd never tell. More than their job was worth, and he'd make sure they never worked in this business again, they must know that.

But there on her shoulders are the beady wide-angle buttons of Legion, and on her sleeves, and maybe on her pant seams too, for all he knows. Maybe she's the one testing out the dye packs. Maybe he would be vilified, maybe he'd look ridiculous. He hesitates, not wanting to give in, not wanting to be caught. And then, before he can decide, they are coming out into the sunlight.

Saad Z. Hossain

VARGA WORE A TALL BLACK COAT. IT HUNG THREE INCHES BELOW HIS KNEES, AND was buttoned up to his chin, even in this murderous heat. The skirt of the coat was narrow and hampered his movement somewhat, but he wasn't a gun fighter or anything, so he didn't need all that swashbuckling grace. It was more important that his skin didn't get contaminated.

From drone cameras, he knew he looked like a crow. His coat had a chemical layer on it that gave it a worn, slightly speckled look, and he wore a black cowl with a ragged scarf around it, making him appear like some dusty stranger come to town for no good. He would have preferred something else, something brightly colored perhaps, but this was the uniform. People had expectations.

When he arrived at a house it was always mournful. He was not invited for jovial occasions, after all. It was a street of prefabricated houses, the walls printed on-site, cheap but well maintained, the pavement spotless. These were solid middle-class people, he would say, stalwart shareholders of the City, who would never acquire any true wealth, but were too proud to take the bare minimum. They had curtains on their windows, old, polished vehicles, savings, heirlooms, books, and plenty of education; everything a long scream proclaiming they weren't part of the *headcount*, not part of the cardless[1] scum whose only contribution to society was the nanotech they made in their bodies to clean the air.

They were too rich to accept the City's largess, too poor to join the elite in space. Varga pitied them, almost as much as they pitied him.

The air quality here was fine but he kept his cowl on. No one wanted to see his face, after all. There was a crowd outside the front door, neighbors

---

1. In the early days of city incorporation, shareholders were given a card. Nonshareholders had no voting rights and were "given" a bare minimum of services in return for the implants in their bodies churning good nanotech into the air, the so-called air tax, which was a necessity for pockets of humanity to survive the polluted atmosphere.

and friends come to pay respects, wearing their best whites. The body was Mr. Kashem, taking pride of place just inside the foyer, looking more handsome than he ever had in life. The family had done a good job. He lay in the death cot in perfect repose, dignified, the tips of his moustache waxed to a fine curl, flowers all around him, filling the empty spaces.

Varga made sure to lower his van around the corner, out of sight. He moved respectfully to the back of the crowd, staying a little behind. He would never enter the house, but he peered in through the open doors and windows, trying to gauge when he could get to work. He recognized the big man Halder, whose mother he had picked up two years ago, the last death in the area. The man had a perpetually mournful look about him, and did not acknowledge Varga at all.

Someone's pet dog found him and started barking, objecting to his suspicious posturing. The lady of the house strode out, looking for her errant retriever. She stopped short when she saw him, her face turning instinctively to revulsion.

"What are you doing here? Peering through windows? Can't you see we haven't finished?" she said with venom that lit up her haughty eyes.

Varga took a step back to avoid the spit coming out of her mouth. Her eyelids were puffy with grief. He could tell she was looking for any slight provocation to blow up, the anger in her growing exponentially as each second ticked by. She was Mr. Kashem's daughter, in a crisp white dress, coiffed, ready to kill.

Death was a humiliation these days, an economic failure, admission that you couldn't afford immortality. Mr. Kashem had only been seventy, he could have lived twice that long at least. The sight of Varga threw that failure in the face of the family, made him the target of all their humiliation and rage.

For some reason, they always blamed him.

"Wait in the corner please," the lady said, regaining control. She had an educated accent. "We will send for you when we're done." She took out a wipe and cleaned her dog's face, even though it had not touched him. The disdain of the act cut Varga, and he retreated a distance. *Even my dog is cleaner than you, corpse collector.*

He wanted to smoke a cigarette but stopped himself. They were keeping an eye on him now, and he didn't want to be abused any more. Sometimes the people were nice. In one house last week they had offered him food and drink, from a real plate and glass. He had declined of course, because he knew they'd be compelled to break the things after. It was the ingrained habit of caste after all. There was no one as unclean as the handler of bodies.

More often they threw money at him, a few chips for a cup of tea if he had to wait long, maybe a spot in the shade. The key was to keep your eyes down, make yourself small. Speak when spoken to. Yes sir no sir.

Mr. Kashem's family were from a good caste. He had been the math teacher at the neighborhood school. Many of his students had come to the funeral, so it was taking longer than usual. Varga was wary of the students. Young boys were rambunctious and might decide to throw things at him. He had been cut by a bottle last year, boys drinking beer and deciding it would be fun to fight the man in black.

Eventually the crowd dissipated without incident and Mr. Kashem's daughter beckoned imperiously.

"Vultures," she said as he approached. "Not a tear on them. They just came to see what he died of. And why I couldn't pay." Her friends had already pushed the coffin out onto the sidewalk.

Varga nodded noncommittally. Deaths were an event these days.

"Level 3 upgrade on the PMD," she said bitterly. "I couldn't beg or borrow enough for that in a hundred years. Hell, I couldn't earn that much even if I spread my legs all day up in space." She covered her mouth with her hand as if objecting to her own vulgarity. The space stations were notorious for high-paid consorts of either sex.

Varga personally did not find her that attractive and thought that she was perhaps overestimating her earning capacity in this manner, but he thought it wise not to comment.

The two great pieces of human engineering of the era, the PMD and the ECHO, were genius biotech devices that everyone carried, even the cardless. The PMD was the Personal Medical Device, implanted into every citizen's spine: part doctor, part nanotech controller, part cure. The PMD also helped pay the air tax, directing the body to make those tiny biological molecules, little machines humans exhaled into the air to fight destructive pollution. Enough good nanotech created a microclimate, a little blue-skied oasis dense with people. It was why the City tolerated the poor in the first place, why the cardless were packed into tiny spaces and "nurtured." It was why the hinterland had been ceded to the wilderness.

The ECHO was a brain implant, a silver filigree that grew with each passing year, part augment, part communication device; it let you play in the Virtuality, the cloud of technology that enveloped the entire world, turning the grey utilitarian existence to paradise, pixels over paint, every stimulant and experience delivered directly to the brain, bypassing the mundane botheration of brick and mortar altogether.

These were cornucopia tech, transforming humanity or enslaving them, depending on whom you asked, the answer to death and disease, to the wreckage of the world. Ironically, it was the failure of these two implants that most often caused death these days.

"First death in the row this year," Ms. Kashem said. "I'm going to get this false sympathy for months. Ughhh. I'll be like poor Halder. Halder's wife left him, you know that? Couldn't take all the little jokes. I have no other family. I'll be alone now for the rest of my life."

Old lady Halder and Banne were two sisters a few grids over, both dead at sixty of a rare genetic defect. He remembered taking the bodies, Halder's inconsolable grief at losing both mother and aunt so close together.

Varga worked while she carried on prattling. Often people spoke their minds to him, unloading their thoughts as if he were a mute priest. Religion had faded from the death rituals, until outcasts like him were the only custodians left to manage all the little aspects of the passing. She was worried about the afterlife, of course; modern mysticism had pushed away heaven and hell, but left an amorphous vacancy, a lack of clear expectations. Where did souls go, after the body demised? It was theoretically possible for the body not to demise, after all. And there were virtual heavens for the rich, iced bodies up in space, were they inferior to the real thing?

The City had given him a handbook to prepare for every situation, but he found that just shutting up and listening was the best course. Meanwhile he packed the body into a bag, and onto the little scooter he had unclipped from his belt, a simple axle on a stick. There was a hook at the top that went into the eyelet of the body bag, and let him carry the corpse upright. The wheels were tiny, but with mag lift, suited for rough ground. He had never spilled a body, not even when pelted with stones by neighborhood boys.

He finally spoke, his voice coming out scratchy from the cowl.

"What did he die of, madam?" He had to know. If it was contagious he would have to take precautions.

"PMD rejection," she said. "Rare case apparently. They said an exotic upgrade would fix that, but well you understand. We're only nominal shareholders of the City. One share, my dad was born with, and one lousy share more he got for teaching kids all his life. They doubled him up, he said. He was pretty happy. Guess how many shares he needed for a free upgrade just to stay alive? Twenty. Ten times what he had. Otherwise it was cash bitto, or a butcher's black market shop, neither of which we could afford."

Twenty shares in the City Corporation gave unlimited care, as far as Varga knew. Hell, they'd grow you a brand new body if they had to.

"So now he's dead and I get his chips," the lady continued. "I'm at three. I teach at the university. So maybe when I'm his age I'll have four, and you'll carry me out the front door too."

Varga wondered why everyone thought he was immortal. It must be the coat.

"But no, you don't have to worry, it's not the plague." She glanced at him with contempt, as if cowardice was his only quality.

"There's no plague in the Free City, Madam," Varga said. It was the party line, and true, as far as he knew. The bodies weren't piling up here like some other places.

"What's your name?"

"Varga."

"Just Varga?"

"Varga the corpse collector," Varga said. *Do you think the cardless have last names?* "I am sorry about your father, sorry he could not be saved. I saw him sometimes, outside the school. He was a kind man, I think."

"Did he teach you?" she asked.

"My . . . my father was also a corpse collector," Varga said. "I was not allowed to attend the school. The other parents would not have liked it. But the teachers were kind. They sent the lessons online to me, and a certificate at the end, so there would be proof I was lettered."

"You were lucky," Ms. Kashem said. "I'm surprised they bothered. You don't need letters to burn bodies, surely. Wasting their time, if you ask me. But that was my dad, head in the clouds, utopian till the end."

"I was very grateful, madam," Varga said. "It was thoughtful of them. Without the certificate I would not have been permitted my current job." *I'd have stayed apprentice, and been given a pittance.*

"The City pays you, right? A good salary, place to live," Ms. Kashem said. "What more do you need? But I bet when you've saved enough you'll throw away that coat and run off. Teaching you people anything is a mistake, I always say."

An interesting stance for an educator. "I am good at my job," Varga said with a little pride. "And someone has to do it."

"Well, I suppose you want a tip," Ms. Kashem said, noticing he was done.

"Madam, there is no need, I cannot accept," Varga said.

"Oh shut up," Ms. Kashem said. "I know your type. All false humility and then you'll go around saying to everyone that I'm a miser. Just wait here."

She went inside for a few minutes, returned with a brown bottle, cold and already sweating in the heat. "Here. I suppose you want alcohol, but it's only lemonade. I don't have any spare change in the house."

She thrust it into his hands, and glanced at his face, but of course he was cowled and invisible, his features just a black smudge. By the time he had thanked her she had already stomped back inside. He drank the lemonade on the way to his vehicle. It was good.

In the cemetery he worked alone. There had been three of them before, his father and Uncle Rummy, the two veterans. Varga's mother had left them when he was young, done exactly what Ms. Kashem had suggested, run away and changed her name and tried to break her caste. He often wondered what had become of her, whether she had managed to pull off the fraud. His father never spoke of her, and did not attempt a second marriage. Uncle Rummy, when drunk, had once mentioned that she had been very pretty and that he feared that in her attempt to get away from corpse collection, she had slid into the other indispensable profession, prostitution. It was not clear to Varga which was better, being a prostitute or a corpse collector, and Uncle Rummy had not further elaborated.

Sadly, age and illness had removed both his mentors, his father first, followed shortly by his uncle. He had gotten a notice one day, informing him that the City Corporation was affirming his employment and salary as chief caretaker of the cemetery and processor of bodies. Should he finish his full term of service (which ended with death), he would posthumously receive a single share of citizenship. He might not enjoy it, but perhaps his progeny would. There would be no new apprentices.

The cemetery was unkempt and largely abandoned. There had been burials before, but no one bothered to visit graves anymore, or even collect the ashes in case of cremation. All the death rituals had gradually faded, when death itself had faded, with the undying rich living in space, and high-end PMDs keeping people alive for untold decades. It was difficult to take it seriously when advertisements kept hitting you with immortality, ever young, ever beautiful.

Varga processed bodies, a job no one wanted to do. He collected the dead and gave the family a commemorative coin, which the City sent to him. He had a whole stack of them in his office, and a little stamp to put in the name and date. Office was a bit misleading. He actually worked in a morgue, with modest living quarters to the side. He had taken over his father and uncle's rooms, after he had processed their bodies, and following a respectful interlude, had converted one into a sitting room and another into a library. There was a small kitchen and bathroom besides, and a small kitchen garden.

His library was his main consolation. Physical books were rare but still possible to find, and many times he had collected bodies of the very old who had no family or friends, people left dead and stinking for a week before some neighbor got around to calling for him.

In those situations, with no heirs, the City reclaimed the possessions and in an unadvertised process, attempted to auction them before calling the scrap men. Most of the time no one bothered to sort through the belongings of the dead. If you died of old age, it meant you were poor anyway, deficient, unable to afford new body parts or rejuvenation. Varga always bid for the books, and the City allowed it even though it was strictly speaking for citizens only; perhaps some petty bureaucrat was throwing him a bone, cognizant that he was doing a vital, unpleasant job.

He fit Mr. Kashem on the cold table and did his preliminary work with the auto surgeon, the first vital tasks that had to be done immediately. Afterward, it was too late to continue so he lit a candle outside, and knocked off for the night. The City didn't pay for it, but candles were cheap, and the chandler knew what it was for and gave him a bulk discount. He keyed a quick dinner of noodle soup into the kitchen machine and ate it mechanically. He fell asleep on the sofa with his Balzac on his lap.

The next morning he went to the morgue at eight. On corpse days he did not eat breakfast. The worst part was extracting the PMD. This required some surgical skill because it was fused into the spine, delicate, and different each time because the device adjusted to each body, like all good biotech. The remaining organs were also useful, and he was expected to salvage everything. Most people didn't want to know, and never asked, but if anyone did, he would have told them that the City expected all shareholders to be "donors," that it was in the fine print somewhere, and unless someone objected specifically in writing (in triplicate), it was deemed acceptable to harvest them.

He was about to get to work when he saw a shadow on the front gate cam. He was expecting no one. The shadow moved around, and finally the camera got a clear look at a veiled face, vaguely familiar. It was Ms. Kashem, this time in a navy blue suit.

He hurried to the gate.

"Oh, it's you," she said awkwardly through the wrought iron bars. "I thought there was a whole team here."

"I work alone," Varga said. He wanted her to leave, and so did not open the door.

"I want to see my father."

"He's in the cold room."

"Why can't I see him?"

"No one is allowed back there. It's very unusual. I already gave you the coin."

"Yes, thanks for the coin," she said. "It was a great consolation. Should I put it up on the wall? Like a trophy? Or maybe wear it around my neck?" She was unpleasantly sarcastic. Varga regretted feeling sorry for her.

"I'm sorry, the City makes me give them," Varga said. "Most people are glad to have them after the grief has lessened."

"Let me in," she said. "Or do you want me to call the police?"

Varga was forced to open the gate. In truth he had no authority to deny a citizen access to the cemetery. He led her to the back. They stood in front of the morgue door awkwardly. Waves of cold were coming from the steel door. He hoped this was far enough. No one had ever wanted to see the actual body. Yet.

"He's in there," Varga said. "Everything is done."

"I thought the City incinerates."

"Yes."

"So why this big morgue thing?"

"There used to be more deaths. They've been going down. Fewer births, fewer deaths. It used to be full."

"So have you burned him already? I want to see the ashes."

"I will," Varga said finally, admitting defeat. "First I um have to process the body."

"What?"

"I have to take the PMD out. They have rare metals. I have to give it back to the City."

"You're going to cut up my father?"

"It's part of the job," Varga said.

"What else?"

"What?"

"I can tell by your face that it gets worse."

180

"The organs. Everyone is an organ donor by default. I'm supposed to send those to the hospital."

"Default organ donor. You're a piece of shit, you know that?"

Varga hung his head in silence.

"So then you just burn whatever garbage is left, huh?"

"Madam, this is what the City pays me to do. I can assure you, everything is by the book here."

"I want to see him. I don't trust you."

She pushed past him, slammed open the door.

Mr. Kashem was on the table. She whipped off the plastic sheet and then screamed, as he knew she would. He wanted to grab her but he was conditioned not to touch anyone so he just stood back, feeling his world collapsing. He had known this day would come, sooner or later. He willed her not to call the police. He had no delusions about what they would do to him.

"Where's his head?" she asked finally.

"I can explain."

"Where is my father's head, Varga?" Her voice was hoarse, drained of all emotion, eyes glassy with shock. She was shivering.

He took her to the back of the morgue, to a partitioned room. Uncle Rummy had built it lovingly, out of scavenged scrap metal. There was a glass tank inside full of nanotech broth. Inside it lay fifteen topless skulls, each one with a preserved brain inside, all of them intact, inlaid with the silver veins of the ECHO. On closer inspection, the brains at the far end of the tank were almost entirely silver, as if the ECHO filaments had replaced the meat altogether, while the nearer ones were pinker. Varga pointed wordlessly at the freshest one.

"That's your father."

"Why?" Her face was almost white.

He quickly pulled a stool over and made her sit. She gripped the sides as if she was about to fall over, but then visibly pulled herself together and shook it off. She had no intention of fainting in a morgue, not matter how bizarre the business.

Varga pointed at the farthest one, which was almost entirely silver. "That's my uncle, Rummy. He worked here for the longest time, taught my father and me the ropes. He is the one who worked it out. Let me tell you the story. Then you can call the police."

Uncle Rummy had been so old even he didn't know his true age. He said he stopped counting birthdays after eighty. He had no family. He had

181

taken in Varga's father, trained him in the work of corpse tending. He was an educated man. Quite how he had fallen into this abhorred caste was unknown. Whatever the case, he had an encyclopedic knowledge of the human body. He was the one who had noted that the ECHO, implanted into the brain at youth, continued to grow its semibiological filaments as long as the person lived, far beyond original operating protocols.

It was Rummy's belief that given the right conditions, the ECHO could keep the brain going indefinitely, that in fact it could one day *replace* the higher functions of the brain in all meaningful ways, losing only those vestigial reptilian parts.

When he became terminally ill from PMD rejection syndrome, he made a simple last request. Put my brain in a high-nutrient nanotech gel, and feed the correct electrical pulses to make the ECHO grow, he said. Let's do one last, grand experiment.

Drunk, he told Varga that he was afraid to die, afraid of the afterlife, or rather, the entire lack of one. To lose this beautiful experience and turn to dust was unpalatable to him. Varga asked him about god, but Uncle Rummy could not place his faith in that far-off deity, not when there was a solution for him close at hand. God can have me in the end, he said, what does He care if I steal a few extra years?

The morgue had come with an auto surgeon with full scanners and a sarcophagus, meant for the safe removal of organs without butchering the body. It was easy to remove the brain. Varga set an auto program, and the machine did the rest. Later, he put it in the high-nutrient gel, with a nano-tech bath that kept everything alive. The brain in the tank was gruesome, but he quickly became used to it.

Varga thought nothing of it until, on the seventh day, Uncle Rummy spoke.

"He actually *spoke*?" Ms. Kashem asked, breaking his tale.

Varga nodded. "In the Virtuality."

"And my father will . . . ?"

"In a few days maybe," Varga said. "Uncle Rummy will help him."

"Why did you do this crazy thing?"

"Because there's nothing for us," Varga said. "There wasn't for my father when he died, no priest, no prayer, no hope. It's just reclaiming parts from the body. You get a button. I didn't even get that. I'm not a citizen. We just get erased. They don't care anymore, don't you see that? They live in the sky, they think they've beaten death. The Egyptian Pharaoh used to take all of his attendants with him, to serve him in the afterlife. He took his pets, his wives, his soldiers. But the Pharaoh doesn't die anymore. So what happens to us?"

"But this . . . this is a monstrosity."

"They're alive," Varga said. "They're alive in the Virtuality. You can't tell they don't have bodies. They're doing whatever they want, free, wandering around like a billion other people. Please. Don't take it away from them."

"Who are the others?" Ms. Kashem asked.

"Uncle Rummy is the first, of course. The second is Mr. Pala, who was once the cemetery auditor. He found out, and wanted to join in. He's still the auditor, the City thinks he's still alive. Then there is Mrs. Halder, and Mrs. Banne, from the same enclave as you." Varga stopped. "The rest are cardless like me, low caste. I asked them, madam, if they minded sharing the tank with us. No one said no. They are all very happy. If anyone dislikes it, they can just fade away. No one has. Please ma'am."

Ms. Kashem stood up. "I will return tomorrow. I expect to speak to my father."

She came back that night though. There was a mob with her, eight other men and women, including Halder and his cousin Banne, both strapping large men armed with electric truncheons. They broke into the cemetery and caught him just as he was leaving the morgue.

Halder slammed the door into him, trapping him half in, half out. Some others kicked him in the head and torso, and as he slumped, they started stomping on him with relish. He looked around frantically for a way out, eyes glazing over with blood. He grabbed someone's ankle, trying to curl into a defensive posture. In the distance he saw Ms. Kashem's legs, wearing the same clothes she had earlier.

Halder whipped the baton down on his temple. The electric charge twitched through his spine and cancelled out the rush of adrenalin his PMD was mustering. He became limp, and the two men dragged him fully out of the doorway. He felt a moment of relief that they had not seen what was inside the morgue. Halder flipped him over and hit him in the face, right across the mouth, splintering his teeth and jaw. The pain made him bleat like a butchered goat. They began to beat him in earnest, great methodical kicks, until his bones started to crack and his flesh turned to pulp. The electric batons burned him everywhere they touched, his face and hands melting entirely black, the air bubbling with the stench of broiled meat.

He could hear yelling, the men whooping in rage and Ms. Kashem telling them to stop. There was a momentary pause, for how long he could not

183

count, the sounds of intelligible argument and then Halder held the truncheon to his eyes and burnt them out, liquefying the eyeballs. He screamed one last time and died.

Later, he woke up on the table. He couldn't see or feel anything. Then he remembered his eyes were burnt out, but there was no pain. Voices murmured around him, and then came into focus. It was Uncle Rummy talking to . . . Ms. Kashem?

"What now?" she asked. Her voice was choked and scarred, as if she had cried herself hoarse.

"We wait. The mind should coalesce around the ECHO."

"Can he hear? Is he awake?"

"He might be, but he will not be able to communicate yet," Uncle Rummy said. "If you speak close to the brain the ECHO can translate the vibrations into words."

"Varga, I'm sorry," she said. "I told them you had misbehaved with me. I didn't say anything about the brains. I thought they'd scare you a little . . . Not kill you. I . . . I couldn't stop Halder. I put you in the auto surgeon. Your ECHO is in the bath now. Your Uncle Rummy helped me."

"You did very well, Samarra."

A new voice, one he had not heard before. Mr. Kashem, then? He had managed to find his way online. Varga gave a small cheer. Sometimes it took many days for a lost soul to get into the Virtuality.

"Varga, you have to try and find connections," Uncle Rummy said. "Right now your brain is lacking any inputs. Your ECHO can process sounds and fill in sights, but you don't have a physical body. You can't use your blink commands, for example, or hand motions to get into the Virtuality. However, your brain works the same way, so at first, you have to imagine blinking and it should work. You must keep trying."

Varga tried. He thought about the countless times he had blinked in. He thought about waving his hands to move virtual objects, of walking down the street in augmented reality, using gestures or even simply his glance to affect the environment. His vision stayed stubbornly black. He panicked. Perhaps the truncheon had burned away his brain. If there was ECHO damage, sometimes the afterlife did not take.

He heard Ms. Kashem's low voice cutting through the fugue, words coalesced into Balzac, and he relaxed into the half-finished story. She read for an extraordinarily long time, chapter after chapter, her voice expressive and full, until his anxiety went away, so much so that he forgot to practice blinking and unthinkingly blinked into the Virtuality.

The Virtuality encompassed the entire surface world. It was a second skein of life, stretched and ethereal, and one could walk it live or in avatar form. Varga found he had a body again, an approximation made from his mental image of himself, colorful and handsome. He was in his own morgue, bizarrely overlaid with a cocktail party, where others circled in evening dress.

An older man approached him with a bottle of champagne.

"Welcome, my boy!"

"Uncle Rummy?"

"Yes. It's a bit of a tradition now. The first time someone comes in, we greet them here with a party."

The others gathered around him, all of them overjoyed, full of revelry, beautiful. There were hugs and many words of gratitude. He was the ferryman, after all, who had sent them all here.

"You can go anywhere with a blink," Uncle Rummy said. "Anywhere at all. We have a common fund, for places or things you need money for. But for the most part, there's always a hack. We meet back here every three months, just to check in. Where is Mrs. Banne?"

"She's in Egypt, she will come soon," a statuesque lady said. She touched Varga's shoulder lightly. "I'm so sorry, my dear. My son did that to you. I am Mrs. Halder."

"I am dead then?" Varga asked, finding that he could speak again. He looked at his hands. The fingers were no longer broken.

"Welcome to the afterlife," Uncle Rummy said.

"What am I supposed to do?" he asked.

"Go out and explore the world, Varga!" Rummy said. "You are free. Be whoever you want. Do whatever you want. Your avatar form can feel everything or nothing, it is up to you. You can fall in love, you can dive off a cliff, you can climb a mountain. You can go to Mars, Varga, or to space!"

"I can't," Varga said. "There's no one at the cemetery. What if the ECHOes go off? Or the City sends a new person who turns off the project?"

"I'm the new person, Varga." Ms. Kashem came behind him and gave him a hug. She was surprisingly strong. "This morning I went to the City and explained that a mob broke in and killed you. I offered to take your place."

"*You* will be a corpse collector?"

"At much better terms mind you. I will have a drone assistant, triple your salary, and two extra shares now, double that upon end of service," Ms. Kashem said. "I will also train an apprentice."

"People hate corpse collectors, ma'am," Varga felt compelled to point out. "*You* hate us. We are below caste. No one will receive you. You'll be alone for the rest of your life. It's not right . . ."

"What's not right was leading a mob here to break your skull. What's not right is that you've made this wonderful, selfless thing, and died for it. So I'll take a turn doing your job. I will spend time with my father, and all of you, in the Virtuality," she said. "I will read your wonderful books. I will enjoy the peace and quiet of this forgotten cemetery. I will offer the choice to every person who crosses the threshold. And when I die, I'd like to join all of you. Are you satisfied?"

"Yes, ma'am."

"And will you come speak to me, when you are free?" she asked. "Tell me all the things you've done?"

"Yes, ma'am."

"Thank you, Varga." She leaned her head on his shoulder. "Call me Samarra."

11 AFTER THE STORM

James Bradley

CHARLIE KNEW SHE'D MADE A MISTAKE THE MOMENT SHE SAID HER FATHER WAS coming for her birthday. Her grandmother, Helen, made a face, then caught herself.

"Did he say when?"

Charlie shook her head, her brief pleasure at her father's message already draining away.

"Just that he had a new place, and a present for me."

Helen regarded Charlie with a look somewhere between sympathy and irritation.

"What?" Charlie demanded.

"Just don't get your hopes up," Helen said.

"No danger of that with you around."

"Charlie . . ." her grandmother began, but Charlie had already picked up her bag and was heading for the door.

"I have to get to the co-op," she said.

She was out on the road before she stopped wanting to run. Clenching her fists she blinked back tears, and calling up her overlays, scrolled furiously through her feeds, trying to lose herself, to forget her anger. The annoying thing was that Helen was right: her father had let her down before, more than once. But this time was different. This time he'd said he was coming to get her, that he'd take her away from here. And even if he was going to let her down again she wanted to be able to believe in that for a minute, to imagine there might be a way for her to be somewhere else, somewhere people didn't know her.

Breen was standing outside the co-op when Charlie arrived, sucking on her vape in the shade by the wall, her red cap pulled down over her wide, charmless face. She and Charlie's monthly community contribution shifts had overlapped for most of the past year, a fact Charlie had given up letting upset her. Breen watched Charlie approach with bland hostility.

"You're late."

Charlie's eyes flicked to the clock in her overlays before she could stop herself.

"No, I'm not."

Breen snorted. "Mike wants to see you."

Mike was the co-op supervisor, a former engineer who managed the coastal restoration and protection projects for the Council.

Charlie nodded. "What about?"

Breen shrugged. "Dunno. Didn't say."

Charlie walked through the co-op building to the yard at the back. Making her way through the pallets of fertilizers and saplings in black planting tubes she found Mike loading gear into his ute with a kid she didn't recognize. Mike looked up as she approached.

"Hey, Charlie," he said.

"Breen said you were looking for me."

Mike pushed his cap up and wiped the sweat on his forehead. "You're out on the replanting project again today," he said. "I'll drop you out there, but I've got to head over to the nursery to pick up some more seedlings, so I thought you could keep an eye on Aaron, show him the ropes."

As Mike spoke the kid stepped forward. He was about Charlie's age, and thin beneath an old T-shirt and shorts, his dark hair hanging long over his face. From the Displacement Camp, Charlie guessed. Why else would he be here?

Mike glanced from one of them to the other. "That okay with you?"

Charlie nodded. "Sure."

"Aaron?"

Aaron gave Charlie an uncertain look. Then he nodded as well. "I suppose."

Aaron sat in the back as they drove out to the regeneration site. Charlie did her best to ignore him, instead scrolling through her feeds while staring out at the passing landscape. Just past the outskirts of town they passed the turnoff to the Camp, the low roofs visible on the far side of the cyclone wire fence, then they were out onto the new road along the coast, the bright blue of St. Vincent's Gulf on their right, the low folds of the hills blue in the distance on their left. This stretch of coast had been vineyards once; before that it had been fields and paddocks, before that scrub and forest, Kaurna Country, but as the sea had risen and the fires and the heat had killed the vines it had grown harder, barer. In recent years the government and the Council had been trying to win it back, planting drawdown plantations of gene-spliced mallee trees, their faded green leaves and dark, twisting limbs rising from the empty fields like a ghost of the world destroyed by European invasion, or perhaps a presentiment of another that was yet to come. Meanwhile offshore the frames of the fish farms glinted in the sun, their yellow metal bright against the blue.

Mike stopped near the entrance to the regeneration site. Clambering out, he dropped the back on the ute and started passing out the trays of seedlings to Charlie and Aaron. When the last tray was on the ground he handed them a pair of water bottles each.

"I'll be back at lunchtime. Don't forget to hydrate," he said.

As Mike drove away Charlie turned and stared out over the regeneration site. It was one of several dozen just like it along this stretch of coast, a football field–sized patch of what had once been fields or grassland but which now abutted the intertidal, the drowned space swallowed by the rising water. For decades the government had been trying to build seawalls to stop the encroaching sea, bulldozing earth into ridges to build levees in the hope of keeping it out, of slowing down the erosion. But as the ocean had risen higher and the storms had grown worse these fortifications had proved insufficient, and so they had turned to natural solutions, planting mangroves in the hope they might stabilize the ground and form a natural barrier capable of withstanding waves and flooding.

Charlie pointed across to the far side of the space. "Let's start over there," she said, picking up the first tray of the seedlings. While she waited for Aaron to do the same she nodded toward the Portaloo and the tin shelter beside it. "You can take a break under there if it gets too hot, but I don't recommend it: the toilet stinks."

Charlie turned away without waiting for an answer. She knew she was being a bitch but she didn't want to think about this new kid or the Displacement Camp today.

For the next hour the two of them worked in silence, digging narrow holes and dropping the seedlings into them one by one, the sun burning Charlie's neck and back, the sweat running down her face. At some point the sea had invaded this area, and as Charlie dug down into the parched soil she could smell the thick smell of rotting seaweed and salt.

When she finished the third tray of seedlings she stood up, her head spinning in the heat. Opening her bottle of water she took a long sip and began to walk toward the trees on the edge of the regeneration site. Behind her Aaron stood up as well, and after a moment, began to follow her.

Charlie slumped down in the shade. Aaron stood a little way off, as if waiting for permission to approach. At first Charlie ignored him, but then she shook her head and slid to one side.

"Come sit in the shade," she said.

Aaron sat down beside her. Although he was careful not to come too close or invade her space, she could smell he needed a wash.

"Is this your first shift?" she asked.

Aaron nodded.

"So your family are in the camp?" she asked.

Aaron nodded again, slower this time.

"How's that?" she asked, although she knew the answer.

Aaron shrugged. "It's okay."

"Is it just you?"

He hesitated. "And my mum and sister. We came from Brisbane."

Charlie took a breath. She knew what that meant. She knew she could begin a search for him, check out his feeds, but she knew that if she did that their profiles would connect, and she didn't want to be bound to him, bound to any of this.

"When did you get here?"

"A few weeks ago. If my mum can find work she wants to find a place up in the city, but for now this is it."

"Have you met anybody?"

Aaron glanced at her. "Not really. Most of the kids in the camp are my sister's age, and the ones who aren't . . ." He shrugged.

"What about in town?"

Aaron shook his head. "Not so far."

Charlie picked up a stick and flicked it out into the sun. "You're not missing much," she said, hearing the bitterness in her voice too late to catch herself.

Aaron hesitated, and then to her surprise, smiled. "That bad?"

Charlie laughed, surprising herself. "Worse."

Aaron smiled again. "And you? Did you grow up here?"

Charlie shook her head. "I only got here a year or so ago. I'm living with my grandmother."

"Your parents aren't with you?" Aaron asked.

"My father is looking for work. My mum . . ." She hesitated. "She died."

Aaron looked at her. "I'm sorry."

Charlie stood up, dusting off her shorts with an abrupt motion. "That's okay. It was a long time ago," she said, her voice not catching on the lie.

"I'm going down to the intertidal," she said, and headed toward the scrub that ran along the seaward side of the regeneration site without giving Aaron time to answer.

It was only a hundred meters to the water but as she pushed her way through the dead scrub it seemed further. Underneath Charlie's feet the ground was soft and treacherous, and a foul, marshy smell lingered in the air. It was only when she was almost at the water that she realized she had been here before, and stopped, startled she hadn't made the connection earlier. For a moment or two she didn't move, just stood, staring ahead. Then she started forward again. After a couple of minutes the ground beneath her feet grew damp, the scrub giving way to low mangroves, the legacy of a replanting project a decade or two ago, until suddenly she stepped out into the open to find the house.

She stopped, staring at it. More than a year had passed since she was last here, and it looked more dilapidated than she remembered. On one side part of the roof had fallen in, while a storm had pushed a tree through one of the back windows, its rotting roots tilted upward into the air.

Part of her wanted to go forward, look inside, but mostly she just wanted to turn around and walk away. Before she could, though, she heard a sound behind her, and turning, found Aaron standing there.

"Hi," he said. "I just wanted to check you were alright."

She nodded, not looking at him. "I'm fine," she said.

He stepped past her, looking at the house.

"Do you know this place?"

She followed his gaze and shrugged. "Kind of," she said, then turned around. "Come on. We need to get back."

WHEN MIKE PICKED THEM UP CHARLIE ASKED IF HE COULD DROP HER AT THE mini-mart in town; as he pulled up Aaron said he'd get out there as well. Charlie tensed.

"If you don't mind," he said.

She sighed. "Sure," she said.

As Mike drove away she walked toward the entrance of the mini-mart, Aaron following her, but just as she reached it, the door opened, and Breen emerged. Seeing Charlie, Breen stopped dead, a mocking smile stealing across her face.

"Back already?" she asked, then looked past Charlie to Aaron.

"How'd you go?" she asked.

Aaron smiled warily. "Fine," he said.

Breen ignored him and turned to Charlie. "Did you see the video of Hugo?"

Charlie felt her stomach lurch. She shook her head.

Breen grinned. "It's killer. You need to see it."

"It's okay," Charlie said, already backing away.

Breen ignored her. "Nah, come on." As she spoke her eyes flickered behind her lenses, and an alert appeared in Charlie's overlays. Next to her Aaron had fallen still, presumably because he had received the same alert. Already knowing she was going to regret it, Charlie opened the link. The video was POV, and underwater, the field of vision filled with the massing bodies of thousands of whiting, their speckled forms darting frantically from side to side and up and down, as if trying to evade a predator. In the overlay comments were spilling in, pinging and flashing as people upvoted and downvoted the footage, love hearts and angry faces and animated emojis popping and fading.

"It's out in one of Hugo's dad's farms," Breen said to Aaron, and tensed. "Wait . . . now!"

As she spoke the swirling fish parted like a curtain, suddenly affording a view of the reason for their agitation. The pale shape of a shark, its long form sleek, aerodynamic, its pointed nose and blank eyes like a child's drawing.

Aaron started, and behind her lenses Breen smiled. With a flick of its tail the shark shot after a straggling ribbon of fish, its jaws snapping wildly, but the whiting were too fast; scattering wildly they shot away, so its mouth closed on nothing, the violence of its movement releasing a stream of bubbles that shot upward toward the shimmering surface. The shark arced around again, its long body lunging toward another group of whiting hanging in the water behind it. Again the fish shot away, but then, from the other side, a diver appeared, his long body wrapped in a black springsuit, what looked like a gun in one hand, and propelled himself toward the shark with two powerful kicks of the huge flippers on his feet. The movement of his body so immediately familiar Charlie didn't need to see his face to know it was Hugo.

Breen snorted delightedly. "Here he is!"

The shark jerked sideways and rolled to one side, but Hugo was already below it. Panicking, the shark tried to change course again, snapping wildly at the water, but Hugo was too quick, and as the shark tried to pull away he was already in front of it. Despite herself Charlie recoiled: the shark's pale, torpedo-like body was longer than Hugo was tall, its powerful head large enough to tear a chunk out of him or sever a limb. But despite that it wasn't

Hugo who looked afraid, but the shark, which was rolling and thrashing in its attempt to get away from its pursuer.

Breen opened her mouth in excited anticipation as Hugo raised the gun and there was a sudden discharge of bubbles. For a split second nothing happened, then the shark jerked backward, its head suddenly exploding in a cloud of red. Charlie flinched, lifting a hand to turn the video off, but before she could the image began to repeat itself, slowed down this time, so it was possible to see the snub shaft of the explosive dart leave the gun and disappear into the shark's head, sinking into it like a stone striking water, the impact followed by a split second of stillness before the shark's head swelled up and burst, like a piece of overripe fruit, throwing the shark backward. Half its head gone, the shark's body writhed and shook in slow motion, still fighting as it rolled and tumbled downward through the red-misted water. In the overlay people were arguing, either delighted or appalled, and Charlie could see subthreads already appearing about whether it was okay to film animals suffering. With one angry motion of her hand she waved the video away, furious with herself for having watched it. Seeing Charlie's expression, Breen laughed, exultant.

"Fuckin' A," she said. "Hugo showed that fishy fuck."

Charlie didn't reply, the slow jerk of the dying animal's sinking body still playing out in her mind.

She turned to Aaron, expecting to see her distress mirrored on his face, but he was still shocked, his eyes wide and bright.

"Was that here?" he asked.

Breen nodded. "This morning. Sweet, huh?"

"Wasn't he frightened being in the pen with the shark?"

Breen shook her head. "Hugo's dad owns the farm. He sends him out to chase sharks all the time."

Aaron turned to Charlie. "This happens all the time?"

But Charlie shook her head and backed away. "Screw you, Breen," she said.

Breen grinned. "What's wrong? Sorry you made a fool of yourself?"

But Charlie was already walking away, her face burning. Behind her she heard Aaron say her name, ask if she was alright, but Breen told him to leave it, that Charlie was a stuck-up bitch who wasn't worth it.

CHARLIE MET HUGO THE WEEK SHE ARRIVED IN TOWN. HE WAS SITTING ON THE SEAT outside the mini-mart with Josh and Tiger. She kept her head down as she walked past, but even so she could feel them watching her.

It was Josh who spoke first. "Hey!" he said. "Nice hat."

Charlie hesitated, her cheeks reddening. Then, surprising herself, she stopped.

"It was my Dad's," she said, touching the brim of the cap, which came from one of the windfarms.

Josh smirked. "Is he out there now?"

She hesitated, then shook her head.

"Pity," Josh said, fixing her with a libidinous stare. Tiger laughed, tipping his head back and slapping his dark brown leg, but then Hugo tipped his chin in her direction.

"Don't be a dick, man," he said, and smiled at her.

Later she would realize this was the dynamic that defined the trio: while Hugo was the leader, it was Josh who was the risktaker, the one who pushed limits, made things happen, thereby allowing Hugo to act as a voice of moderation, and Tiger to play the appreciative audience, the one who found everything hilarious. That day, though, what she mostly saw was Hugo himself, his lean, gracefully muscled body barely covered by board shorts and a singlet, his golden hair and skin. He had a long face, with almost feminine lips, and his marginally too-large nose was slightly crooked, the imperfection lending his looks a particularity they might otherwise lack.

"He's a pig," Hugo said. "Ignore him. What's your name?"

She hesitated. It had been three days since her father left and she knew nobody in town but Helen.

"Charlie."

Hugo nodded. "Cool name."

Charlie reddened. "And you?"

"I'm Hugo. And these miscreants"—he elbowed Josh, suddenly playful—"are Josh and Tiger."

Josh pushed Hugo's arm away. Although he smiled there was something harder behind his eyes. Tiger grinned.

"Is your Dad here with you?" Hugo asked.

Charlie shook her head. "My grandmother. Helen. She lives out on Catherine Street."

"That old bitch," said Josh. Hugo didn't respond but Tiger sniggered.

Charlie's mouth tightened. She didn't love her grandmother's company, but something about the way the three of them spoke about her made her uneasy.

"Some of us are going to hang out tonight," Hugo said. "You should come."

To her surprise Charlie found herself nodding. "Okay," she said. "Maybe."

SHE DIDN'T LOOK BACK, NOT WILLING TO GIVE BREEN THE SATISFACTION OF A response. Instead she kept walking until the road ran out at the water's edge. It was quiet, the only sound the movement of the water against the shore. Even through her lenses the glare was overwhelming, annihilating: she wished she could disappear into it, no longer be. Kicking off her shoes she waded out. Once there would have been sand here, a beach of some sort; she had heard it was still out there, a hundred meters offshore and two meters down, a pale band on the sea bottom. What sand there was along the water's edge was grey, a silty carpet over the stumps and sea-blackened branches that protruded from the water; she could feel it rising around her feet.

In the heat it was tempting to imagine diving in, swimming out into the empty space of the Gulf, but she knew she couldn't, that the shark in the video was just one of many.

Calling up the message from her father in her overlays she read it again. *Coming Friday for your birthday. Got new place, thought you could come stay. Maybe for good?* With it a couple of badly framed photos of a small living space, empty save for a bag and a pair of boots.

Sounds good, she messaged back, and then closed her eyes. Once, before she came here, her father took her out to the turbines off the southern coast. A guy he had met in the pub was working on them, and had told her father there might be a job going. The job never happened, and her father and the guy fell out not long afterward, but before they did his new friend offered to take her father out to the turbines to see them.

On the day of the trip her father was in a buoyant mood, talking fast and making plans for what they would do once he had work again. At the last moment he asked Charlie whether she'd like to come as well. Her mother didn't like the idea, and told him so, but he wouldn't listen, and so, an hour later, Charlie was down at the wharf being loaded onto the boat with her father and his new mates. She knew some of them by sight— back then her father still had friends in the town—and they had joked and laughed with her, teasing her father that he had better watch out, she had an eye on the job he wanted. Charlie had enjoyed it, feeling special, wanted, but she had also enjoyed the boat ride, staring over the side at the beds of seagrass as they passed over them, watching as they receded downward, and then vanished altogether, replaced by the occluding water, the sea

197

AFTER THE STORM

wind. The space and silence of the ocean had made her feel different some-how, as if she was dissolving into the space.

The turbines were five kilometers offshore; as they grew closer she found herself marveling at the scale of them, the way they kept getting taller and thicker until finally the white bulk of the nearest loomed over them like a skyscraper.

Her father led her off the boat and up the ladder to a platform twenty meters above the water. Above her the huge blades spun slowly, slicing through the air with a sound so deep and resonant it vibrated though her.

"Pretty cool, huh?" her father said, but she wasn't really listening to him. Instead she stared out at the vast space of the ocean, the long line of the turbines receding toward the horizon. Those huge machines out here alone, running without any human presence like something constant that would outlast them all. Standing there at the road's end she tried to remember how that felt, to hold onto it, to find a way to feel safe.

BY THE TIME SHE GOT HOME, SHE WAS HOT AND TIRED, HER NECK AND ARMS sunburned. Helen was waiting in the kitchen; she asked Charlie where she'd been, but Charlie ignored her and went through to her room and lay on the bed. Calling up her father's message once again she fired off another reply, asking whether he was still coming the next day; in the silence after her message had gone she sat staring at her overlays, willing him to answer but he did not.

She was still there an hour later when Helen knocked on the door and asked whether she wanted something to eat.

Charlie didn't look up from the video she was watching. Helen stepped through the door.

"I'm going to make some tofu."

Charlie ignored her again.

Helen sighed, and sat down on the bed beside her. Charlie slid away from her.

"I'm sorry we fought this morning."

"It's fine," Charlie said.

"I understand how difficult it's been for you here, and how much you miss them both. But I don't want you to get hurt again."

Charlie snorted. "I won't."

Helen was quiet for a moment. Then she composed herself and sat up in the way Charlie found so irritating.

"Have you seen the forecast?"

Charlie shook her head.

"There are storms on the way."

Charlie nodded.

"We need to get out in the morning, make sure things are secure."

"Sure," she said. "Whatever."

After Helen was gone she lay down again, scrolling miserably through her feeds in search of distraction. Until finally, after midnight, a message arrived. *Looking forward to seeing you tomorrow. Dad.*

ONCE, NOT LONG AFTER SHE CAME TO LIVE IN SOUTH AUSTRALIA, HELEN HAD SAID Charlie's mother was never really happy, that she was always looking for something she couldn't find. At the time Charlie hadn't understood what her grandmother meant, and when she'd asked her to explain Helen just shook her head and looked away, in the way she usually did when Charlie tried to talk to her about Charlie's mother.

But as the months passed Charlie began to think she understood. Until she was seven her parents had lived in a commune near Tathra on the east coast, a straggling collection of houses spread through the trees. Years later, her mother had said, they had been asked to leave because her father's drinking had been causing tension with some of the other community members, a process that culminated in a fight with one of their neighbors, a game designer called Patrick. "It was stupid," her mother said. "He knew Patrick didn't like him, but he kept riding him, until finally things blew up."

Her mother used to talk about the fires in Tathra, the constant fear they would be caught up in one, but that wasn't what Charlie remembered about those years. Instead, when she thought about the community, she mostly recalled the forest, the creek where they used to swim, the cries of the bell miners and whipbirds pealing through the smoky air.

After that they moved further south to Eden for a while. Her mother worked in a crystal store, selling incense and tumbled stones, and later doing readings for tourists and people from the area. Charlie remembered the shop, the bell at the door, her mother's slightly glazed expression. After that they kept moving, bouncing from place to place, until Charlie was thirteen, when her mother got sick. At first the news was reassuring: the cancer was beatable, and her prospects were good. But then the gene therapy failed and they moved her onto chemo, and then more and different chemo, and then the news wasn't so positive, and then the talk turned to managing pain and quality of life, and at each step her mother seemed more diminished, more worn away, more fragile, as if she was being gradually erased from the world.

In the middle of it all Charlie's other grandmother, Aisha, got sick as well. Charlie's mother went to visit Helen and Aisha, but within a few weeks it was over, and Aisha was gone. Not long after that Charlie's mother started reading the Bible, and then she found the Church, and after that it was almost as if she forgot about Charlie. Most days there was some event she needed to be at—services or prayer group or Bible study class—and she would leave already distracted and return exultant, glassy-eyed. Charlie hated her mother a bit then: Didn't she know that Charlie needed her? At one point Helen came to stay for a few weeks, sleeping in a room at the back of the house and helping Charlie with her homework after school; and then one afternoon when her mother wasn't there when Charlie got home from school, Helen took her hand and told Charlie that she knew she was angry, and that she had a right to be angry, but her mother was frightened, and frightened people didn't always do the right thing. But Charlie had shouted at Helen, and stormed out. When she came back it was already dark, and Helen was sitting alone in the kitchen. Charlie knew Helen was waiting for her, but Helen hadn't said anything; instead she'd put food in front of Charlie and her father, and filled Charlie's father's silence with practical chat about jobs that needed doing around the house. The next day she was gone.

Five months later, after Charlie's mother died Helen had come back, and sat with her while she cried. On the night after the funeral she heard Helen and her father arguing about what would happen to her: Helen wanted them to come live with her, but Charlie's father wouldn't hear of it: he hated Helen, and now Charlie's mother was dead he didn't want anything else to do with her. But as his drinking got worse he started coming home drunk, or not coming home at all, and then, one day, Charlie got back from school to find their things on the street, and the house locked up. That night her father loaded her and everything they could carry into his car, and they headed for South Australia; Charlie remembered looking back at their furniture on the roadside and wondering who would get it.

Two days later they pulled up outside Helen's place. Charlie waited outside while Helen and her father talked, their voices tense, until finally her father stormed out, and began to pull her things out of the car and pile them on the ground. When he was done he told her he'd be back later, and after one more angry exchange with Helen, drove away. But he didn't come back, not that night or the next, and although Charlie messaged him, he didn't reply. A week later, he sent her a message to say he was in Adelaide, and although he'd be back he needed to sort some things out first.

Since then she hadn't seen him, although he'd called a few times, and sent messages occasionally. For a while he was in a program; after that he told her he was trying really hard, and messaged her most days, but then he disappeared again, and the next time she heard from him he was back in hospital. Since then he'd been out of contact until this latest message, his socials offline. Helen refused to talk about him, cutting Charlie off if she brought him up in the same way she did if Charlie tried to talk about her mother, her face closing down or assuming the false brightness that Charlie hated. But since nobody else here had ever met either of them that meant Charlie had nobody she could talk to about her parents, nobody who knew what they had been like, or how much she had lost.

THE NEXT MORNING DAWNED HOT AND STILL, THE SKY HUGE AND BLUE, INNOCENT of the approaching storm. By the time Charlie emerged from her room Helen was out in the yard moving pots around, a tarpaulin spread on the ground in front of her. Charlie stopped on the step and watched her. Helen was almost eighty, but her steely manner made it easy to forget her age. Once, years before, she had been a mathematician, but when everything hit the wall in the 2040s she'd lost her job, and she and Charlie's other grandmother, Aisha, had moved down here because it was cheaper, and things were getting bad in the cities. Charlie's mother was four when they arrived, and had grown up around here; she hadn't liked to talk about it, but Charlie knew they had been hard years, not just for Helen and Aisha and her mother, but for everybody.

She didn't know how Helen felt about that time, about the way she'd ended up here. The one time she'd tried asking Helen had frozen up. But a few days later they had passed a group of people walking beside the highway on foot. They were a family, a woman carrying a baby and a man walking behind her with a little boy, and as Charlie watched them recede in the mirror she'd said something about people being vulnerable, and Helen had said people had always been vulnerable, it's just that for a while the world had been organized so some of us could ignore it, at least until we couldn't anymore. She kept her eyes on the road as she spoke, but there was something about her tone that gave Charlie pause, a brittleness that made her wonder whether Helen's blunt manner was a way of masking her own sense of loss, the double blow of losing first Aisha and then Charlie's mother in the space of just a few years. Or had she always been like this?

Charlie was just about to go back inside when Helen turned to face her. There was a brief moment when she hesitated, then she smiled awkwardly and said, "Happy birthday."

Charlie forced herself to smile as well. "Thanks."

"I made breakfast."

Charlie sighed. "Thanks, but I'm not hungry."

Helen ignored her and hurried back in. She opened the fridge and took out a plate of fruit and a bowl of yogurt and placed them on the table. Charlie stared at them and then, conceding defeat, sat down.

Helen sat down opposite and watched her spoon the berries into her mouth. "Have you got plans?"

Charlie shook her head.

"You don't want to see some of the other kids? Is everything okay?"

She folded her arms and exhaled. "It's fine."

Helen pursed her lips. Charlie knew that look: it meant there was something she wanted to say.

"What?"

Helen hesitated. "Did you hear from your father again?"

Charlie didn't reply.

"Charlie?"

"He's coming," she said, the words hot in her mouth.

Helen looked like she was about to say more but thought better of it. Instead she just tightened her mouth and nodded.

WHEN CHARLIE ARRIVED AT THE MINI-MART THAT FIRST NIGHT HUGO WASN'T THERE; instead it was just Josh and Tiger and a girl she didn't know.

As she approached the three of them stopped talking, Josh and the girl regarding her coldly. But Tiger grinned.

"Hey. You came."

She stopped a meter or so away from them. Part of her wanted to flee. "I did."

"Your grandmother let you out?" Josh said.

She nodded. Helen had wanted to know where she was going and when she'd be back, but when Charlie said she was meeting a kid called Hugo her grandmother relaxed and said she knew his parents.

Tiger grinned. "Hugo will be here soon," he said. Then he turned to the other girl. "This is Breen."

Charlie smiled at her but Breen stared back coldly. Charlie felt the urge to flee again, but before she could Tiger looked past her up the road.

"Here he is," he said, as Hugo slid his electric board in beside them.

At Josh's urging they set off down the path toward the shoreline, where they clambered through the mangroves until they came to the shell of a house, its darkened windows broken and walls stained with mud and seawater.

Josh flicked on a light on his lenses and led them in, stepping through the open doorway, the old front door twisted and swollen on its hinges. In the stark white of the LED the space looked like the set of a game, some immersive shooter that mimicked the look of security footage. Charlie tried to put the association to one side.

In one of the rooms an old mattress and a sofa were pressed against the wall; Josh and Tiger flopped down on the sofa, while Breen and Hugo sat on the mattress. Reaching behind the sofa Josh pulled out a filthy plastic bong, and began to pack it. Charlie sat down on one end of the mattress, Hugo between her and Breen, trying to ignore the stink of mildew and sweat that rose off it. The bong packed, Josh lit it and took a hit, then passed it across to Charlie.

"Here," he said.

It was after two before Charlie got back to Helen's. Hugo and Breen walked her home, Breen waiting by the gate while Hugo helped her open the door and stumble into the kitchen in the warm dark. As Charlie said goodbye to him she could see Breen standing by the gate, watching her.

After that night they went to the house several times a week. Sometimes other kids from the area came along, but usually it was just the five of them. After that first night Charlie knew there was something between her and Hugo, but there was a diffidence in his manner, a sense that while he was interested he was too lazy to make the first move. Yet despite that he seemed to take pleasure in her presence, and would sometimes message her during the days, sending her funny memes or offbeat jokes, but when she replied he would fall silent, ghosting her. Finally, one night a fortnight after they first met she fell into him as she was going inside, pressing herself against his long body, and they kissed, Hugo's mouth sickly sweet with beer and dope, before he disappeared, swaying, into the darkness.

The next night Hugo acted as if nothing had happened, leaving Charlie afraid she had made a mistake, so she went home and lay on her bed, rigid with embarrassment and shame. But the night after she was woken by a knock on her window just after midnight, and looking out found him standing there in the dark.

Even then she knew it didn't mean what she wanted it to mean. Not knowing when Hugo would turn up, or whether he would let her be with him any particular night made her feel worthless, repulsive, so when he did appear she felt grateful in a way that embarrassed her. Because of his father Hugo had money, freedom, an assuredness the rest of them lacked; no doubt that confidence was part of his tendency to assume he could have what he wanted when he wanted it, Charlie included: even when they were alone together he let her do the work, lying back and letting things happen.

And then there was the question of Josh and Breen. That Breen disliked Charlie was no secret: she never missed an opportunity to sneer at her or make some unpleasant comment. One night Charlie asked Hugo if he'd ever been with Breen and he laughed and shrugged, as if he didn't care, although something in the way he avoided the question told her all she needed to know. But Josh was more circumspect, especially once Charlie and Hugo were together. But Charlie saw the way he looked at her, the dislike behind his barbed jokes. And though she wished she didn't, she also saw the way he watched Hugo, that he saw her as competition, or a threat.

FOR THE NEXT FEW HOURS CHARLIE HUNG AROUND THE HOUSE, LYING ON HER BED and watching videos. From her window she could see the street, and she kept glancing up, looking for some sign of her father's arrival. Once or twice cars went past, or people wandered by; each time she sat up, staring out, before subsiding back onto the bed, a hollow, nervy feeling in her stomach. When she woke up the first thing she had done was check her messages, expecting him to have sent something for her birthday, or perhaps an indication of when he might arrive, but there was nothing, and neither was there as the morning drifted on.

Finally, in the midafternoon, she fired off another message, asking him when he was coming, but when there was no reply she got out of bed and pulled on her hat and headed out. The weather feed said the storm would arrive in the evening, but outside it was still and hot, the only sign of the approaching weather system a heaviness in the air and white streaks of hazy cloud out to the west.

She stopped at the water's edge again. The water was still, shimmering in the heat. Picking up a stone she flicked it out over the water, watching as it disappeared with a heavy plop. The summer before the co-op had laid a new reef on the sea floor a few hundred meters out from where she stood. Charlie had worked alongside the others from the town, standing in the hot sun and heaving pieces of broken concrete and stone over the side into the water, and later, hovering nearby as the marine biologists emptied the racks of oysters down after them.

The idea was the oysters would spread across the stones, their sharp, dark shells growing one on top of the other, accreting upward toward the light, until the reef was covered in them. Once they had they would begin to clean the water, to absorb the nutrients, and create food for fish and crabs and worms, as well as fertilizer for seagrass beds. But that wasn't the whole point of them. Once there had been reefs everywhere along this coastline, their massing weight helping slow the waves when the storms washed in, protecting the beaches and the shoreline. Those reefs had been there for thousands of years, but when Europeans arrived they had been destroyed in the space of a few decades, the oysters devoured, their shells dredged up to make lime for the invaders to use in the cement they used in their buildings and roads, until finally nobody even remembered the reefs had existed. But now, as the seas rose ever higher and the storms ever more powerful, the hope was these new reefs would help protect the new coast, to diffuse the power of the waves while the mangroves regrew. To hold the line against the encroaching sea.

Some days Charlie believed it might work, that the bodies of the oysters might bind together, somehow hold back the ocean and stop the shore disappearing. Helen said the reefs grew upward faster than the sea could rise, and the mangroves and seagrass were spreading fast. But other days it seemed impossible, a fool's errand. The moment the icecaps could have been saved passed decades ago, and that meant that no matter what they did, the water would keep rising, year after year, for centuries or even longer. And as it did the land—this land—would be swept away, piece by piece, a little more with every passing decade. Charlie had seen projections, simulations of the sea level, the water rising above the roofs of the town, all of it gone. Sometimes it made her happy, to think of this shitty place swept away, gone forever; other times it just filled her with sadness.

Turning she headed back up the road, passing the silent houses on the empty streets. Up near Wakefield Street a girl of about eight was rolling up and down a concrete driveway on a metal scooter, followed by a boy a few years younger on a smaller scooter. The girl wore short denim overalls over a yellow T-shirt, her dark hair pulled back neatly. Something in the way the girl wore the outfit told Charlie it had been carefully assembled, but that wasn't what made Charlie stop to watch them. Instead it was the girl's careful concentration on what she was doing, the way she kept glancing back to check on her little brother. No doubt they fought, but in that moment it was obvious they had each other, and that mattered.

By the time she got back to Helen's it was after six, the sun already low in the west, the ranges in the distance deep purple, the sky above them shimmering, colorless. When she opened the back door Helen was seated at the kitchen table, her hands in front of her. Something about the way she was sitting, her immobility, told Charlie she had been sitting there for a while. Seeing Charlie she looked up and smiled. Charlie stopped just inside in the doorway.

"What is it?"

"Have you heard from your father?"

Charlie shook her head. "No. Why? Has something happened?"

Helen leaned back in her seat and sighed.

"Sit down," she said, gesturing to the seat beside her.

Charlie shook her head. "No. Just tell me what's going on."

"I'm sorry," Helen said. "I didn't want to be the one to tell you. He promised me he'd call you, tell you himself."

"Tell me what?"

"He's not coming."

"What? How do you know?"

"I called him," Helen said. "I can't believe he didn't call you. He said he would."

"What did you say to him?"

Helen shook her head. "Nothing."

Charlie took a step back. "Did you tell him not to come? That you didn't want him here?"

"Of course not. I just didn't want you to be left waiting if he wasn't going to turn up."

"I don't believe you," Charlie said, tears filling her eyes. "He said he was coming. He promised."

Helen pressed her lips together and regarded Charlie sadly. "I'm really sorry."

"No you're not," Charlie said, her voice rising.

"This is why I wanted him to call you," Helen said, her voice rising in annoyance. "It shouldn't be me having to do this."

"Right. So good of you."

Helen shook her head. "You know what happened. Don't pretend you don't. He was drunk."

Charlie stared at her. "No. You hate him, you've always hated him."

Helen hesitated, but Charlie felt something unlock inside her. "They hated you as well, you know. Not just him, but Mum as well. They used to talk about it, about how happy they were you were over here and they didn't need to see you. That time you came, Mum was glad you left. Glad."

At the table Helen had fallen still, the blood draining out of her cheeks, her face suddenly slack and old. Charlie stared at her. Her anger still sung inside of her, but she also knew she had gone too far. Turning she stormed back out the door into the gathering dusk. When she was halfway to the gate she heard the door open again, Helen's voice calling after her, but she didn't slow down or turn around, instead she began to run, pushing herself away down the hot asphalt of the road, the smell of the dust and the salt and the road thick around her, glad she was in motion, frightened about what would happen when she stopped.

207

THE END WITH HUGO CAME TWO DAYS BEFORE THE START OF THE SCHOOL YEAR. The five of them had planned to meet at the house in the intertidal, intending to get messed up one last time before school went back. As usual Hugo and Josh had weed, but Hugo had also brought a bottle of vodka he had stolen from his parents' cupboard. Charlie drank it quickly, ignoring the burning in her throat as she chugged it back, and by the time she realized how drunk she was it was too late. At some point Josh offered her some weed as well, telling her it might help straighten her out, and she had drawn the smoke down into her lungs, coughing as it burned until tears streamed down her face. Slumping back on the mattress she leaned her head back and closed her eyes, and when she opened them Josh was lying beside her. She was so drunk his face loomed and swayed in front of her, but he was smiling, and stroking her hair, so she leaned her head on his shoulder.

"Hi, Josh," she murmured drunkenly.

"Hi, Charlie," he replied, which for some reason she found impossibly funny.

Josh rearranged her head on his shoulder.

"Why are you being so nice to me?" Charlie asked.

"Why wouldn't I be nice to you?"

"I thought you hated me."

Josh didn't reply. Charlie stroked his cheek.

"You're very handsome," she said.

Josh laughed at that, and leaned closer. Charlie stared at his face. His mouth, eye, hair a jumble through the haze of the alcohol.

"Do you want to kiss me?" Josh asked.

Charlie tried to consider the question, but found she couldn't. "What about Hugo?" she said at last.

"Why don't you ask him?" Josh said.

Charlie moved her head and saw Hugo lying on the other side of her, watching with amused interest. "Would you mind?" she said as solemnly as she could.

Hugo shrugged, and Charlie turned back, letting her lips meet Josh's. And as they did he pushed her away, sending her sprawling onto the floor. She tried to say something, to apologize, or protest, but the words wouldn't arrange themselves. Looking up she saw Breen watching, her lenses recording, while Tiger sat, looking away, and after that she remembered nothing, at least until she awoke the next morning, her mouth thick and claggy, the word "Slut" written on her forehead, and the certainty the video was already out there humming through her mind.

SHE WAS STILL WEEPING WHEN SHE PASSED THE MINI-MART, SO SHE DIDN'T SEE Aaron until he stepped out into the road behind her and called after her. She stopped and looked back. He had a pack full of groceries on his back and a plastic container of water in one hand; behind him a younger girl she didn't recognize stood with a bag in one hand.

"Charlie," Aaron said again. "Are you alright?"

Charlie stared at him for a moment or two.

Aaron put down the water and took a step toward her. "Did something happen?"

She shook her head. "I'm fine," she said, backing away.

"Charlie?" Aaron said.

"Leave me alone!" Charlie hissed.

By the time she reached the shoreline it was dark, but out over the Gulf weird, greenish clouds were gathering, lightning moving in them in the distance, its dance of light unsettlingly silent. Charlie stared at it, feeling the fitful wind against her face. Pulling up her weather app she saw the storm was still a couple of hours away, but she knew she needed to find somewhere to shelter, so she set off along the shoreline until she came to the house. She stared at it, the memory of that night a year ago making her shake, but finally she walked to the doorway and went in.

Inside it was much the same, although at some point somebody had set the sofa on fire, leaving it blackened and scorch marks on the wall and ceiling. Charlie lay down on the mattress. In the half-light something clanked

208

and rattled beside it; reaching out toward it her hand closed around a half-empty bottle of vodka. For a few seconds she lay staring at it, the liquid clear in the white light of her lenses, then she twisted the lid and lifted the bottle to her lips.

The vodka burned her throat and chest, sending a warmth spreading through her, so when the rain started she wasn't frightened; instead she smiled, a wanton, careless pleasure filling her, so she drank some more, and then some more, until finally the room began to spin, and she lay back, and closed her eyes, relieved to lose touch with herself.

She didn't remember exactly when she fell asleep, only that she must have, because she was jolted awake by a crash of thunder, so close it shook the room. Blearily she sat up, still swaying from the vodka, wincing at the roar of the rain and the keening wind, trying to remember where she was, how she'd got there; it was only as lightning lit the room, revealing the stained walls and scorched ceiling, that she remembered. The house.

She stood up, her feet sinking into water. Another flash of lightning and she saw the floor was covered, a black tide. She called up her overlays, but there was no response, either because the network was down or it was overloaded. Frantically she flicked through various interfaces, looking for some sign of life, but there was nothing. Stumbling toward the front door she opened it, and recoiled as the force of the rain and the roar of the wind slamming into her. At first she thought the ground was moving, and was unable to make sense of what she was seeing; then with a prickle of fear she realized the house was surrounded by moving water. There was a groan, as if the house was moving on its foundations. She started, panic rising in her chest, and then, steeling herself, stepped out the door, and sank up to her waist in the moving water. Almost losing her balance she tried to steady herself against the side of the house. In the darkness and the sheeting rain it was difficult to make out where she should go. She took a step forward, but the water was moving fast, and she felt herself slipping sideways. Just in time she managed to regain her equilibrium, but only for a few seconds, because a moment later she stumbled, and fell sideways into the surging water. She was moving now as well, her body borne along by the racing water, branches and other refuse around her.

Then she heard something over the din of the storm, and a moment later a figure appeared above her in the darkness. Lightning flashed, and she saw Aaron's face, his mouth open, whatever words he was speaking drowned out by the wind and the thunder. Reaching her he grabbed her arm and brought his face close to hers.

"Charlie!" he shouted, his voice hoarse. "Are you okay?"

She shook her head. "The water."

Aaron nodded. "It's a surge. It's everywhere. We need to get somewhere safe."

Together they waded through the trees toward the regeneration site. The water was shallower there, but the wind was higher, branches and leaves blowing past them, sometimes striking them, the rain so hard it stung. For what seemed a long time they stumbled along the road, until finally they reached a gate, and beyond it a line of prefab huts. Aaron stopped in front of one and bashed on the door, the sound almost inaudible over the roar of the storm. A moment later the door opened and they stumbled inside.

The space within was small, barely enough for the three camp beds that stood across the far end, its narrow space illuminated by a bare LED on one wall. The girl she had seen outside the shop was sitting on a bed against one wall, dressed in a blue nightie with a picture of a dolphin on the front. Aaron helped Charlie to the nearest bed and then pointed back at a small bench by the door.

"Get her some water," he said. The girl did as she was asked, placing a plastic mug in Charlie's hand. She drank it gratefully. Pulling a blanket off the bed behind her Aaron wrapped it around Charlie. A puddle was forming by her feet. She glanced down at it, but Aaron shook his head.

"Don't worry about it," he said.

Charlie fought the sudden impulse to burst into tears.

"Thank you," she said. She looked around again. "Where are we?"

"Our cabin. My mum had to go into the city, and couldn't get back, so it's just me and my sister." He glanced at the girl, who had the same thin face and dark hair as Aaron. "Say hi, Siobhan."

Siobhan looked at Charlie, her face solemn. "Are you okay?"

Charlie nodded, but as she did there was a peal of thunder so loud it shook the cabin. They all started, and looked around in fear. There was another crash, and the cabin creaked and groaned.

Siobhan had gone pale. Aaron reached out and drew her toward him and Charlie. "It's okay," he said. "Don't think about it."

But Siobhan was shaking. Charlie put her arms around her. "What's wrong?" Charlie asked.

Next to her, Aaron hesitated. When he spoke his voice was low. "We were in the cyclone that went through Brisbane a few months ago. Our house . . . my father." He shook his head and looked away.

Charlie didn't reply. For a moment all she could think about was the relentlessness of the wind and the water, the way it kept rising, the fantasy the oyster reefs might be enough to hold them back. About Helen, about her father, about Aaron and Siobhan. About how they were all bound together, however fragile that sometimes seemed. About how much they had already lost, about all the loss that lay ahead. In her arms Siobhan trembled, her child's body warm, vulnerable, and she pressed her face into Charlie's chest. Charlie leaned down and pressed her lips to the child's head.

"It's okay," she said, trying to keep her voice steady. "We're here. We'll keep you safe."

And as she spoke she felt the weight of that impossible promise, the need to make it true. And the fear they might not.

ARTWORK: SEAN BODLEY

IN THE ANTHROPOCENE, ART WILL HELP DECIDE THE FATE OF HUMANITY, JUST AS IT did in the Holocene. Art has always been about visions; envisioning the past or the unseeable, fully observing the present moment, and imagining the future. I believe our ability to use our imagination is what will determine humanity's fate on the spectrum of survival to extinction.

Art lives in the space between the routine and the unimaginable. Stories help us cross boundaries into new types of awareness. From the beginning of my art journey, stories from games, fantasy books, and movies inspired me to daydream and draw.

When I first learned to draw I felt that I could take fantasies, dreams, visions, and share them, through pictures. I doodled, studied plein air painting, figure drawing, vehicle design, game design, and many other subjects over the years to convey the visions in my head.

The first time I heard about climate change I didn't believe it. It was beyond my understanding of the rhythm of the seasons. I knew that each season was different, but I couldn't imagine how they could change beyond my scope of familiarity. But my initial disbelief was overpowered by curiosity and as I began to read on the subject, I felt that climate change was the biggest transformation on the planet that no one was seeing.

I soon discovered, many people were already thinking, concerned and organizing around environmental justice, and so after college I joined the chorus of artists focused on the environment.

In my sketchbooks you will find an equal weight of apocalyptic and utopian drawings. I am a paranoid optimist. Early on in my art journey I was inspired by books like *Utopia or Oblivion* by Buckminster Fuller, and *The Left Hand of Darkness* by Ursula K. Le Guin. These visionaries taught me that the ability to imagine, to break out of the current mode of thinking, is invaluable and that artists have a lot of great tools to do this. It's also fun!

In each new artwork I make, whether fantastical or realistic, I am imagining and thinking about how life in this new era will look. Books like *Visualizing Climate Change* by Stephen Sheppard, *Doughnut Economics* by Kate Raworth, and *Dire Predictions* by Dr. Michael Mann deeply inform my work.

My ultimate goal is to be part of a community of artists and creatives who are passionate about visualizing climate change through stories. Stories and drawings can encode so many types of information and I think these are the tools that will help our culture transition to new ways of life in the Anthropocene. Artists like Swoon are foundational in teaching how artists can create art for Earth by embracing their climate grief and at the same time acknowledging the things they're good at.

Initially I felt alone creating this type of "climate art" because the reality of global warming was denied by society, there was no viable market for employment at the time, and there were few venues for displaying such work. Now, however, there are buzzing communities of artists, like Artists vs. Extinction, who are constantly engaged with each other and exposing each other to different types of art, including 3D modeling, animation, and game design.

Groups like Water Is Life and Movement for Black Lives are on the front lines of environmental justice and are a major source of inspiration for my work. My latest vision is for hundreds and thousands of artists to create art centered on climate justice in the hope that together we can slow down and eventually stop the ecocide that defines this era.

You will often read that climate solutions are relative to local regions. One of my dreams is of a decentralized network of artists across the world serving as Resilience Visionaries in their local communities. They could help the community visualize changes that are coming to help people adapt and respond.

At the root of my art creation is my amazing mother, who nurtured my love for drawing. Also my grandmother, Caroline Greenwald, who exposed me to many wonders of nature and in whose footsteps I follow as a career artist. My wife, Dr. Stephanie Bora, constantly inspires me with her ideas, both scientific and culinary, alongside her wonder for the world!

I was born and raised in Madison, Wisconsin, and currently work in Los Angeles, California, as a background designer in the animation industry. For fun I love painting en plein air with the Warrior Painters and hiking in the mountains with my family.

Thank you for looking at the work, and I hope it inspires you to use your own imagination!

Wind Walkers

IN THE FUTURE, WIND WALKERS BRAVE HOSTILE WEATHER SYSTEMS TO ACQUIRE data that is as valuable as gold. This data allows the villages back home to better prepare for megastorms that get worse and worse each year. It's a lonely existence, trekking for hundreds of miles in solitude, but Wind Walkers are a strange type, and you'll rarely find one who has settled down.

Neo Germination

SCAVENGER OAKS STARTED SPROUTING UP AFTER THE HUMANS HAD GONE AWAY. The technoprimordial soup of e-waste landfills had sat long enough that new life forms began to evolve. After generations of acorns from a nearby grove spilled into the landfill, it brought about a digital fermentation of sorts that sparked new life. Now, many species of metallic plant life thrive on a transformed Earth.

ACKNOWLEDGMENTS

ANY PROJECT LIKE *TOMORROW'S PARTIES* IS THE PRODUCT OF A TEAM OF HARD-working, talented people doing their best to create something special. I'm indebted to Susan Buckley at the MIT Press, who has been incredibly supportive and a delight to work with, and to Gideon Lichfield, who was wonderful early on before moving on to even bigger things, for the chance to work on this volume and become part of the *Twelve Tomorrows* team.

I'd also like to thank Sean Bodley, James Bradley, Greg Egan, Meg Elison, Sarah Gailey, Daryl Gregory, Saad Z. Hossain, Emily Jin, Malka Older, Chen Qiufan, Justina Robson, and Tade Thompson for the fantastic work they have done, and for being inspiring to work with over the past six months. Special thanks to Stan Robinson for agreeing to the interview that opens the volume. My thanks to everyone for their work on copyediting and completing *Tomorrow's Parties*, and to the whole MIT Press team.

CONTRIBUTORS

Sean Bodley is inspired and motivated by the impact of human caused climate change. He studied Drawing and Painting at University of Wisconsin–Milwaukee, completing a BFA in 2010. In 2011 he moved to Lemont, Pennsylvania, and started Mount Nittany Studio where he worked as a freelance illustrator, fine art painter, and teacher. Currently he lives and works in Los Angeles, California, where he is a background designer for Rick and Morty. In his free time he loves being outside, plein air painting, and video games.

James Bradley is a writer and critic. His books include the novels *Wrack*, *The Deep Field*, *The Resurrectionist*, and *Clade*, all of which have won or been nominated for major literary awards; a book of poetry, *Paper Nautilus*; and *The Penguin Book of the Ocean*. In 2012 he won the Pascall Prize for Australia's Critic of the Year. His newest novel, *Ghost Species*, is published by Hodder Studio. He lives on Gadigal Land in Sydney, Australia.

Greg Egan has published fourteen novels and more than sixty works of short fiction, including the Hugo Award–winning novella "Oceanic." His latest collection is *Instantiation* and his most recent novel is *The Book of All Skies*. He lives in Perth, Australia.

Meg Elison is a science fiction author and feminist essayist. Her series The Road to Nowhere won the 2014 Philip K. Dick award. She is a Hugo, Nebula, and Otherwise awards finalist. In 2020, she published her first collection, *Big Girl*, with PM Press, containing the Locus Award–winning novelette, *The Pill*. Elison's first young adult novel, *Find Layla*, was published in 2020 by Skyscape. Meg has been published in *McSweeney's*, *Fantasy & Science Fiction*, *Fangoria*, *Uncanny*, *Lightspeed*, *Nightmare*, and many other places. Elison is a high school dropout and a graduate of UC Berkeley.

Hugo Award winner and best-selling author **Sarah Gailey** is an internationally published writer of fiction and nonfiction. Their nonfiction has been published by *Mashable* and the *Boston Globe*. Their short fiction credits include *Vice* and *The Atlantic*. Their debut novella, *River of Teeth*, was a 2018 Hugo and Nebula award finalist. Their best-selling adult novel debut, *Magic for Liars*, was published in 2019. Their most recent novel is *The Echo Wife*.

Daryl Gregory's novels and short stories have been translated into a dozen languages and have won multiple awards, including the World Fantasy and Shirley Jackson awards, and have been nominated for the Hugo, Nebula, Locus, Lambda, and Sturgeon awards. His latest books are the novel *Revelator* (Knopf) and the novella *The Album of Dr. Moreau* (Tordotcom). His eight other books include *Spoonbenders*, *We Are All Completely Fine*, *Afterparty*, the Crawford Award–winning novel *Pandemonium*, and the collection *Unpossible and Other Stories*, a *Publishers Weekly* book of the year. He also teaches writing and is a regular instructor at the Viable Paradise writing workshop.

Saad Z. Hossain is the author of three novels, *Escape from Baghdad!*, *Djinn City*, and *Cybermage*. His science fantasy novella, *The Gurkha and the Lord of Tuesday*, was published in 2019 and was followed by *Kundo Wakes Up* earlier this year. He lives in Dhaka, Bangladesh.

Malka Older is a writer, academic, and aid worker. She is currently a faculty associate at Arizona State University's School for the Future of Innovation in Society, where she teaches on the humanitarian-development spectrum and on predictive fiction, and an associate researcher at the Centre de Sociologie des Organisations.

Her science fiction political thriller *Infomocracy* was named one of the best books of 2016 by *Kirkus*, Book Riot, and the *Washington Post*. She is also the author of the sequels *Null States* (2017) and *State Tectonics* (2018), and the full trilogy was nominated for a Hugo Award. She is also the creator of the serial *Ninth Step Station* and lead writer for the licensed sequel to *Orphan Black*, both currently running on Realm. Her short story and poetry collection *. . . and Other Disasters* came out in late 2019. Her short fiction and poetry can be found at *WIRED*, *Slate Future Tense*, *Leveler*, *Sundog Lit*, *Reservoir Lit*, *Inkscrawl*, *Rogue Agent*, *Tor.com*, *Fireside Magazine*, and others. She has written opinion pieces for the *New York Times*, *The Nation*, *Foreign Policy*, and NBC News THINK.

Chen Qiufan (a.k.a. Stanley Chan) is an award-winning Chinese speculative fiction author, translator, creative producer, and curator. He is the honorary president of the Chinese Science Fiction Writers Association and has a seat on the XPRIZE Foundation Science Fiction Advisory Council. His works include the novel *Waste Tide* and, coauthored with Kai-Fu Lee, the book *AI 2041: Ten Visions for Our Future*. He currently lives in Shanghai and is the founder of Thema Mundi Studio.

Justina Robson is the author of eleven published science fiction novels and many short stories. She was the winner of the 2000 Amazon Writers' Bursary for her first two novels, which explored AI and human engineering, respectively. Her later work continued to explore science fiction and to merge it with fantasy, culminating in the popular Quantum Gravity series. In addition to her original work, she has also written *Transformers: The Covenant of Primus* and a fantasy novel in the After the War shared world series from Solaris.

Tade Thompson is the author of the Rosewater novels, the Molly Southbourne books, *Making Wolf,* and *Far from the Light of Heaven*. He has won the Arthur C. Clarke Award, the Nommo Award, the Prix Julia-Verlange, and been a finalist for the John W. Campbell Award, the Locus Award, the Shirley Jackson Award, and the Hugo Award, among others. He lives and works on the south coast of England.

Jonathan Strahan (www.jonathanstrahan.com.au) is a World Fantasy Award–winning editor, anthologist, and podcaster and has been nominated for the Hugo Award nineteen times. He has edited more than ninety books, is the reviews editor for *Locus*, a consulting editor for *Tor.com* and Tordotcom Publishing, and cohost and producer of the Hugo-winning *Coode Street Podcast*. 221